THE ARISTOCRACY OF ART IN JOYCE AND WOLFE

THE ARISTOCRACY OF ART IN

JOYCE AND WOLFE

MARGARET MILLS HARPER

LOUISIANA STATE UNIVERSITY PRESS BATON ROUGE AND LONDON

Manufactured in the United States of America
First printing

99 98 97 96 95 94 93 92 91 90   5 4 3 2 1

Designer: *Amanda McDonald Key*
Typeface: *Baskerville*
Typesetter: *G&S Typesetters, Inc.*
Printer and binder: *Thomson-Shore, Inc.*

Library of Congress Cataloging-in-Publication Data

Harper, Margaret Mills, 1957–
The aristocracy of art in Joyce and Wolfe / Margaret Mills Harper.
p. cm.
Includes bibliographical references and index.
ISBN 0-8071-1596-7 (alk. paper)
1. Joyce, James, 1882–1941—Criticism and interpretation.
2. Wolfe, Thomas, 1900–1938—Criticism and interpretation.
3. Autobiographical fiction, English—History and criticism.
4. Autobiographical fiction, American—History and criticism.
5. Literature, Comparative—English and American. 6. Literature, Comparative—American and English. 7. Artists in literature.
8. Self in literature. 9. Art in literature. I. Title.
PR6019.09Z5755 1991
823'.912—dc20 90-33949
CIP

The author is grateful to Harper and Row for permission to quote from Thomas Wolfe's novels *The Web and the Rock*, © 1939, and *You Can't Go Home Again*, © 1940. Excerpts are reprinted with permission of Charles Scribner's Sons, an imprint of Macmillan Publishing Company, from *Look Homeward, Angel*, by Thomas Wolfe. Copyright 1929 by Charles Scribner's Sons; renewal copyright © 1957 by Edward C. Aswell, Administrator, C.T.A.; and/or Fred W. Wolfe; and from *Of Time and the River*, by Thomas Wolfe, copyright 1935 by Charles Scribner's Sons; renewal copyright © 1963 by Paul Gitlin, Administrator, C.T.A.

The author is also grateful to Viking Penguin, Inc., for permission to quote from *A Portrait of the Artist as a Young Man* by James Joyce. Copyright 1916 by B. W. Huebsch, Inc., by Nora Joyce. Copyright © 1964 by the Estate of James Joyce. All rights reserved. Reprinted by permission of Viking Penguin, a division of Penguin Books USA, Inc.; and from *Finnegans Wake* by James Joyce. Copyright 1939 by James Joyce. Copyright renewed © 1967 by the Estate of James Joyce. All rights reserved. Reprinted by permission of Viking Penguin, a division of Penguin Books USA, Inc. She thanks Random House, Inc., and the Bodley Head, Ltd., for permission to quote from Joyce's novel *Ulysses*, © 1986; Jonathan Cape and the executors of the James Joyce Estate for permission to quote from his novels *Stephen Hero* and *A Portrait of the Artist as a Young Man*; and the Society of Authors as the literary representative of the Estate of James Joyce for permission to quote from *Stephen Hero, A Portrait of the Artist as a Young Man, Ulysses*, and *Finnegans Wake*.

The author also thanks the editors of the *Thomas Wolfe Review* for permission to reprint in a somewhat different form material from her essay "*Of Time and the River* and the Problem of Authority," which appeared in the Autumn, 1987, issue of that journal.

The paper in this book meets the guidelines for permanence and durability of the Committee on Production Guidelines for Book Longevity of the Council on Library Resources. ∞

To Pierce, who had faith

Contents

Preface

Autobiographical art is usually a very early or a very late phenomenon in a writer's oeuvre, serving either to exorcise self, "get it out of one's system," or to keep it permanently, warding off the inevitability of death by investing a past or passing life with meaning. We do not often encounter writers who devote entire careers to considering self in their works. But James Joyce and Thomas Wolfe did so, and this point of connection between two otherwise different men and novelists is the starting point of this study. Although the products of their lifelong interest in fictionalizing themselves were in many respects as different as the two individuals, many of the differences, as well as quite a few similarities, between the writers and their works can be made intelligible if we examine the works in the context of Joyce's and Wolfe's continuing interest in a similar kind of literary endeavor.

In the first novels of both writers there is what at first appears a coincidental pattern of an artistic sensibility growing from difficult social and economic circumstances into recognition of the artist's vocation. Both men applied to their earlier lives the formula of artistic potential triumphing over the chaos of an alcoholic home in which social status is a continual source of anxiety, and this formula generated for both Joyce and Wolfe fruitful, lifelong explorations in fiction of such topics as the relation of art and artists to society and the question of individual identity in terms of one's past versus timeless or mythic qualities in the human personality. In addition, the equation of artists with a transcendent elite contributed to both authors' abiding interest in technical matters such as rhetorical distance and the presumed presence or absence of narrating voices. I will examine this complex of ideas in both Joyce and Wolfe from the double perspective of an abiding theme and an underlying structural assumption. Doing so will allow me to show by example an essential quality of books such as Joyce's and Wolfe's—the distinctive way in which events in the story and elements of the discourse mirror each other.

I will be using the term *autobiographical fiction* to describe their projects, for we must take into account the two elements to which this term refers, as well as the ways in which both elements interact, if we are to read Joyce and Wolfe well. Both writers began their novelistic careers by producing an autobiographical version of the apprenticeship novel. *A Portrait of the Artist as a Young Man* and *Look Homeward, Angel* depend, first of all, upon the development of the individual at the emotional center of the text and, second, upon our recognition of the relationship between the protagonist and the narrating voice whom we are meant to identify as the author. Character and writer both move toward the moment (which presumably will occur beyond the novel's time) when one will become the other and when the trajectory of the developing skill of one will meet the skill of the other. By then, the artist's skill will have proved itself in the writing of the novel we are reading. We read these novels as if they were autobiographical not because they are, but because they tell us they are. They make the identification between writer and text clear, because that identification is an important determinant of their meaning.

As I use the term, *autobiographical fiction* does not apply only to the portrait-of-the-artist kind of novel. Indeed it cannot be so restricted if I intend to discuss writers who continued to indulge in an autobiographical mode, for it is impossible to write successfully more than one work like *A Portrait* or *Look Homeward, Angel.* The dependence of text on extratextual reality prevents such an undertaking: these novels have been propelled forward by the real situation of an unproven writer creating the story of his own potential, in addition to the represented drama of the protagonist. Once the first novel has been written, the relationship between remembering narrator and remembered version of self alters. A subsequent novel, then, will lack the rhetorical tension that gave the first its dramatic interest unless both character and narrating voice develop further.

The necessity of changing both character and expression underlies the later work of both Joyce and Wolfe, and Joyce's success illuminates Wolfe's ultimate failure to realize such change. In fact, each highlights the other: we can see more clearly why *Ulysses* and *Finnegans Wake* were required for the continuation of Joyce's exploration of self in fiction by looking at Wolfe's frustrating attempts to conceive and carry out his later projects (attempts that were defeated by a sad combination of personal weakness, notoriously bad editing, and his early death). Likewise, the unwieldy mass of Wolfe's work also becomes more comprehensible when viewed in the context of Joyce's texts.

Autobiographical fiction for both Joyce and Wolfe led to the larger question of making and remaking ways to join the actual with the possible, and truth with artistic falsehood. Both writers continued to use linguistic representations of the self, that simultaneously fictional and autobiographical entity, as the best means to accomplish this end. I intend here to follow them in this enterprise as closely as I can by following the versions of themselves I see in their work.

This book would never have been written without the help, encouragement, and example of Louis D. Rubin, Jr. I am deeply in his debt. I am also grateful for the patient reading and suggestions of Charles Edge, Jerry Leath Mills, Albrecht B. Strauss, Weldon Thornton, and Morris Beja. My father, George Mills Harper, "cast a cold eye" on my prose, as he has done since I wrote my first "book" at age five; my mother, Mary Jane Harper, gave invaluable grandmotherly help while I revised the manuscript. The Ohio State University at Marion graciously provided a summer research grant and a quarter's leave from my teaching duties there.

Zhenya Kurashova Wine gave of her time and affection as few can while I worked on the manuscript and entered the world of motherhood simultaneously. I wish to thank her especially.

My greatest debt is to Pierce Pettis and to our children, Rayvon and Grace, who support me in untold ways.

Abbreviations

DD	David Herbert Donald. *Look Homeward: A Life of Thomas Wolfe*. Boston, 1987.
FW	James Joyce. *Finnegans Wake*. New York, 1939. Quotations noted by page and line number.
LHA	Thomas Wolfe. *Look Homeward, Angel: A Story of the Buried Life*. New York, 1929.
LJJ	*Letters of James Joyce*. Vol. I edited by Stuart Gilbert, Vols. II and III edited by Richard Ellmann. New York, 1966.
LTW	*The Letters of Thomas Wolfe*. Edited by Elizabeth Nowell. New York, 1956.
OTTR	Thomas Wolfe. *Of Time and the River: A Legend of a Man's Hunger in His Youth*. New York, 1935.
P	James Joyce. *"A Portrait of the Artist as a Young Man": Text, Criticism, and Notes*. Edited by Chester G. Anderson. New York, 1968.
RE	Richard Ellmann. *James Joyce*. Rev. ed. New York, 1982.
RSK	Richard S. Kennedy. *The Window of Memory: The Literary Career of Thomas Wolfe*. Chapel Hill, 1962.
SH	James Joyce. *Stephen Hero*. Edited by John J. Slocum and Herbert Cahoon. New York, 1963.

U	James Joyce. *Ulysses*. Edited by Hans Walter Gabler. New York, 1986.
WR	Thomas Wolfe. *The Web and the Rock*. New York, 1939.
YCGHA	Thomas Wolfe. *You Can't Go Home Again*. New York, 1940.

THE ARISTOCRACY OF ART IN JOYCE AND WOLFE

Introduction: Cracked Lookingglasses

In *Stephen Hero*, the fragmentary early draft of James Joyce's first novel, a character named Mr. Fulham is mentioned several times. He is Stephen Dedalus' godfather, a country gentleman from Mullingar, County Westmeath. He appears in only one episode in *Stephen Hero* but serves an interesting function as the wealthy patron who sends the Dedaluses the money for their son's tuition at the university.[1] Near the end of Stephen's first year, "the youth was given to understand that if he did not succeed brilliantly at the coming examination his career at the University would come to a close." But Stephen "was not greatly troubled by this warning for he knew that his fate was, in this respect, with his godfather and not with his father" (*SH*, 48). The godfather, although he has no dramatic role in the main fragment, is a significant figure because of the power he has over the hero's "fate." Stephen's father, who is as willing to assert power (even if it is not properly his own) as

1. Joyce spelled his protagonist's surname *Daedalus* in *Stephen Hero* but changed it to *Dedalus* when he revised his novel. Although the two Stephens are in some respects different characters (as the Stephen of *A Portrait* is different from the Stephen of *Ulysses*), I have used the later spelling throughout this study for the sake of consistency.

Stephen is to rebel against it, uses Mr. Fulham as a threat whenever the youth seems to not take proper advantage of his education. When it looks as though Stephen will not accept the help of the Jesuits to "get on," Simon Dedalus informs him that "he's not going to fool me nor his godfather, either. With the help of God I won't be long till I let *him* know what a bloody nice atheist this fellow has turned out." Stephen promptly answers "that he did not want his godfather's help either" (228).

A fragment discovered after the first edition of *Stephen Hero* was published, included in new editions beginning in 1955, describes a trip Stephen makes to the home of his wealthy patron at Mullingar. Little happens during this episode: Stephen spends his time enjoying the comfort of his godfather's country estate, observing the local peasantry with some distaste, and arguing at dinner with Mr. Fulham and a neighbor about such favorite topics as politics and religion. The manuscript breaks off abruptly after twenty-five pages, in the middle of a rather strange, undeveloped scene in which, during a walk, Stephen and two companions come upon a crowd gathered around the corpse of a drowned woman. Fulham is presented as a typical country squire, a bit sententious and opinionated but eminently respectable. Fulham grills Stephen about his conduct at the university, but there is no apparent threat of cutting off his funds.

John J. Slocum and Herbert Cahoon speculate in the foreword to the later edition that Joyce chose not to include the Mullingar episode in *A Portrait of the Artist as a Young Man* "perhaps because he came to feel that the role of Stephen showing off against the provincials had something disagreeable in it." They also speculate that Joyce originally intended for Mr. Fulham to play a fuller role in the novel than he does in the final version but that the Mullingar episode became "a little irrelevant" when Joyce decided to rewrite the novel with a radically different structure (*SH*, 5).

Why might Joyce have decided to do away with Mr. Fulham? One possible reason is simply artistic economy. Joyce heeded the advice that he put into the mouth of one of Stephen's Mullingar acquaintances: a Mr. Garvey, on hearing that Stephen "was inclined for writing," recommends to him, "You take my tip: shorthand" (251). The author of *A Portrait* had learned some shorthand since he wrote *Stephen Hero*. Joyce did a lot of cutting as he rewrote, and *A Portrait* is much sparer and leaner than its first draft. He may have decided that Mr. Fulham, like Maurice Dedalus, Stephen's younger brother in the early version, simply detracted from the novel's focus on Stephen himself. But Mr. Fulham is hardly in the same category as Maurice, a fully developed character whose presence in the Dedalus family keeps readers of *Stephen Hero* from feeling the important alienation of the protagonist from his family, thus diminishing the sympathy we extend to Stephen alone. When Joyce rewrote his novel, he pared down or eliminated not only Maurice but also most of the other Dedalus children. In *A Portrait*, Stephen cannot remember even the exact number of his brothers and sisters. Their names are mentioned only in passing, and none is given a definite character.

The excision of Stephen's benefactor, Mr. Fulham, from *A Portrait* is only one example of the authorial silence in this novel concerning potentially compromising financial situations. A similar detail involves Stephen's earlier schooling. John Joyce, the writer's father, was forced in 1893 to take his son out of Clongowes Wood College, a respectable Jesuit institution, and enroll him in a less expensive but also less prestigious Christian Brothers' school. As Richard Ellmann notes in his biography, however, Joyce "chose never to remember this interlude with the Christian Brothers in his writings, preferring to have his hero spend the period in two years of reverie." Even more telling is the fact that Joyce neglected to tell Herbert Gorman, his first biographer, anything about his "one break with Jesuit education" (RE, 35).

Both Mr. Fulham and the Christian Brothers would have compromised a curious elitism in Stephen Dedalus' upbringing—an attitude that clearly was present in the Joyce household as well. Despite the family's decline into penury and squalor as James grew from childhood to young manhood, the Joyces apparently never admitted that they were no longer in a position to think of themselves as members of a socially distinguished class. Ellmann notes that in his opinion of himself, John Joyce "was never a poor man, always a rich man who had suffered reverses. His family accepted the state of poverty without ever accepting the word" (RE, 34). Of course James Joyce did not hesitate, in *Stephen Hero* and *A Portrait*, to show the Dedaluses in dire poverty. His sense of his own superiority to others had taken a different turn from his father's by the time he wrote his first novel. It was aesthetic rather than social or economic, but in his convictions about his place in society we can see a family resemblance. In *Stephen Hero*, Stephen also rejects his parents' delusions of gentility as he rejects their plans "that he would at once follow the path of remunerative respectability and save the situation"—"but he could not satisfy his family" (49). He does not reject the notion of aristocracy altogether, however; he replaces the ideas of his family with his own definition, in which we plainly hear echoes of the attitudes that surrounded him from childhood. We are told that Simon Dedalus' "son's notion of aristocracy was not the one which he [Simon] could sympathize with" (111).

The artist, as Stephen conceives him, is a member of an aesthetic aristocracy, although not in the usual sense of an aristocratic elite—the attitude that we find, for example, in Virginia Woolf or Marcel Proust. Stephen's aristocracy is almost entirely abstract: as an artist, he will be part of a rarefied company that transcends physical considerations such as material circumstances, and any others, including language, culture, or even time. But he does assume the existence of an elite group, differing in outward characteristics but not in essential quality from any other group claiming superiority over the common run of humanity. And so Joyce punctuates the sentence that informs us of Stephen's artistic intentions with a colon to indicate that the qualities of snobbery and pride that follow the punctuation mark are characteristics of the artist as Stephen defines him. "Stephen had begun to regard himself seriously as a literary artist: he professed scorn for the rabblement and contempt for authority" (*SH*, 122–23). Later, this view of the artist is made obvious when Stephen engages in a revealing debate with himself about the question of leaving the Church. "During the train of these reflections," we are told, "the Church sent an embassy of nimble pleaders into his ears. . . . They addressed every side of his nature in turn" (204). One of these "ambassadors'" most nimble arguments rests upon Stephen's recognition of his "aristocratic intelligence and passion for a supremely satisfying order in all the fervours of artistic creation." They say, "You believe in an aristocracy: believe also in the eminence of the aristocratic class and in the order of society which secures that eminence"—the "patrician order" of the Church. "With us you can exercise your contemptuous faculties when you are recognized as one of the patrician order" (205–206).

This kind of nobility is threatened by the Christian Brothers' usurping the rightful place of the Jesuits as teachers of the young aristocrat. It is also, finally, threatened by the solid, well-to-do "burgher," Mr. Fulham, and his superior attitude toward those in his debt. Although in much of the manuscript Stephen is clearly pleased to be under the patronage of his godfather rather than of his natural father, the Mullingar episode reveals a slight uneasiness on Stephen's part that parallels Joyce's own artistic judgment in deciding to edit Mr. Fulham out of the finished novel.

Stephen seems at first to find the home of the country gentleman a pleasant place. His enjoyment of fruit and milk on the lawn of the orchard, a game of cards after dinner in the evening, and a tennis tournament is anything but consistent with what we know of the protagonist of *A Portrait*. But the earlier Stephen also begins to chafe a bit toward the end of the fragment. At dinner one evening he studies his godfather. Perceiving initially that Mr. Fulham's "championing of the Irish peasant was full of zealous patronage" and that "his ardour for the Church was implicit with his respect for feudal distinctions," Stephen soon realizes that "his conceptions of human relations" are feudal. If he had lived "in the ages when the earth was thought to be scaphoid," the young man sarcastically thinks, "he might have been reputed the most . . . enlightened of slave-owners" (*SH*, 249–50). And Stephen, the favored poor relation, is one of the happy slaves.

So the good godfather was deleted from the manuscript. Joyce seems in this instance, as in others, to have clarified his fictional intentions as he revised, in order to emphasize the specific kind of aristocracy to which his "hero" would belong. Interestingly, this example is a clear illustration of the extent to which Joyce's decisions as he wrote his first novel were from the beginning made for fictional and not confessional or autobiographical purposes. Mr. Fulham has no model in Joyce's extraliterary life who has been discovered. He was not based on Joyce's actual godfather, a distant relative named Philip McCann, a ship's chandler. According to

Ellmann, McCann is unlikely to have paid Joyce's bills, since he "died in 1898, and does not seem to have left money for the purpose" (RE, 23). Nor did Joyce's brother Stanislaus know after whom Mr. Fulham was patterned. As a matter of fact, he asked Joyce if the godfather was David Sheehy, whose family both brothers visited regularly. Joyce replied, in a letter reprinted in Ellmann's biography, that "Fulham is not old Sheehy—he comes in later" (*LJJ*, II, 79; RE, 191).

Both the inclusion and the exclusion of Mr. Fulham, then, illustrate Joyce's fictionalizing. First the writer invented him, perhaps from whole cloth, and then he omitted him from the novel. In both cases, Joyce acted on artistic principle. One of the clear and primary requisites for Joyce's figure of the young artist is distance (hence the need for exile that is a pervasive theme in Joyce's work and life). In first forming his story of the development of an artist, he seems to have envisioned that Stephen Dedalus needed the support of a superior social context in order to distance himself from his family and their social class. When revising the manuscript, however, Joyce became increasingly aware that the aristocracy to which his hero had to belong was the aristocracy of art alone. In *A Portrait*, Stephen must reject not only his family and the nobility of the Church but also the worldly patriciate if he is to achieve his purpose. The young man must realize that "his destiny was to be elusive of social or religious orders" a few pages before he can be granted the vision of the wading girl that confirms his vocation at the end of Chapter 4 (*P*, 162, 171).

The creation of a self-image as an abstractly aristocratic artist as a way of satisfying a desire to escape from a lower-class background is intrinsic to *A Portrait*, on both thematic and structural levels. Almost as soon as Stephen becomes conscious of himself and the world around him, in the opening pages of the novel, he is confronted with the issue of gentility. The ubiquitous concern with social status that characterizes the Dedalus household forms an early and deep impression on their eldest son. With cruel irony, however, Stephen also soon learns that as long as he is a member of his family and a part of their world, he will never be able to attain the status he longs for. The anxiety that this situation creates propels him in one direction and then another until he discovers art as a vocation and a means to an aristocracy to which he can securely belong. We watch him begin to see the squalor surrounding him as a lack of beauty; the crassness, the lack of a desire for the beautiful. Once he is in sure command of beauty, he will have the perspective he needs: as an artist he will reside in an unchanging palace from which to look down on the disordered, ugly world of his family and Dublin.

A reading of *A Portrait* from the perspective of this theme also illuminates its expression, for it is not only Stephen Dedalus who appropriates a personal theory of art that will presumably raise him into aesthetic nobility out of a social position he finds degrading. The formal equivalent of this urge can be felt in a distinctive intensity in *A Portrait.* The narrator's great distance from the autobiographical protagonist and the story wars with the implicit rhetorical engagement of the form Joyce chose for his work, a *Bildungsroman* that is closely autobiographical.[2] Stephen may not have grown past being young in his artistic calling, but he knows enough to realize that he will prove himself worthy to be among the august company of true artists by returning *as* an artist to the low life he has transcended—returning in a work of art, in other words. Thus it would be appropriate for him to do what his creator does in writing the novel—attempt to remake the actual history of a desire-ridden, unsettled, disunified self in a work of impersonal, static, beautifully ordered art. The disparity between the actual predicament and the artistic project might be expected to result in some instability and tension, which we do find in *A Portrait,* but the paradox also causes a dynamic quality that is one reason for the pleasure we have in reading the book.

Like Joyce, who wrote a play before settling on prose fiction as the genre that best suited him, Thomas Wolfe also attempted to write drama before discovering (actually, being forced to recognize) that his talent lay elsewhere. As he began work on the novel

2. In *The Way of the World: The "Bildungsroman" in European Culture* (London, 1987), Franco Moretti attributes this tension to the *Bildungsroman* itself, which as a form has the paradoxical goal of bringing the protagonist to both self-determination and integration into society. See also Steven Helmling, "Joyce the Irresponsible," *Sewanee Review,* XCIV (1986), 466–68, for a biographical interpretation of this tension.

that would become *Look Homeward, Angel,* he was still sending the script of his play *Mannerhouse,* the last work he had finished, to New York producers, hoping to establish a career as a dramatist. *Mannerhouse* features an autobiographical protagonist named Eugene, a sensitive, cynical young intellectual out of step with the uncomprehending society around him—much as the Eugene Gant of *Look Homeward, Angel* would be alienated from the shallow culture of Altamont, his hometown. But the Eugene of the play, unlike the middle-class Eugene Gant, is a genuine patrician, the son and heir to an antebellum southern plantation threatened and finally destroyed by the Civil War. He is aware that the Confederate cause, along with the grand rhetoric surrounding it, is an attempt to preserve a false style of life—a manner, in other words, instead of a genuine encounter with unruly reality. Nevertheless, Eugene is "to the manner born," and he joins his father in fighting for it, in his words, "striking a blow for my own disbelief."[3] His spiritual renunciation of the values of his society cannot prevent him from joining in the inevitable collapse of his family, their house, and their aristocratic southern way of life, which the play chronicles.

Mannerhouse is not an accomplished piece of writing, but it is interesting, like the rather uninspiring *Stephen Hero,* for the progress it represents toward its author's first novel. In *Mannerhouse,* as in *Look Homeward, Angel,* Wolfe presented a refined young protagonist in conflict with the world of which he is a part. Wolfe had not yet, however, taken the step of making Eugene an aristocrat only in the abstract sense of belonging to an artistic nobility with which he, like Stephen Dedalus, senses a kinship. Like Joyce, Wolfe decided early on to use a focusing character in his work whose sensibilities make him innately superior to those around him. Also like Joyce, Wolfe experimented with more than one way to present his protagonist's superiority before he decided to banish him from all but an artistic elite. In *Look Homeward, Angel,* the tension between Eugene Gant and his environment increases the drama of his search for his place as an artist. This search, in turn, translates the tension into the structure and narrative texture of the novel,

3. Thomas Wolfe, *Mannerhouse: A Play in a Prologue and Four Acts,* ed. Louis D. Rubin, Jr., and John L. Idol, Jr. (Baton Rouge, 1985), 68.

which also presents a drama—the progress of the protagonist toward the author of the work. In both *Look Homeward, Angel* and *A Portrait*, a longing for refinement, in both a social and an emotional sense, is integral to the birth and growth of the artist. In both works, too, unsatisfied desire propels forward the story and characterizes the narrating voice, unifying and energizing the text.

Look Homeward, Angel, like *A Portrait*, depicts a sensitive child who perceives at an early age both that the issue of social class is vitally important to his family and the world around him and that his people do not belong to the desired class. The Gants do not lose respectability, as the Dedaluses do. Instead, they never quite attain it. There are a number of reasons for this failure: W. O. Gant, Eugene's father, is a flamboyant alcoholic, and his wife is a miserly businesswoman whose boardinghouse has been known to accept guests of doubtful morality. The Gants do not live together, and their children reside with one or the other as they please. Eugene, their youngest son, ultimately resolves to join an abstract aristocracy of art, similar to that conceived by Stephen Dedalus, as a solution to the conflict created by the chaos and unsatisfied longing for status that characterize his youth.[4] In Wolfe's novel, as in Joyce's, we can trace the thread of the protagonist's desire, at first unconscious, then increasingly well defined, to be superior to and separate from the world in which he finds himself as a child.

Wolfe's novel has a much looser structure than Joyce's elaborately constructed one, but it yields to a more or less systematic analysis if we begin by watching Eugene's developing awareness of caste. As he grows he abstracts an almost intuitive perception of status from a personal into an aesthetic issue, while the novel draws our attention stylistically to the presence of an artist who is in confident control of the events being narrated but who also remembers and rejoins the past rhetorically and poetically. As Eugene becomes convinced that he must leave Altamont in order to return to it imaginatively, the distance at which the narrative voice stands from

4. Louis D. Rubin, Jr., first noticed the close link between Thomas Wolfe's art and his cultural and social background; Rubin's arguments for the importance of Wolfe's background have influenced my own ideas considerably. See Rubin, *The Faraway Country: Writers of the Modern South* (Seattle, 1963), 97–104; and Rubin, *A Gallery of Southerners* (Baton Rouge, 1982), 82–83 and esp. 85–106.

the action gradually lessens. The expressionist conclusion, which is meant to join Eugene and his author in an overcoming of time and loss, fuses the realms of past and future, and fact and fiction.

Approaching *Look Homeward, Angel* in this way reveals the considerable artistry of a novel that has not often fared well under formalistic analysis, written by a novelist whose literary reputation remains insecure. The notion of Wolfe as a passionate but totally undisciplined writer, indulging alternately in rodomontade and self-pity, is still popular enough to warrant a reading of his first novel that will indicate the experiment in fictional form that it presents.[5] The dynamic relationship between author and autobiographical character is unusually important in Wolfe's work, and to read *Look Homeward, Angel* without taking into account the attempt to find radical organic unity between artifact and extraliterary truth that it dramatizes is to misread it seriously.

By the end of *Look Homeward, Angel,* Eugene Gant's search for his vocation is well under way, although he does not recognize and respond to his calling until the end of Wolfe's second novel, *Of Time and the River.* The triumphant tone of the ending of *Look Homeward, Angel* is designed to show that Eugene will find his way into the art he desires so passionately to create. However, even though Eugene comes much closer to being the artist he desires to be than Stephen does in *A Portrait* or *Ulysses,* it is still the passion of Eugene's search for art, rather than the art we are told he makes, that is the focus of the novels. We can see by comparing Eugene's quest with Stephen's parallel search that Wolfe's tendency to emphasize the close relationship between the text and the authorial voice injects a tone of incompleteness even over the success that the climax of *Look Homeward, Angel* claims for Eugene. Joyce's novel, on the other hand, constantly stresses the separateness of the events in the protagonist's life and the creation or re-creation of them by the

5. Recent criticism of Wolfe as caustic as that of Bernard DeVoto ("Genius Is Not Enough," reprinted in Louis D. Rubin, Jr. [ed.], *Thomas Wolfe: A Collection of Critical Essays* [Englewood Cliffs, N.J., 1973], 72–79) is rare. More often, one encounters the attitude Eugene Gant noticed in discussions of "aht" among graduate students: "I'm sorry," an acquaintance remarks about a writer who has gone out of fashion, "I can't read him. I've tried it—but it simply can't be done" (*OTTR*, 114). Leo Gurko summarizes stereotypes often applied to Wolfe's writing in *Thomas Wolfe: Beyond the Romantic Ego* (New York, 1975), 1–8.

author. This stress is a significant difference between *A Portrait* and *Look Homeward, Angel*, for *A Portrait* moves toward an aesthetic "stasis," an impression of artistic control (so that even though we may not agree on what the authorial attitude toward Stephen is, we do not often hesitate to assume that that attitude is set).[6] In Wolfe's novel, however, the stance of the author often seems to shift with the dramatic movement of the story.

Significantly, then, the conspicuous patronymic of Joyce's hero recalls the nobility to which he belongs—the descendants of the mythological artist Daedalus. His given name, Stephen, suggests the certainty of the first Christian martyr's faith in his calling. Wolfe's autobiographical protagonist, on the other hand, is called by a name that, we are told, "means 'well born,' but which, as any one will be able to testify, does not mean, has never meant, 'well bred'" (*LHA*, 35). His surname, Gant (spelled *Gaunt* by his English grandfather, we learn from the opening page of the book), denotes hunger and yearning but not fulfillment or confidence. The names of the protagonists, like the patterns that their lives make in *A Portrait* and *Look Homeward, Angel*, reveal an important difference between the approaches to autobiographical art taken by Joyce and Wolfe.

By examining what Stephen and Eugene have in common and how they differ from each other, I will find myself viewing the novels that contain them in generic terms. Both *A Portrait* and *Look Homeward, Angel* are a variety of *Bildungsroman* or, more exactly, of *Künstlerroman*, focusing as they do on artistic development.[7] They

6. Joyce once told his friend Frank Budgen that Stephen Dedalus "has a shape that can't be changed." See Budgen, *James Joyce and the Making of "Ulysses"* (1934; rpr. Bloomington, 1960), 107. Just what that authorial attitude is has been a subject of considerable debate. Hugh Kenner has made the greatest use of the argument that because Joyce "had his eye constantly on the epic sequel" by the time he finished *A Portrait*, he viewed Stephen with distaste. Kenner, *Dublin's Joyce* (Bloomington, Ind., 1956), 120.

7. Maurice Beebe, *Ivory Towers and Sacred Founts: The Artist as Hero in Fiction from Goethe to Joyce* (New York, 1964); Jerome Hamilton Buckley, *Season of Youth: The Bildungsroman from Dickens to Golding* (Cambridge, Mass., 1974), 225–47; and Richard S. Kennedy, "Wolfe's *Look Homeward, Angel* as a Novel of Development," in Paschal Reeves (ed.), *The Merrill Studies in "Look Homeward, Angel"* (Columbus, Ohio, 1970), 82–90, treat these novels as *Bildungsromane*. See also John Hagan, "Thomas Wolfe's *Of Time and the River*: The Quest for Transcendence," in Richard S. Kennedy

are also autobiographical, a qualification that is at least equally important in defining what is distinctive about them.[8] This study emphasizes the latter quality, regarding the novels as *autobiographical fiction* (as opposed, perhaps, to *fictional autobiography*, which does not emphasize the term that both Joyce and Wolfe would prefer).[9] For I am convinced that we must distinguish autobiographical fiction from fiction in general if we are to penetrate certain key aspects of texts such as *A Portrait* or *Look Homeward, Angel*—just as we are usually careful to separate autobiographical novels from autobiography.

It is significant to our reading of their first novels that Joyce and Wolfe both created characters out of relatively direct images of themselves and placed the characters in stories meant to express something about the larger world, using the remembered stories of their own lives as a starting point. This is not to say that the plots of the novels coincide exactly with the mythoi that we have created about the lives of James Joyce and Thomas Wolfe or that they assigned to themselves. But there is a relationship between their lives and their works that we ignore at the risk of missing part of the distinctive character of the texts.[10]

It is true, of course, that the personal and the artistic join in all literary art: the transforming of private need into something more or less fictional is part of the human activity of writing. The impulse to create and the urge to reveal and justify are closely aligned.

(ed.), *Thomas Wolfe: A Harvard Perspective* (Athens, Ohio, 1983), 3–20, for a discussion of *Of Time and the River*, Wolfe's second novel, in similar terms.

8. There have been relatively few studies treating *A Portrait* as autobiographical fiction, as Avrom Fleishman notes in *Figures of Autobiography: The Language of Self-Writing in Victorian and Modern England* (Berkeley, 1983), 411. They include Louis D. Rubin, Jr., *The Teller in the Tale* (Seattle, 1967), 122–26, 141–77; Hélène Cixous, *The Exile of James Joyce*, trans. Sally A. J. Purcell (London, 1976); Ralph W. Rader, "Defoe, Richardson, Joyce, and the Concept of Form in the Novel," in William Matthews and Ralph W. Rader, *Autobiography, Biography, and the Novel* (Los Angeles, 1973), 31–72; and C. Hugh Holman, *The Loneliness at the Core: Studies in Thomas Wolfe* (Baton Rouge, 1975), Chapter 2.

9. O. Alan Weltzien, in "*Look Homeward, Angel* and Wolfe's Autobiographical Imperative," *CEA Critic*, XLIX (Winter, 1986–Summer, 1987), 89–101, approaches Wolfe's work as fictional autobiography.

10. *Cf.* the explanation of autobiography as myth in James Olney, *Metaphors of Self: The Meaning of Autobiography* (Princeton, 1972).

More particularly, first novels (or any first works) are especially likely to draw their subject matter fairly directly from the life of their author. According to common wisdom, a writer often first focuses on his or her own life and, then, having exhausted the material or resolved the personal issues that prevented attention elsewhere, turns in other directions for subsequent works.

But the autobiographical elements in *A Portrait* and *Look Homeward, Angel* are considerably more than mere sources for the subject matter from which the setting, plot, or characters of the novels are derived. Nor do they serve merely a psychological function, as catharsis or confession for the authors. Rather, they are integral to the works of art: without the assumption of the autobiographical relationship between the authorial voice and the main character, many considerations that are fundamental in fiction, such as structure, narrative technique, character development, and dramatic tension, cease to make good sense. The autobiographical aspect of the text is vital to our understanding of it in formal terms.

The autobiographical relationship between author and protagonist exerts rhetorical pressure on the novels of Joyce and Wolfe, straining the surface of the narrative and challenging the author to create fictional techniques to contain and control it. The source of this pressure is the fact that the burden of proof for the aesthetic assumptions underlying both works lies to a considerable extent in the artists whom we suppose that the two principal characters will become—in other words, in James Joyce and Thomas Wolfe, the young men writing the books. Wolfe also found, as Ellmann has said of Joyce, that "he could become an artist by writing about the process of becoming an artist, his life legitimizing his portrait by supplying the sitter, while the portrait vindicated the sitter by its evident admiration for him" (RE, 144–45), tempered though that admiration might seem in the attitude toward the subject projected at times by the narrating voice. Both *A Portrait* and *Look Homeward, Angel* are technical experiments that undertake to resolve at once two distinct aesthetic purposes the novels are called upon to serve.

The artistry that both novels demonstrate rests primarily upon a working assumption that the artist is superior to and detached from his environment, an environment that includes the subject matter of his autobiographical art. Yet the work of art also presupposes an act of self-creation. It is a rhetorical piece meant to convince its readers of the artistic validity of the voice we identify with its author (whose worth as a novelist, incidentally, is as yet unproven, since both *A Portrait* and *Look Homeward, Angel* are first—or first-published—novels). And rhetoric, as theorists from Aristotle onward have insisted, demands that the audience sense the speaker's involvement with his subject.[11] The works are asked to function both as "forged artifacts," to speak in Joycean terms, and as "works in progress." They are products, finished objects separated temporally as well as emotionally from their authors, and processes, acts of persuasion taking place at the time of their writing and again at the time they are read.

These terms are familiar ones. Northrop Frye used them to distinguish between a novel like *Tom Jones*, in which "the suspense is thrown forward until it reaches the end, and is based on our confidence that the author knows what is coming next," and a text such as *Tristram Shandy*, in which "we are not being led into a story, but into the process of writing a story: we wonder, not what is coming next, but what the author will think of next."[12] The narrator of Fielding's novel stands apart from and maintains constant control of his story. Tristram, on the other hand, as both recorder and participant, is at no such safe remove from the action. We are meant to sense that he has much more at stake from his authorship than does the narrator of *Tom Jones*. One crucial distinction between these two kinds of novel, then, is the difference in the distance from the story at which the narrator stands.

Both *Tom Jones* and *Tristram Shandy*, unlike *A Portrait* and *Look Homeward, Angel*, use a personified "author," who functions almost as a character in the novel, to relate the story to the reader. But the presence of an author is a created construct in every novel: there is always what Mikhail Bakhtin called a "posited author" and Wayne Booth called an "implied author" arranging and selecting events as

11. See Aristotle *Rhetoric*, 1356a1–13, in Jonathan Barnes (ed.), *The Complete Works of Aristotle: The Revised Oxford Translation* (2 vols.; Princeton, 1984), II. See also Wayne C. Booth, *The Rhetoric of Fiction* (Rev. ed.; Chicago, 1983).

12. Northrop Frye, "Towards Defining an Age of Sensibility," *Journal of English Literary History*, XXIII (1956), 145.

well as imputing values and asserting cultural norms in the text.[13]

In any novel, the level of involvement of the author with his or her work is a determinant of meaning that the reader must gauge. As readers we instinctively form an assumption about the position of the author vis-à-vis the work. In doing so, of course, we actually rely on the "implied author" for our perceptions of the real author, who is not actually present in the text. But our reasons for wondering about the created author implicate the human being who wrote the book, to whose writing we are being asked to respond. Formal concerns are derived from human ones. When we address the issue of aesthetic distance, we should not forget that this novelistic convention plays with the issue of interpersonal communication and leads, intentional fallacy or no, to the question of how closely the "implied author" resembles an actual man or woman. We may not be able to answer the questions that the novel implicitly raises by reading the book, but we must not forget that it does raise them.

The question of aesthetic distance is particularly appropriate to autobiographical fiction. It is a crucial, if irresolvable, issue with reference to *A Portrait*, and *Look Homeward, Angel* stands or falls due largely to the vacillating distance caused by its uneasy joining of process and product. The relationship between authorial voice and protagonist is vitally important in these novels. The development that Stephen Dedalus and Eugene Gant undergo, as we have seen, is progress toward a goal of being able to do what their creators are presumably doing by writing. As we read *A Portrait* or *Look Homeward, Angel*, we sense at almost any point the character's inability and need to be an artist and the author's ability and satisfaction at being one. We feel, too, the inevitable hesitation in this rhetorical relationship: the level of certainty that the narrating voice projects is manifested in various ways in his interpretation of events and his attitude toward the character whom we know has been created from his former self. Thus the authorial presence is at once objective and subjective, separate from and involved in his story.

13. M. M. Bakhtin mentions the "posited author" in "Discourse in the Novel," in *The Dialogic Imagination*, trans. Caryl Emerson and Michael Holquist, ed. Michael Holquist (Austin, Tex., 1981), 311–15. See also Booth, *The Rhetoric of Fiction*, 70–77 and *passim*.

It is no accident, then, that these novels are conspicuously autobiographical. They actively encourage us to infer that the action once actually happened to their writers, even in parts that are not strictly autobiographical (so that unwary readers, particularly before much biographical data about Joyce and Wolfe had been gathered, might have been expected to read the novels as if they were more factual than they are, a phenomenon that troubled critical interpretation of both texts). Our knowledge of Joyce's and Wolfe's lives, then, is by no means the only source of our tendency to identify *A Portrait* and *Look Homeward, Angel* as works based directly on their authors' experiences. The novels do not employ the same stylistic means to ensure that we make this identification (as they draw directly upon fact to differing degrees), but they do so for a common purpose.

Examining what this purpose is leads us ultimately closer to the "real" authors than we might otherwise get: to the convictions about art that Wolfe and Joyce held. We cannot necessarily deduce the author's working assumptions from the artistic credos espoused by the narrators or characters, but we can do so with some justification from the kind of art we see in the novels. These underlying assumptions determine the extent to which the novels are factual. Thus, what the text seems to indicate about what its creator was attempting by writing it more directly represents his life than what happens in the plot. The same premises also determine to what extent the novels are ironic, providing the only rule by which we can measure authorial attitude with any reliability. Therefore, noticing that both *A Portrait* and *Look Homeward, Angel* draw our attention to their protagonists' newly formed artistic creeds, to their own artistry as novels, and to the resemblance between the two, we may recognize an invitation to connect the economic and social environments that Joyce and Wolfe encountered as children with their own art, just as we do for Stephen Dedalus and Eugene Gant.

The connection between the question of social status and the creation of art becomes more complex as it continues to be made and developed, on thematic and expressive levels, in both writers' later works. Interestingly, both Joyce and Wolfe continued to write fiction that was patterned heavily after their own lives. We cannot, however, describe Joyce's later work as *autobiographical fiction* in a restricted sense of the term: neither the central character of *Ulysses*, Leopold Bloom, nor the personage we sense at the center of *Finnegans Wake* is based in a conventional way on Joyce himself. In these books and in Wolfe's writing after *Look Homeward, Angel*, we can see a pattern emerging from the unrepeatable relationship between a relatively unknown author and his earliest publishable autobiographical novel. This pattern was transformed into structures of great importance throughout the oeuvres of both Joyce and Wolfe. The outlines of the pattern take shape from the unusually "kinetic" (to use Stephen's term from his aesthetic theory in *A Portrait*) artistic circumstance mentioned above: the drama in the work, of the birth and growth of the writer, is presumably occurring in the writer's life at the time of the writing, as well as in the protagonist's life in the past tense of the narrative. It is a central aspect of the novel's form as well that its author's artistry seems to be proven because he has written/is writing the book. The work itself validates its implied author's thesis about his own artistic development: its form implies that it justifies life.

In this proposition of art justifying life, we can of course hear echoes of the aesthetic theories of Romantic and Victorian writers and thinkers who influenced Joyce's and Wolfe's youth. Such ideas as Blake's insistence upon the redemptive imagination or Coleridge's theory of the direct link between the human mind and the world outside it were part of the intellectual climate in which both Joyce and Wolfe lived and breathed at school and university. Joyce's contribution to these aesthetic ideas derives from the emphasis he placed on literalness in connecting the realms of the beautiful and the mundane—symbolic, or mythic, and naturalistic ways of viewing reality. He seems to have concurred with the aesthetic theories he passed on to Stephen in *Stephen Hero, A Portrait*, and *Ulysses* insofar as they claimed that artistic truth can be apprehended in ordinary reality and that art made from fact has the greatest potential for representing that truth. By the time Joyce wrote *Finnegans Wake*, that "farced epistol to the hibruws" (*FW*. 228.33–34), his convictions about literalness had led to the almost fantastic proposition that art was to be created from the linguistic debris that lingers in the ordinary human subconscious or unconscious—bits of music-hall ballads, nursery rhymes, bad poetry, advertisements, radio broadcasters' lingo, and so on. For Wolfe as well, truth in art seems to have demanded a basis in literal fact, although he did not resolve the issues facing an autobiographical novelist as successfully as Joyce did, either theoretically or formally, in his novels. For Wolfe as well as Joyce, however, the relationship between art and life and the possibilities for representing that relationship in fiction were lifelong obsessions.

The question of later works is something of a problem when we consider autobiographical fiction. An author can write only one "portrait of the artist." If a writer's interest in this kind of work, and the exploration of the relationship between self and world that it depicts, continues after the first novel, the complexity of the undertaking increases significantly. As Gérard Genette has noted, the autobiographical *Bildungsroman* must in effect become a new form.[14] If the second work continues the first chronologically, for instance, aesthetic distance becomes more difficult to control as portrayed time approaches the actual time of writing (a phenomenon we notice at the ends of both *A Portrait* and *Look Homeward, Angel*). Likewise, the relationship between author and character that characterizes this kind of novel must grow in sophistication, to reflect the implied author's development in skill and range, if a second work is to succeed as a sequel. We must have a sense of the artist improving, and we must be convinced that the author is confidently in control of the lessons the protagonist will learn. Second works, and third or fourth works, are also likely to reflect the multiple nature of self, since the history they reflect is the history not only of a person but also of an autobiographical work about that person. Thus we might expect to encounter the kinds of experiments that we find in the later novels of both Joyce and Wolfe: a more intrusive narrating voice (or voices) demanding awareness of the artificiality of the project; expansion of the canvas on which the events take place, including alterations in the presentation of time and space; and varying or additional self-images that depict multiple relationships between self and literary representation, among other technical and thematic variations.

14. Gérard Genette, *Narrative Discourse: An Essay in Method*, trans. Jane E. Lewin (Ithaca, N.Y., 1980), 226–27.

So the need for aristocratic identity that Joyce and Wolfe translated, in Stephen Dedalus and Eugene Gant, into the desire to be an artist can ultimately be associated with both authors' lifelong preoccupation with writing fiction in which autobiographical elements (including the formal and theoretical issues that attend them) play a centrally important role. In the opening scene of *Ulysses*, Stephen calls Irish art "the cracked lookingglass of a servant" (*U*, 6), a phrase that is particularly appropriate to the literary genre he has the potential to engage in someday. For we may regard Joyce's and Wolfe's autobiographical fiction as such a mirror. What Stephen does not know, of course, is that the looking glass gives back, in the multiple images it reflects of its seemingly unfortunate owner, patterns of great interest and beauty.

1

I Shall Try to Fly by Those Nets

In an episode from the last chapter of *A Portrait of the Artist as a Young Man,* Stephen Dedalus wanders into the day's lectures at the university. A rather lackadaisical student, he is "late as usual" today and has also forgotten to bring paper along. But he does have quite a reputation among his fellow students as a freethinking intellectual. After the lecture, "a little ring of listeners" gathers in the hallway around a fellow student and him to hear the verbal volleys that are sure to be exchanged when Stephen is approached to sign a testimonial on some popular issue. MacCann energetically espouses the cause at hand, something vaguely concerned with "general disarmament, arbitration in cases of international disputes . . . the signs of the times . . . the new humanity and the new gospel of life" (*P*, 196), and Stephen is expected to provide an entertaining opposition.

After a brief "war of wits" about universal peace, which consists for the most part of Stephen's refusing to engage the "wooden sword" of MacCann's rhetoric, informal talk continues with several fellow students and friends as they walk outside together. Among other topics, religion and Irish nationalism are touched on briefly, but Stephen never allows himself to be engaged in any one subject for long. The others do most of the talking until Davin, whose family are peasants, admits how much it bothers him that his friend "Stevie" lives the way he does in his "private life."

At this, "a tide began to surge beneath the calm surface of Stephen's friendliness" (203). Soon he pauses, "following his own thought," then speaks: "The soul is born, he said vaguely, first in those moments I told you of. It has a slow and dark birth, more mysterious than the birth of the body. When the soul of a man is born in this country there are nets flung at it to hold it back from flight. You talk to me of nationality, language, religion. I shall try to fly by those nets" (203).

One wonders if "those moments I told you of" in this well-known passage are the same moments that so upset Davin's simple ethics. At any rate, Stephen states here one of the central credos of the vocation he has recently discovered: the artist he will try to become must be free of any soul-entangling loyalties to social institutions. Like the birds that appear throughout the novel's imagery, Stephen must fly past his immediate surroundings into a bigger world. He must ascend, as he did imaginatively as a small child in primary school when he wrote "himself, his name and where he was" in the flyleaf of one of his textbooks:

Stephen Dedalus
Class of Elements
Clongowes Wood College
Sallins
County Kildare
Ireland
Europe
The World
The Universe (15)

Both of these passages illustrate an impulse that undergirds *A Portrait* from beginning to end. As we shall see, Stephen's resolve to discard the social structure in which he finds himself has important consequences both for his artistic calling and for the work of art in which he exists. A central reason for his urge to be an artist is his need to escape the life he leads at home and in his native city. This connection between art and escape is also, to an important degree, a connection between art and refinement. Thus it is possible for Stephen to imagine that he can shed the unpleasantness of his background by taking on the persona of an artist. We shall find that he believes that artists are fundamentally superior to other people, and his notion of superiority has distinct class-related overtones. Artists are their own aristocracy.

Whether or not Stephen actually manages to join that aristocracy, or fly by the nets he intends to elude by taking off for Holyhead at the end of the novel, is a difficult question to answer, as almost all critical readers notice. The irony with which especially the last chapters are laced may make it impossible for us to be certain about the likelihood of Stephen's becoming the artist he is determined to be.[1] I shall return to the ending and its ineluctable question, not so much to answer it as to show how important it is to Joyce's autobiographical and fictional project that it hang in the air. For now let us remember two clear implications of Stephen's attempt at aviation. First, the question of Stephen's eventual success, outside the pages of the novel, is a proper one to ask. From the title onward, *A Portrait of the Artist as a Young Man* encourages us to imagine Stephen later—to ask if he will indeed be "the artist" and to wonder just what "the artist" is. Second, whether or not Stephen manages to become this artist, entanglements will exist from which he cannot or will not free himself. Stephen's story shows that he will remain an Irish-born, English-speaking, Roman Catholic–thinking artist no matter how far he flies. Furthermore, by the end of the novel he has clearly come to realize this. In typical

1. For two summaries of critical discussion of this question see Thomas F. Staley, "Strings in the Labyrinth: Sixty Years with Joyce's *Portrait*," in Thomas F. Staley and Bernard Benstock (eds.), *Approaches to Joyce's "Portrait"* (Pittsburgh, 1976), 3–24; and James J. Sosnoski, "Reading Acts and Reading Warrants: Some Implications for Readers Responding to Joyce's Portrait of Stephen," *James Joyce Quarterly*, XVI (1978–79), 43–63, esp. Sosnoski's year-by-year bibliography of the controversy (59–63). The most widely known participants are Hugh Kenner (who first called Stephen a "prig") and Wayne C. Booth (who suggested that we cannot know from internal evidence whether he is one or not). See Kenner, "The *Portrait* in Perspective," in *Dublin's Joyce* (Bloomington, Ind., 1956), 109–33; and Booth, *The Rhetoric of Fiction* (Rev. ed.; Chicago, 1983). James J. Sosnoski and Charles Rossman discuss the implications of poststructuralist theory on the ongoing debate in "The Reader's Role in *A Portrait*," in Suheil Badi Bushrui and Bernard Benstock (eds.), *James Joyce: An International Perspective* (Totowa, N.J., 1982), 19–37.

fashion, Joyce worded the comment about the nets so that it can have a double meaning: when Stephen flies by those nets he must fly *by means of* as well as *past* them.

When we recognize that Joyce means for us to ask about Stephen's future, we have run squarely into the question of how closely that future will approximate the life of Joyce himself after his university career. We are asking about the special character of *A Portrait*, a work of fiction that is openly autobiographical. And when we ask about the influence of those nets around Stephen's soul, we are asking also about the nets around Joyce's, to what extent they enmeshed him and how they influenced his artistic beliefs and practices. As Joyce worked and reworked his personal memories into this novel, a pattern emerged that would continue throughout his life and career. The truth of the matter, as *A Portrait, Ulysses*, and *Finnegans Wake* show with increasing intensity, is that the artist's soul is characterized both by what he is free of and what he is not free of. The influences and bonds he cannot overcome or break can help him as much as they hinder.

Furthermore, those nets of nationality, language, and religion are by no means the only or, in a sense, the greatest of the snares laid for Stephen's soul—or for Joyce's either. Irish nationalism, the Irish language movement, and the Catholic Church can be avoided, as Stephen nimbly does, to the extent that they are all political forces imposed upon an individual by external agents. Despite Joyce's professed interest in socialism and his lifelong fascination with the Church, neither what *Finnegans Wake* terms "idiology" (352.19) nor religion in an external sense was a genuine issue of the heart for him. He managed quite easily to avoid becoming involved in such major political events as the Irish revolution (or even World War I) and was not uncomfortable with severing his ties with Rome.

To the extent that patriotism and religion affect basic human urges such as consciousness of place and concern with metaphysical reality, however, they influenced Joyce deeply, as they do Stephen. The distinction between external forces that remain "other" and forces that answer genuine internal needs and so become an inextricable part of the psyche is important to remember. It is clear, for instance, that the nets that Stephen discusses with Davin are of both varieties. We are justified, I believe, in imagining that Stephen will fly by the external ones, as Joyce did. Issues of Irish political independence, the proper language for an Irish citizen or writer to use, and the theological consequences of living outside the ordinances of the Holy Roman church do not seem to trouble Stephen much by the end of the novel. Nor is he particularly concerned with them on a literal or political level when we meet him again in *Ulysses*.

This is not to say, incidentally, that a certain amount of anxiety does not accompany his decisions, especially his renunciation of Catholicism. As Richard M. Kain remarked in an early study of *Ulysses*, "One may question whether it is ever entirely possible to break away from the Catholic Church." Stephen reveals as much to Cranly in a discussion near the end of *A Portrait*, admitting he is still afraid that Jesus "is more like a son of God than a son of Mary" to him and that "the host too may be the body and blood of the son of God and not a wafer of bread." He also fears the elements of communion because, he says, "I imagine . . . that there is a malevolent reality behind those things I say I fear." Kain explained this passage by noting that "Joyce, like Dostoevski before him, will be acutely aware of the ambivalence of the human mind, of the drawing-power of the forces which he wishes to reject or escape."[2] Whatever the reason for Stephen's doubts about rejecting what may be metaphysical truth, however, his doubts are outweighed by his certainty that he should run from the "net" of the institution: "I fear more than that the chemical action which would be set up in my soul by a false homage to a symbol behind which are massed twenty centuries of authority and veneration" (*P*, 243).

Stephen's deeper problems—the idea of being an artist, the implications of his mother's death, and the issue of sonship and fatherhood—continue long after his famous flight at the end of *A Portrait*. And they originate in good part in a "net" that neither Joyce nor his characters were able to elude—their familial and social backgrounds. The identity of the young man as artist is intricately entwined with his position in society, a position that derives unavoidably from being a member of his family. The aesthetic vo-

2. Richard M. Kain, *Fabulous Voyager: James Joyce's "Ulysses"* (Chicago, 1947), 12–13.

cation and the family's social status are closely linked in both the structure and style of *A Portrait*. Under the pressure of his family's hopeless social and economic decline, Stephen will embrace a conception of art as a new kind of aristocracy, to which the true artist belongs and which allows him safely to separate his identity from that of his family, his class, and his race. The autobiographical nature of the novel, with the manipulations of narrative distance that result from that choice, extends Stephen's concerns into the technical arena of the writing of fiction. In Joyce's style, too, we can see the effects of a link between social class and the kind of art he committed himself to creating.

Although several critics have noticed a relationship between social status and the vocation of art in Joyce's work, to my knowledge no one has yet examined it in detail.[3] But looking closely at *A Portrait* with this relationship in mind will demonstrate how Joyce organized his novel to emphasize its importance to Stephen's conception of art, and how it is central to Joyce's, especially to *A Portrait* as autobiographical fiction.

From the first pages of *A Portrait,* we begin to see this relationship developing. In the remarkable opening section we hear about important events in a little boy's life, told in a child's language—a story his father tells him about a moocow, a song the child learns to sing in his own way, the sensation of wetting the bed, the hornpipe his mother plays on the piano for him to dance to, and so on. In two pages we have been introduced to most of the profound influences on this child's life and to an incipient talent that is probably innate—the fascination with words, sounds, and images.[4] The

3. The earliest mention of this relationship that I have found is Harry Levin's observation of the link between social status and artistic vocation in *A Portrait* and *Sons and Lovers*. See Levin, *James Joyce: A Critical Introduction* (2d ed.; London, 1960), 48. See also James T. Farrell, "Joyce's *Portrait of the Artist,* with a Postscript on *Stephen Hero,*" in Seon Givens (ed.), *James Joyce: Two Decades of Criticism* (2d ed.; New York, 1963), 175–97; and Hélène Cixous, *The Exile of James Joyce*, trans. Sally A. J. Purcell (London, 1976), xii, 4, 396. Several studies of the social and political content of Joyce's works touch on this idea: see Colin McCabe, *James Joyce and the Revolution of the Word* (London, 1979); Dominic Manganiello, *Joyce's Politics* (London, 1980); and Cheryl Herr, *Joyce's Anatomy of Culture* (Urbana, 1986).

4. See Kenner, "The *Portrait* in Perspective"; and Dorothy Van Ghent, "On *A Portrait of the Artist as a Young Man,*" in Thomas E. Connolly (ed.), *Joyce's Portrait: Criticism and Critiques* (New York, 1962), 60–74.

issue of social class first appears immediately after the lyric opening. In the first scene that takes place outside the Dedaluses' home, on the playground at Clongowes Wood College, Stephen learns something about social distinctions at an early age from another boy whose social status—though not his character—is on a higher rung of the ladder than Stephen's. Nasty Roche, "a stink," finds a way to make the new boy uncomfortable by asking about his odd name. Then he finds another point of offense.

> —What is your name?
> Stephen had answered:
> —Stephen Dedalus.
> Then Nasty Roche had said:
> —What kind of a name is that?
> And when Stephen had not been able to answer Nasty Roche had asked:
> —What is your father?
> Stephen had answered:
> —A gentleman.
> Then Nasty Roche had asked:
> —Is he a magistrate? (8–9)

Nasty, of course, asks about magistrates because his father is one. We learn with Stephen a page or two later about certain desirable aspects of social position: he drinks weak tea, but Nasty and another boy drink "cocoa that their people sent them in tins. They said they could not drink the tea; that it was hogwash. Their fathers were magistrates, the fellows said" (13). Stephen also learns to apply the knowledge he has gained in school to his family life. At the Christmas holiday when he sees his parents again, he wonders immediately what his father's status is relative to a magistrate's (20). Already the question has hit home.

The one political figure in whom Stephen shows a recurring and deep interest is Charles Stewart Parnell, the "Uncrowned King of Ireland," whose political career was ruined over a longstanding love affair with a married woman who, to make matters worse, was English. Parnell's spectacular fall ended hopes for Home Rule and seemed to Joyce and many of his contemporaries to throw Ireland into self-pitying hopelessness for twenty years or more after Parnell's death in 1891. The hypocritical mourning for Parnell by the people who "hounded him into his grave" (*P*, 34) and the enervated mood that seemed to settle over Dublin and the rest of the country during the period contribute significantly to the moral paralysis of Joyce's *Dubliners* (most clearly in the story "Ivy Day in the Committee Room").[5] Throughout his life, in fact, Joyce was attracted to (and to some extent identified himself with) the figure of Parnell as a type of the undeserving victim betrayed by his friends.[6]

But Parnell is also important to Stephen in *A Portrait* because he is connected in the boy's mind with the issue of social standing from early in his development. The motifs of betrayal by friends or close associates and of Irish political self-destruction resonate along with Stephen's incipient recognition of his family's class standing. The dead hero comes to represent the failure of the family's political fortunes as well as the country's, and thus Parnell's fall symbolically damages the family's claim to respectability along with family unity. In other words, politics encroach upon the boy's sense of status and so intrude into his sense of self-worth.

While the boy is lying sick in the infirmary at Clongowes, he remembers his father telling him that political involvement put the Dedaluses on a level with those ubiquitous magistrates. It was because of Daniel O'Connell, "the Liberator" who stood for Irish radicalism during the first half of the nineteenth century, that Stephen deserves to be at the school with the others: "He thought of his own father, of how he sang songs while his mother played and of how he always gave him a shilling when he asked for sixpence and he felt sorry for him that he was not a magistrate like the other boys' fathers. Then why was he sent to that place with them? But his father had told him that he would be no stranger there because his granduncle had presented an address to the liberator there fifty years before" (26).

As he begins to pity his father and wonder about the old days, young Stephen falls asleep and dreams about the dead Parnell. Al-

5. See Herbert Howarth, *The Irish Writers, 1880–1940: Literature Under Parnell's Star* (London, 1958), for an early but useful consideration of the influence of Parnell, the myths surrounding his fall, and the effects of his loss on the imaginative lives of Joyce and five other Irish writers.

6. RE, 293, 338. See also Stanislaus Joyce, *My Brother's Keeper: James Joyce's Early Years*, ed. Richard Ellmann (New York, 1958), 168.

ready the shift of loyalty from father to father figure is under way. The stage is being set for the terrible revelation of his father's helpless loyalty at the end of the scene at Christmas dinner, as the argument over Parnell between Simon Dedalus, the family friend John Casey, and Stephen's aunt Dante Riordan ends with Mr. Casey's cry of "Poor Parnell! . . . My dead king!" Stephen is "terror-stricken" to see "that his father's eyes are full of tears" (39): his father is defeated and his family is torn apart by the politics that were, pathetically, supposed to give Stephen a place with the sons of magistrates.

As the boy grows, he begins to learn how to manipulate his surroundings to avoid painful situations like the one with Nasty Roche, and at the same time he comes to realize the precariousness of his family's social standing. In Chapter 2, his talent for making things up and his need to escape from money-related troubles converge, and for the first time Stephen feels not only inclined but also impelled to create. This important moment for his aesthetic vocation arrives without his knowledge: after he begins to realize the implications of the Dedaluses' economic decline, he retreats almost instinctively into an imagined world.

The Count of Monte Cristo, his uncle Charles, and a summer in Blackrock provide the idyllic holiday Stephen is enjoying at the beginning of the chapter. In fact, this year Stephen will attain every schoolboy's dream—a summer vacation that does not end in the fall. At first this is good news: "The coming of September did not trouble him this year for he was not to be sent back to Clongowes" (63). The new and pleasant feelings of anticipation about the future that he has been having, however, gradually begin to fade. Earlier in the summer he thought that "the hour when he too would take part in the life of [the real] world seemed drawing near and in secret he began to make ready for the great part which he felt awaited him the nature of which he only dimly apprehended" (62). But in September any pleasant "vision of the future" is dissipated:

> In a vague way he understood that his father was in trouble and that this was the reason why he himself had not been sent back to Clongowes. For some time he had felt the slight changes in his house; and these changes in what he had deemed unchangeable were so many slight shocks to his

boyish conception of the world. The ambition which he felt astir at times in the darkness of his soul sought no outlet. A dusk like that of the outer world obscured his mind as he heard the mare's hoofs clattering along the tramtrack on the Rock Road and the great can swaying and rattling behind him. (64)

His awareness of some kind of economic trouble immediately precedes the short sentence describing the new, vague "ambition," which is immediately overwhelmed by the clatter of the milkman's car. The "dusk" that "obscured his mind" and the milkman's way of life are joined by more than sentence structure. It is no accident that an occupation that recalls Irish peasantry has a serious effect on Stephen's nascent artistic calling.

Stephen has had conflicting emotional reactions to the occupation of the milkman with whom he has been making the evening rounds. At times the job seems "a pleasant life enough," simple and rustic. But direct contact with an actual cowyard, "with its foul green puddles and clots of liquid dung and steaming brantroughs," provokes an unusually strong response. It "sickened Stephen's heart" so violently that "the cattle which had seemed so beautiful in the country on sunny days revolted him and he could not even look at the milk they yielded" (63). When he is upset by his intuition about his family's fortunes, the sound of peasant life, with all the emotions it evokes, enters his perception. It will do so again, with the same conflict of positive and negative resonances, later in *A Portrait* and also in *Ulysses*. Stephen will often be torn between romantic idealization of Irish peasantry and hypersensitive revulsion at the ugliness of the life of the lower classes. In *Ulysses* a milkwoman symbolizes Ireland itself for him, but the older Stephen cannot regard her with equanimity any more than the boy can befriend the milkman in *A Portrait*. He is incapable of such an emotional attachment. Even in its inchoate form, the ambition that he is just beginning to recognize requires his segregation from common humanity.

So his mind moves in another direction. Instantly "he returned to Mercedes and, as he brooded upon her image, a strange unrest crept into his blood" (64). This "strange unrest" (his awakening sexuality) that will later play an important part in impelling him into the role of the artist immediately follows the moment of first genuine perception of his family's financial troubles. He has seen lower-class life, and he has foreseen it for his own family. And despite his mixed feelings about rural Ireland, "the same foreknowledge which had sickened his heart and made his legs sag suddenly as he raced around the park" has brought darkness, then another vision to replace the first "boyish conception." He feels, "even more keenly than he had felt at Clongowes, that he was different from the others" (64–65). The difference is his vision of Mercedes, an "unsubstantial image" from the world of a novel. He will meet her, suddenly and unexpectedly. When he does, "he would fade into something impalpable under her eyes and then in a moment, he would be transfigured. Weakness and timidity and inexperience would fall from him in that magic moment" (65). Stephen has found a place of refuge, a place where he can be all that he dreams of being, in the world where Mercedes lives. Adolescent sexuality and the magic of art supply him, for the time being, with a new, "transfigured" life.

The flowery rhetoric of his imaginary relationship with Mercedes is soon crushed. The first of a series of moving vans appears at the Dedaluses' Blackrock house, and movers haul furniture "out through the front garden which was strewn with wisps of straw and rope ends and into the huge vans at the gate" (65). It is not the beautiful heroine but Stephen's "redeyed mother" beside whom he sits during the move into Dublin city. Nor can he visualize Mercedes in his new environment: his creative imagination is not strong enough to keep the world out when it intrudes with the vigor of the city. He wanders up and down in "the new and complex sensation," while "the vastness and strangeness of the life suggested to him by the bales of merchandise stocked along the walls or swung aloft out of the holds of steamers wakened again in him the unrest which had sent him wandering in the evening from garden to garden in search of Mercedes." But even under the pressure of an imagination as vivid as Stephen's, Dublin refuses to be sunny, clean Marseilles. So "a vague dissatisfaction grew up within him as he looked on the quays and on the river and on the lowering skies and yet he continued to wander up and down day after day as if he really sought someone that eluded him" (66).

He resolves, in an important passage, to cultivate the imaginative strength he needs—to learn the skill of distancing himself from ugly reality.

> He went once or twice with his mother to visit their relatives: and, though they passed a jovial array of shops lit up and adorned for Christmas, his mood of embittered silence did not leave him. The causes of his embitterment were many, remote and near. He was angry with himself for being young and the prey of restless foolish impulses, angry also with the change of fortune which was reshaping the world about him into a vision of squalor and insincerity. Yet his anger lent nothing to the vision. He chronicled with patience what he saw, detaching himself from it and testing its mortifying flavour in secret. (67)

He will attempt to ease his pain by detachment and to chronicle what is happening. We should remember that this decision, which is of tremendous significance to Stephen's development as an artist, also comes as a direct reaction to the pain he feels because of his family's troubles. For the first time, Stephen's action is deliberate: he has *chosen* to remove himself from his surroundings, and he knows clearly just what he is escaping. The "intuition" and "foreknowledge" of last summer have become—in dear, dirty Dublin—the recognition of plain, present fact.

The pain from which Stephen is fleeing, the "vision of squalor and insincerity," is composed not only of material or social discomforts, the unsettling "thought of the bare cheerless house in which they were now to live" and the perception of "why the servants had often whispered together in the hall" (66), but also of other evils as well. Chief among these, perhaps, is the loss of a home, a stable place where he feels secure.

Later in the novel, and in *Ulysses*, Stephen conceives of an artist who not only belongs to a "true" aristocracy but also has a permanent place in a homeland of art—who can thus, among other things, leave Ireland without qualms. For a true artist, not only are there no ever-shifting social positions and no pretensions to stations beyond one's means, but there is also no interminable series of moving vans. One is always at home, no matter what the country or town or flat. Moving physically is of no consequence. In fact, although Stephen does not travel much in *A Portrait*, it makes sense to suppose that he might in the future. A true artist might even be encouraged to move often, to prove that he truly resides in another realm. Such was the habit of James and Nora Joyce, of course, who moved with amazing frequency (well over 150 times) through nearly ten European countries after they left Ireland in 1904.[7]

Similarly, one of the hallmarks of this kind of aristocrat might be a disregard for the usual signs of class distinction such as proper dress, personal hygiene, and good manners. An unkempt appearance or unconventional behavior might be supposed to prove that this nobility is not of the ordinary kind. Stephen does come to have a decided antipathy toward cleanliness. The first scene after the famous epiphany of the wading girl, which marks the beginning of his artistic vocation, features Mrs. Dedalus scrubbing his head and neck and complaining that "it's a poor case . . . when a university student is so dirty that his mother has to wash him" (175).

The conception of a homeland of art is a key point at which Stephen's idea of the artist differs from a typical nineteenth-century Romantic hero, who is usually homeless. Although Joyce admired Byron and to some extent patterned Stephen after the proud, isolated character of a Childe Harold or a Manfred, he had in mind a more positive role for his protagonist. The romantic hero to which Harry Levin's early and influential study compared Stephen, who stands "like Thomas Mann's outsiders, pressing their noses against the window panes of a bourgeois society from which they feel excluded," is misleading.[8] Stephen does not merely regard himself as an outsider in bourgeois society: he is entering another kind of society. Ellmann makes this distinction, remarking that despite Joyce's regard for Byron, Parnell, and others who gave up everything for a cause, "Stephen's esthetic notions are not renunciant; he becomes an artist because art opens to him 'the fair courts of life' " (RE, 148). Joyce was apparently taken with this phrase from the ecstatic vision of the wading girl, which appears at the end of Chapter 4 of *A Portrait*: he kept it through all the revisions of this scene from his earliest experiment with autobiographical fiction, the narrative essay he wrote in 1904 entitled "A Portrait of the

7. See "James Joyce's Addresses," *LJJ*, II, lv–lxxii.
8. Levin, *James Joyce*, 49.

Artist." We should note, however, that the courts of life are fair only because they are opened from "some new world" (*P*, 172), the world of art. Stephen will try to find life as an artist by escaping the drab life around him and returning to it from the vantage point of a new position, a new home.

After the move to Dublin, Stephen's attitude toward his family is increasingly colored by social and economic as well as personal and familial elements. His mixed feelings toward his improvident father come in large part from the fact that Mr. Dedalus will not support his wife and children. On a trip to Cork city to sell family property in order to pay some of his debts, Simon Dedalus brags incessantly about his gentlemanly background and his youthful exploits. The whole trip is excruciatingly painful to Stephen because he lives in the squalid present and is all too aware of the shameful distance between his father's prosperous past and the current state of affairs. Stephen listens "without sympathy" to Mr. Dedalus' nostalgic talk: he "knew, however, that his father's property was going to be sold by auction and in the manner of his own dispossession he felt the world give the lie rudely to his phantasy" (87). (Interestingly, the ambiguity in pronoun referents in this passage represents on a syntactical level Stephen's confusion about just whose troubles these fundamentally are. The "dispossession" and "phantasy" could be either father's or son's—and are both in Stephen's mind.)

Complicating the emotional turmoil of the trip to Cork is Stephen's shame at his own sexual fantasies, the "recent monstrous reveries" that he cannot control. Finding that the young gentlemen at the Queen's College, where his father had gone to school, hide dirty minds under their well-bred exteriors is the final ironic blow of the journey. The young aristocrats, the "fine decent fellows" with whom his father wants him to associate, are not what they should be, after all. Seeing the word *Foetus* carved into "the dark stained wood" of a desk in the anatomy lecture hall and dwelling in his imagination on the well-groomed students writing it "shocked him" so much that "the spittle in his throat grew bitter and foul to swallow and the faint sickness climbed to his brain so that for a moment he closed his eyes and walked on in darkness" (91).

His strong reaction to the imagined scene shows him torn between conflicting emotions about the upper class to which the "fine decent fellows" belong. On the one hand, they represent all that his father once was, all that Stephen would like to have been but now will never be because of the Dedaluses' economic ruin. But they carelessly indulge in "what he had deemed till then a brutish and individual malady of his own mind" (90) and so cannot be worthy of his respect or emulation. His own position at his new school in Dublin, Belvedere College, is "equivocal," he thinks, defending himself against his own mixed feelings. He belongs to no class but is "a free boy, a leader afraid of his own authority, proud and sensitive and suspicious, battling against the squalor of his life and against the riot of his mind" (90–92). He is battling against his own lost chance to be "fine and decent," to have both sexual purity and social respectability.

In the scene following, Stephen realizes that he cannot win the battle against either "the squalor of his life" or "the riot of his mind" by changing his physical surroundings. Mr. Dedalus and he have gone to the bank to cash the thirty-three-pound exhibition and essay prize he has won. Afterward, his father stands in the front hall reminiscing about Irish heroes. Stephen meanwhile "looked at his thinly clad mother and remembered that a few days before he had seen a mantle priced at twenty guineas in the windows of Barnardo's" (97). He spends his prize money lavishly, trying to use it to establish for himself and his family an ordered and beautiful life. Soon, though, "the season of pleasure came to an end." He runs out of the pink enamel with which he has been repainting, and "the wainscot of his bedroom remained with its unfinished and illplastered coat." His elaborate schemes to superimpose "the rules of life which he had drawn about himself" over the disarray of daily existence also "fell into desuetude" (98). So in retaliation for the way that money betrayed its promise to provide beauty and civilized order, he yields to "his secret riots," which represent for him all that is ugly, brutal, and shameful. He wanders down into "another world," the world of illicit sex. Again connecting sex with the question of social status, he runs from his family's poverty in "iniquitous abandonment" to the brothels in "the quarter of the jews" (100).

After the money has gone, he realizes that the things money can provide could never have brought him the kind of life he needs:

"How foolish his aim had been! He had tried to build a breakwater of order and elegance against the sordid tide of life without him and to dam up, by rules of conduct and active interests and new filial relations, the powerful recurrence of the tides within him. Useless" (98).

Stephen's debaucheries begin to teach him a lesson that will be of great importance to the vocation of art he will eventually embrace. For the first time he is able to divide his life into two coexisting but separate worlds, making secret nightly forays to the brothels and participating simultaneously in the daytime routine of family and school. Since these worlds are completely incompatible, he lives at some distance from them both and is filled with "a certain pride" at his ability to do so (104). He lives in "a cold indifferent knowledge of himself" (103), able to objectify the whores, so that his senses "note keenly all that wounded or shamed them; his eyes, a ring of porter froth on a clothless table or a photograph of two soldiers standing to attention or a gaudy playbill; his ears, the drawling jargon of greeting" (102). Likewise, he indulges in "contempt of his fellows" at school and "the evil of hypocrisy" in church, since he is no longer an innocent companion or communicant (104). An actual descent into what he believes is mortal sin has given him the ability to distance himself from his surroundings as his fantasies of Mercedes could not. Sin by definition is separation, and Stephen welcomes it.

We can see why his alienation does not extend to the Blessed Virgin Mary, why "his sin . . . had led him nearer to the refuge of sinners" (105). The Queen of Heaven, like Mercedes and the birdlike wading girl, represents in her femininity the power of deliverance from Stephen's patrimony of squalor. Once again the boy confuses the sexual attraction of a pure and beautiful woman with escape from his unlovely environment. Ironically, the whores he visits nightly also deliver him in their own way from his daily life, and his mind includes them also in the association: "If ever his soul . . . was turned towards her whose emblem is the morning star . . . it was when her names were murmured softly by lips whereon there still lingered foul and shameful words, the savour itself of a lewd kiss" (105).

Stephen does not understand why he feels this way toward

Mary. It "was strange" to him: "He tried to think how it could be but the dusk, deepening in the schoolroom, covered over his thoughts" (105). To us it is less strange. Mary is a woman; more than that, she is a queen. Stephen's reverence for her also allows him imaginatively to escape his embarrassing social identity and to join her noble realm. He is drawn to this aspect of Mariology, finding respite from "his barren pride" in "the glories of Mary . . . spikenard and myrrh and frankincense, symbolising the preciousness of God's gifts to her soul, rich garments, symbolising her royal lineage, her emblems, the lateflowering plant and lateblossoming tree, symbolising the agelong gradual growth of her cultus among men" (104). It is also appropriate for Stephen that Mary's worth was unrecognized during her lifetime. She was not betrayed by her subjects as was Parnell (and her Son), but she was "lateflowering," a queen in secret who was treated royally only years after her time on earth.

Stephen becomes increasingly ashamed of his surroundings and continues to try to separate himself from them as his adolescence proceeds. The duplicity of his secret life of sin is a heavy burden for a sixteen-year-old to bear, so he is a perfect candidate for an emotional conversion, sparked by the fiery rhetoric of the sermons of a three-day retreat at Belvedere. "God's turn had come," as he recognizes. After the conversion his heartrending repentance seems for a while to purge the world of its ugliness and disarray. He goes to confession at an unfamiliar chapel, and then he walks home and sits "by the fire in the kitchen, not daring to speak for happiness." Everything is what it ought to be, he thinks: "Till that moment he had not known how beautiful and peaceful life could be. The green square of paper pinned round the lamp cast down a tender shade. On the dresser was a plate of sausages and white pudding and on the shelf there were eggs. They would be for the breakfast in the morning after the communion in the college chapel. White pudding and eggs and sausages and cups of tea. How simple and beautiful was life after all! And life lay all before him." (146). We can see the continued appeal of order and beauty.

Certainly religion lures Stephen by its promise of escape from mundane (and thus painful and coarse) daily life. In a state of spiritual exaltation he can feel that "the world for all its solid substance and complexity no longer existed for his soul save as a theorem of divine power and love and universality" (150). His "proud musings" on the possibility of becoming a priest include "accomplishing the vague acts of the priesthood which pleased him by reason of their semblance of reality and of their distance from it" (158). In the ordered beauty of its rituals and symbolism, the Church offers an alternative to the Dedaluses' chaotic, barren home life, and it is with this aspect of religion that Stephen is primarily entranced. The language in which he meditates on spiritual truth is filled with references to theorems, numbers, and symmetry on the one hand, and imagery and symbols on the other.

But even when he is most fervently caught up in religious devotion he is something of a snob. "To merge his life in the common tide of other lives," he has to admit, "was harder for him than any fasting or prayer." Once again it is social discomfort that impels him toward his final vocation by causing "in his soul at last a sensation of spiritual dryness together with a growth of doubts and scruples" (151–52). He has imagined himself a priest but one who holds a minor office so that he could "stand aloof from the altar, forgotten by the people" (158). And he finally realizes that he can never join an order, because of his need to be separate from and superior to any group: "He saw himself sitting at dinner with the community of a college. What, then, had become of that deep-rooted shyness of his which had made him loth to eat or drink under a strange roof? What had come of the pride of his spirit which had always made him conceive himself as a being apart in every order?" (161). The pride is still there, of course. Time passes and he becomes a very complex adolescent, and his frustrated desire for class status is less obvious as he tries to satisfy it in increasingly subtle or indirect ways. But as he searches for a way of life that will fill his soul's requirements, we can still see traces of the little boy who suffered a nameless pain because his father was not a magistrate.

Religion is also directly linked with social status. From the Middle Ages onward the Church has represented for boys of talent an opportunity not only for escape but also for social advancement. Neither Stephen nor his father is immune to this allure, especially as it is embodied by the Jesuits. Since its founding in the sixteenth century, the Society of Jesus has been known for political and social sophistication as well as scholastic excellence. Not only is joining the order itself an attractive possibility, but knowing the Jesuits as influential friends in the lay community is also useful. "There's no mistake about it," one of the characters in "Grace," a story in *Dubliners*, puts it. "If you want a thing well done and no flies about it you go to a Jesuit. They're the boyos have influence. . . . The Jesuits cater for the upper classes."[9] Earlier in *A Portrait*, when Mr. Dedalus could no longer afford to send his son to Clongowes, the idea of entering Stephen in a school run by Christian Brothers had to be entertained. The Christian Brothers, an Irish lay order of Catholic teachers founded in 1804, had schools all over Ireland by the end of the nineteenth century, but both Mr. Dedalus and his wife considered that class of religious education beneath them. When an offer of free tuition at Belvedere arrived, enabling them to afford their pretentiousness, they wasted no time deciding to keep Stephen in the Jesuits' care:

> —I never liked the idea of sending him to the christian brothers myself, said Mrs Dedalus.
>
> —Christian brothers be damned! said Mr Dedalus. Is it with Paddy Stink and Mickey Mud? No, let him stick to the jesuits in God's name since he began with them. They'll be of service to him in after years. Those are the fellows that can get you a position. (71)

Stephen's vision of himself as "a young and silentmannered priest" has at least a touch of this snobbery in it. But he ends in pride and isolation, determined to find a vocation and a fraternity more out of reach of the common herd than one in which "The Reverend Stephen Dedalus, S.J." could become "a mental spectre of the face of one of the jesuits whom some of the boys called Lantern Jaws and others Foxy Campbell" (161).

Almost without realizing it, Stephen moves away from a religious life. The Church seems no longer to offer salvation; now he perceives that joining an order had "threatened to end for ever, in time and in eternity, his freedom" (161–62). It would deliver

9. James Joyce, *"Dubliners": Text, Criticism, and Notes*, ed. Robert Scholes and A. Walton Litz (New York, 1969), 163–64.

him from one kind of society only to immerse him in another, and Stephen now knows that not even Jesuits are noble enough to be unassailable. His sense of shame is so strong that he needs to find a way to separate himself absolutely from the possibility of being scorned. His identity must not rest in any place where it might be possible for someone to look down on him in condescension or ridicule.

Thus he decides that "he was destined to learn his own wisdom apart from others or to learn the wisdom of others himself wandering among the snares of the world." This means, since "the snares of the world were its ways of sin," that "he would fall" back into the confusion and squalor that surrounded him before his conversion (162). But there will be a difference this time. He will develop the notion of living two separate lives, which caused him such conflict during his first fall from grace, into a more satisfactory principle. Now he will live in the world of sin not secretly or shamefully, but precisely because living there is a prerequisite for achieving the superior life he has inwardly chosen. The two realms will not be mutually exclusive even though they are inalterably distinct.[10]

Furthermore, since Stephen will not be merely a resident in one sphere or the other, he can avoid the vulnerability of simple loyalty to either. He can escape the world but still live there—in fact, he can successfully escape it into independent wisdom only because he does live in it and teaches himself its lessons. He begins to formulate for himself a noble calling that also has the virtue of appeasing his own insistent subconscious demand for status.

In the last scenes of Chapter 4 and in Chapter 5 of *A Portrait*, we watch Stephen evolve this principle and try to apply it. In essence, he has discovered irony—how to see from two perspectives simultaneously, to be safe from the embarrassment to which any single angle of vision might expose him. It is not exactly the wisdom that he claims to seek, but Stephen is not the first adolescent to be fooled into thinking that ironic distance gives superiority. He

10. See the discussion of "the divided self" in *Künstlerromane* in Maurice Beebe's study *Ivory Towers and Sacred Founts: The Artist as Hero in Fiction from Goethe to Joyce* (New York, 1964), esp. 21–64.

begins to try to conquer his unsatisfactory environment by achieving an emotional separation, to achieve the doubleness of vision that is his only truly effective shield. Thus in deciding that "his destiny was to be elusive of social or religious orders" (162), he repudiates the Church's equivalent of an aristocratic class and resolves to embrace in triumphant ironic transcendence the vulgarity of the life that envelops his family. Walking home, he is confident of his ability: "The faint sour stink of rotted cabbages came towards him from the kitchengardens on the rising ground above the river. He smiled to think that it was this disorder, the misrule and confusion of his father's house and the stagnation of vegetable life, which was to win the day in his soul. Then a short laugh broke from his lips" (162).

When he arrives, he gets his first chance to embrace in the abstract something that causes immediate pain to those close to him. The Dedalus kitchen, where "tea was nearly over and only the last of the second watered tea remained in the bottoms of the small glassjars and jampots which did service for teacups," provokes "a sudden instinct of remorse in Stephen's heart. All that had been denied them had been freely given to him, the eldest: but the quiet glow of evening showed him in their faces no sign of rancour." News of another move, necessary "becauseboro theboro landboro lordboro willboro putboro usboro outboro," as a young sister tells him, revives a painful memory of a classmate at Belvedere laughing about how often the Dedaluses changed addresses. But soon he generalizes and abstracts his "pain of spirit," retreating several removes from his siblings into a quotation from Virgil, through Newman, about *"children in every time"* (163–64).

He continues to try to transcend poverty and ugliness into abstract thought or art, then to reenter the hated world shielded by his new aristocratic identity. The long walk he takes at the end of Chapter 4, which climaxes in the vision of the wading girl, takes him through several such moments of distancing and reentry. He has gone walking to release some nervous energy, to be doing something besides waiting for his father and his tutor to finish negotiating "something about the university" (perhaps how Stephen's tuition is to be financed). His mind turns to his mother and her hostility to his going to the university, then jumps from the "dim antagonism" that that subject inspires in him to thoughts of the university and how "the end he had been born to serve yet did not see had led him to escape by an unknown path." He hears "notes of fitful music," then the rhythm of pattering feet. These fade into a quotation from Newman: *"whose feet are as the feet of harts and underneath the everlasting arms"* (164–65).

He can then return to musing about his immediate situation, why he has refused the vocation of priest. His senses again register the material world around him, the Clontarf Road and the "thin wooden bridge" he crosses to get to "the Bull" (North Bull Island)—and "a squad of christian brothers" coming back from the Bull. The Christian Brothers immediately evoke the old shame at their lack of gentility, and Stephen is angry at himself for being unable to overcome his class consciousness. "The uncouth faces passed him two by two, stained yellow or red or livid by the sea, and as he strove to look at them with ease and indifference, a faint stain of personal shame and commiseration rose to his own face." He cannot help himself, he thinks, from being insufferably pompous toward them. So

> he drew forth a phrase from his treasure and spoke it softly to himself:
> —A day of dappled seaborne clouds.

Then, immersed in reverie on the beauty and power of words, he can leave the poor Brothers, and his own discomfort, behind. After he is safely removed, his mind returns to the "firm land" of the island and takes in the myriad details of external reality (165–66).

The scene of the walk to the Bull is an example of Stephen's newfound method of escape and victory over his environment. His rapturous epiphany leaps out from an anxious day, on which he will find out whether or not he will be able to attend the university, and it gives him the strength to become the proud, self-sufficient student that he is in the last chapter of the novel. His mother, in the first scene of Chapter 5, thinks that it is the university that has "changed" him, but Stephen, enigmatically "smiling and kissing the tips of his fingers in adieu," knows differently (175).

By now he believes that his salvation will come through art, and his definition of art is clearly one in which the artist becomes a new kind of aristocrat. In his formulation of how art will satisfy his needs, we can hear how powerfully his conviction of its transcendent nature works on his imagination. "His thinking was a dusk of doubt and selfmistrust," but it is "lit up at moments by the lightnings of intuition." These lightnings are "of so clear a splendour that in those moments the world perished about his feet as if it had been fireconsumed," for "he felt that the spirit of beauty had folded him round like a mantle and that in revery at least he had been acquainted with nobility. But, when this brief pride of silence upheld him no longer, he was glad to find himself still in the midst of common lives, passing on his way amid the squalor and noise and sloth of the city fearlessly and with a light heart" (177).

The "light heart" is possible for him because he has been "acquainted with nobility." For all his professed gladness over being in squalor and noise and sloth, the reverie and the yearning for nobility move him more strongly than the gladness we are assured he possesses when he is surrounded by lower-class life. He is much more vitally interested in escape than in rejoining the "common lives" around him. MacCann, like Stephen's other friends at the university, perceives something of this: "Dedalus, you're an antisocial being, wrapped up in yourself. I'm not. I'm a democrat: and I'll work and act for social liberty and equality among all classes and sexes in the United States of the Europe of the future" (177).

Stephen is not, of course, "a democrat" in MacCann's sense. He does want a kind of intimacy with common people and a squalid world, but this desire is rooted in a need to be securely above them. As an artist he wants to "recreate life out of life" (172), and this recreation will involve close observation of and sympathetic engagement with the actual grimy world. It will also require emotional detachment, since accurate vision depends on distance. And the distance is in part the separation of upper class from lower class: aesthetic judgment is intimately connected not only with sympathy and objectivity but also with refinement, of sensibility if not of physical surroundings. Democracy and socialism, like Christianity (the Jesuit elite notwithstanding), tend to oppose this kind of judgment. Stephen knows that he cannot avoid it, and his inability to do so is both a result and a contributory cause of his artistic temperament.

The vocation of art, then, in good *fin de siècle* fashion, is the vocation for Stephen Dedalus. The images that he uses to articulate his intentions in the final pages of the novel often reflect how rarefied he considers his calling. The highest art is "life purified in and reprojected from the human imagination" (215). The artist "remains within or behind or beyond or above his handiwork, invisible, refined out of existence" (215). Stephen as artist will be "a priest of eternal imagination, transmuting the daily bread of experience into the radiant body of everliving life" (221). He confesses to Cranly that "I do not fear to be alone . . . or to leave whatever I have to leave" (247), since, having found his true artistic communion and homeland, he is now free to be physically alone and in exile. And he tells Davin that "the shortest way to Tara was *via* Holyhead" (250). He is determined to find Ireland by leaving it, just as he has decided that he can "encounter . . . the reality of experience" by first extricating himself from it (253).

After we see Stephen off at the end of the novel and read the two places and dates appended to the text proper (Dublin 1904/Trieste 1914), we face the novel's troublesome ending. In fact, the more carefully we read, the more unsettled, even unsettling, its ending is likely to appear. I shall not add to the many scholarly bets on Stephen's chances for success in his chosen vocation, but I will suggest that ambiguity on this point shows how prominently issues associated with autobiographical fiction figure in the novel. The ending troubles us because it demands that we extend the book's implications out of the text to what we imagine of the writer's life. At least it was meant to: Joyce prepared long and carefully, through several drafts of his hero's story, to ensure that we wonder about Stephen's future.

It is of course possible for us to argue by means of several lines of reasoning that this kind of question is unanswerable or should not be asked—that a fictional character who only exists within the pages of a novel can have no "future," that we cannot know whether Joyce himself had decided that Stephen would become a successful artist, that it is improper to include evidence from Joyce's biography or *Ulysses* into a discussion of *A Portrait*, and so on.

But in novels about the growth of a young man or woman, especially in novels that are obviously drawn from the "real life" of a writer, it is perfectly appropriate—in fact, expected—for readers to wonder about what kind of person the young protagonist is becoming (or has become). Rather than avoiding the question, we should ask why our efforts to answer it are frustrated in *A Portrait*. We ought to see that, by writing a novel that raises this question insistently and then toys with readers' expectations of how to find a conclusive answer, Joyce was playing with the generic form of the apprenticeship novel and, in particular, of the novel in which the protagonist is obviously a younger version of the author. In fact, as I shall show, Joyce had worried with the conventions of this form from the outset of his experiments with the story of his young man. By the time he finished *A Portrait*, he was making novelistic use of inherent stresses caused by the necessarily unfixed rhetorical distance between the teller and the tale. These stresses make inevitable certain inconsistencies in the narrating voice, and Joyce continued to experiment with this issue in later works. At the same time, however, he had settled on autobiographical art as the mode that could yield the greatest returns for his life's investment in literary art.

Basically, the question of whether Stephen's resolution to become an artist is realistic reflects tension between generic expectations and narrative style. On the one hand, *A Portrait* clearly announces itself to be autobiographical and is generically similar to the many *Bildungsromane* written in the several generations before its publication. Thus it should be reasonable to suppose that Stephen will become an artist, since his creator might be presumed to be one, and that as other novels of development tend to end with the protagonist's successful entry into maturity and self-knowledge, this one does, too. On the other hand, the narrative of *A Portrait* is decidedly ambiguous in tone, so that the authorial attitude is difficult if not impossible to ascertain. The way the story is told can seem to show us that Stephen is a hopeless aesthete whose posing and hypersensitivity will never yield real artistic productivity. But the same story—even, in some cases, the same passages—can also be read as evidence of a strong potential that will later reach fulfillment.[11]

The tension between the expected progression of the story and the style is not easily resolvable. Nor is it unique to *A Portrait.* In fact, some trouble of this kind is inherent in autobiographical fiction. We know that an autobiographical novel involves a more complex problem with the distance at which the narrator stands from his or her story than other types of fiction, because of the intimate relationship between the writer and the autobiographical protagonist. The narrator can easily seem too openly partisan, too anxious to prove to the reader that the protagonist is capable of one day producing a work that is worthy of reading (like the one being read, presumably). This narrating voice, whom we normally, unless otherwise informed, assume to be the voice of the writer, must be telling a story that is convincing on its own if we are to believe what the voice tells us about the central character. The narrating voice must stand at a sufficient distance from the protagonist to persuade us of its authorial control of the story. Yet the writer of such a novel chooses to exploit the autobiographical relationship between the main character and him- or herself. The novel's plot depends for its forward motion upon the character's growing toward the author's maturity as an artist and a human being. Events are arranged according to the role they play in carrying the protagonist toward what we presume will be his or her ultimate destination, the point at which the protagonists's identity will converge with that of the author. The restless lack of closure at the end of *A Portrait* thus exposes an instability latent in all autobiographical novels.

In a number of ways, *A Portrait* contends conspicuously with matters that are at issue in autobiographical fiction. Joyce was absorbed by the question of what it means to fictionalize self, and his book is plainly autobiographical even as it is also clearly novelistic and fictional. The title of the book is the first of a series of signals

11. The passage that is most often cited as evidence for both sides of the argument about irony in *A Portrait* is the villanelle Stephen composes in Chapter 5 (223–24). Others include his romantic exaltation at the vision of the wading girl (171), birds in flight (224–25), and his own vocation (252–53).

of its dual character, even though, appropriately enough for the fiction inside the cover, the title is a bit ambiguous. Is "the artist" an abstract generalization—"the one who creates art" in any place or time—or, more particularly, is it "the man who wrote this book" (even if the book does depict him as a young man, not yet capable of writing it)?[12] Beyond the title page are countless messages that cannot be received if we do not perceive that the text is autobiographical.

Luckily, we do read *A Portrait* autobiographically, I think, even if we do not do so consciously. Twenty years ago Louis D. Rubin, Jr., presented detailed evidence of how *A Portrait* announces its autobiographical character from its beginning sequence, and his work remains one of the only significant studies of the novel as an example of this distinctive kind of fiction, whose autobiographical nature is central to its form and meaning.[13] As Rubin pointed out, we read the opening collage of early memories as if it were a recollection from a narrator's childhood, in a writer's words but from the perspective of a child. The child is a little boy whose interest in stories and songs and whose tendency to make them up probably indicate that he will be the artist of the title, reinforcing the impression that he will also be the writer of this novel. After the opening section, a narrative pattern begins in which the narrator's and the boy's ways of speaking alternate in close conjunction. Adult literary language is interrupted by childlike expression, as in the paragraphs just after the opening that begin by describing a football practice in conventional novelistic language ("the greasy leather orb flew like a heavy bird through the grey light") but end in a boy's phrasing ("Rody Kickham was a decent fellow but Nasty Roche was a stink").[14] Recurrent image patterns throughout the

12. Hugh Kenner, reading the novel's title ironically, has argued that "the artist" may be merely "the artistic type, the sort of person who sets up as an artist, or acts the artist, or is even described by irreverent friends as The Artist, or as 'bullock-befriending bard'" (as Stephen imagines Mulligan doing in *Ulysses* [36]). See Kenner, "The Cubist *Portrait,*" in Staley and Benstock (eds.), *Approaches to Joyce's "Portrait,"* 171–84. Joyce's fondness for such characters is described by Morris Beja in "A Poor Trait of the Artless: The Artist Manqué in James Joyce," *James Joyce Quarterly*, XXVI (1988), 89–104.

13. See Louis D. Rubin, Jr., *The Teller in the Tale* (Seattle, 1967), 141–77.

14. *Ibid.*, 153–58.

novel also suggest kinship between author and character (series of birds, for example, culminate in the association of "the hawklike man whose name [Stephen] bore" and "Thoth, the god of writers" [225]). The very kinds of discourse in which the ending is couched should give us pause: we hear prayer within a diary, optative mood embedded in confessional form, that expresses Stephen's simultaneous hesitancy about and confidence in his ability to affect and express the world outside himself. Furthermore, the ending is unrestricted in time, so that it is not clear whether this is an end or a beginning: invocations, we know, occur at the start of enterprises; journals record and define the past. Stephen's prayerful journal is at once a wishful and faithful construction, like any remaking or making of a self. He tries imaginatively to possess his past and shape his future through words, an activity that parallels the action of the author of *A Portrait* itself and implies that the novel's context includes the act of its writing.

In other words, in several distinct ways the book invites us to think that James Joyce as a young man is Stephen Dedalus, just as the story at the beginning of the novel invited Stephen to think that "he was baby tuckoo."[15] James Joyce, like Stephen's father, has told his story in such a way that we make the identification and continue to see it right on through to the last words of the text—the dates that suggest that the young man who left Dublin at the end of the story finished this book ten years later. We should not miss the ambiguity here, however; it is possible that the dates reflect merely that it took the writer ten years to finish the novel, that 1904 is when Joyce began to write, not when Stephen sailed from Ireland. In fact, as we know from Joyce's biography, his initial flight from Dublin to Paris in order to "try myself against the powers of the world," as he wrote to Lady Gregory, occurred in 1902 (*LJJ*, I, 53; RE, 107). But his far more successful leave-taking did occur in 1904, when he departed again, this time with Nora Barnacle, the woman he had met on the day that *Ulysses* commemorates, secretly aboard the same boat. It is likely that Joyce conflated the two departures for the ending of his novel, as Ellmann asserts (RE, 109).

15. See Fritz Senn, *Joyce's Dislocutions: Essays on Reading as Translation*, ed. John Paul Riquelme (Baltimore, 1984), 102–103, for a discussion of linguistic nuances of this phrase.

In fact, the novel's narrative structure is so clearly autobiographical that we can be led to suppose that events and ideas in the book are more exact representations of things that occurred in Joyce's youth than they actually are. It was reasonable for early readers of the novel to assume that *A Portrait* was taken almost directly from Joyce's life (especially since little biographical data about Joyce was available). In recent years, much critical and theoretical emphasis has been placed on fictional elements of the book. But we should not allow our interest in Joyce's fictionalizing to distract us from the multiplex ways that this portrait depicts its sitter and its artist, who are versions of one subject. Some issues, like the notion of an aristocracy of art that is the focus of this study, cannot be fully engaged if the dual nature of the form is not taken into account. The question of a young would-be artist's acquaintance with nobility exerts pressure on the text in two usually separate contexts: it is an autobiographical issue, concerned with textual traces of the life of the writer, and it is also fictional in its implications, with aesthetic and formal aspects.

Like many of Stephen's concepts and beliefs, his idea of artistic gentility has its roots in Joyce's interpretation of his actual upbringing. Like his fictional counterpart, Joyce defined the term *artist* originally by the lexicon of his personal needs. In his relationships with family, class, country, and church he endured many of the same frustrations that he pictured for Stephen Dedalus. By his late teens he too seems to have decided to overcome them by conceiving for himself a new, separate, and superior identity.

The misfortunes of the Dedalus family are for the most part a faithful reproduction of the Joyces' decline. Like Simon Dedalus, Joyce's father John was, in Ellmann's words, a "reckless, talented man, convinced that he was the victim of circumstances, never at a loss for a retort, fearfully sentimental and acid by turns, drinking, spending, talking, singing" (RE, 21–22). He was an inveterate loser of money and a zealous proclaimer of his family's fast-disappearing prestige. Stephen's list of his father's occupations in *A Portrait* closely resembles a résumé of John Joyce's career: "a medical student, an oarsman, a tenor, an amateur actor, a shouting politician, a small landlord, a small investor, a drinker, a good fellow, a storyteller, somebody's secretary, something in a distillery, a taxgatherer, a bankrupt and at present a praiser of his own past" (241). Joyce's brother Stanislaus, whose recollections of the family are often bitterly accusatory, wrote of his father that he "belonged to the class of the deserving poor, that is to say, the class of people who richly deserve to be poor."[16]

Like Stephen, Joyce grew up in a home—or, rather, a series of houses—characterized by chaos, unfulfilled desires, and a distinct absence of gentility or even dignity. The simultaneously claustrophobic and unstable atmosphere of the Joyce household was acutely sensed by both adults and children. Not only was the family in constant financial decline, but John Joyce was also temperamentally incapable of relinquishing the appearance of social position, even after any basis in reality for that status had long since disappeared. The children were caught between mother and father in frequent domestic squabbles (John Joyce became violent on at least one occasion), which most often pitted Mrs. Joyce's determined Catholicism against her husband's equally obstinate love of liquor and uncontrollable temper. Their eldest son, however, apparently learned at an early age how to survive amid the material and emotional wreckage of his home. Ellmann writes that "the sense of home life as a continual crisis, averted from disaster by pawnbroker, obliging friend, or sudden job, became fixed in James Joyce's mind," but by the time he was twelve years old Joyce "was warily cultivating indifference to such matters, and already . . . was learning to pick his way among the family ruins as nimbly as an archaeologist" (RE, 41).

Joyce achieved his distance more effectively than his younger brother seems to have been able to do and more completely than he pictured Stephen Dedalus as doing. In an early love letter to Nora Barnacle, he wrote that "my home was simply a middle-class affair ruined by spendthrift habits which I have inherited," although he asked rhetorically, "How could I like the idea of home?" admitting that he could not be anything but estranged from it (*LJJ*, II, 48). In a similar spirit, Shem, an autobiographical apparition in

16. Stanislaus Joyce, *My Brother's Keeper*, 21.

Finnegans Wake, shares what seems to have been Joyce's ambivalence toward his father. Shem is always "one moment tarabooming great blunderguns (poh!) about his farfamed fine Poppamore, Mr Humhum, whom history, climate and entertainment made the first of his sept and always up to debt, though Eavens ears ow many fines he faces, and another moment visanvrerssas, cruaching three jeers (pah!) for his rotten little ghost of a Peppybeg, Mr Himmyshimmy, a blighty, a reeky, a lighty, a scrapy, a babbly, a ninny, dirty seventh among thieves and always bottom sawyer" (*FW*, 173.21–29).

Joyce's unmixed antipathy, however, was reserved neither for the Joyce family nor the lower class into which they were descending. He replaced the shame of being the target of social disapproval with distaste for the class from which it came—the class whose approval his father was equally eager to court. It was of course the upper middle class to which the Joyces were denied membership as their fortunes sank and whose scorn must have stung especially the older children in the family, who could remember a more prosperous time. Joyce seems to have cultivated a clear sense of his superiority in status to this group as he grew away from his family. A letter of September 6, 1906, speaks of his "detestation of the stupid, dishonest, tyrannical and cowardly burgher class" (*LJJ*, II, 158). The Irish bourgeoisie, with its absurd pretensions to cultural sophistication and its inveterate tendency to meddle in the lives of artists and works of art, was to be fought at every opportunity. "His great passion," Stanislaus Joyce records of his brother (with his own characteristic fervor) in his *Dublin Diary*, "is a fierce scorn of what he calls the 'rabblement'—a tigerlike, insatiable hatred."[17] The term *rabblement* recalls Joyce's defiant essay "The Day of the Rabblement," written when he was nineteen to condemn the Irish Literary Theatre for its chauvinism in producing only Irish plays.

A good part of Joyce's venom in "The Day of the Rabblement" is directed at the unendurable Irishness of the theater. Throughout his life Joyce, in his attitude toward his native land, despite the comic equanimity that is the reigning mood of *Ulysses* and to an

17. George H. Healy (ed.), *The Complete Dublin Diary of Stanislaus Joyce* (Ithaca, N.Y., 1971), 3.

even greater extent of *Finnegans Wake,* retained vestiges of the tension of being a member of a "lower" class or race. He kept a certain loyalty to Ireland, although he, like Stephen, left the country permanently in 1904, but he also kept some of the repugnance at Ireland's smallmindedness and lack of sophistication he had felt in his adolescence. In his attitude toward England and continental Europe we can perceive a note of envy mingled with his loyal refusal to realign his spiritual citizenship. Ellmann relates that Joyce lectured Arthur Power, a young Irishman with an interest in "letters" whom he met in 1921: "You are an Irishman and you must write in your own tradition. . . . You must write what is in your blood and not what is in your brain." Nonetheless, he admitted that he regretted being Irish, if only "for the temperament it has given me" (RE, 505). Joyce joked continually about the English, that nation of literal-minded, merchant-class imperialists whose greatest claim to world influence, he said, was the invention of the toilet, and his humor has the defensive ring common to Irish writers since Swift. His repertory of Irish jokes is self-denigrating ethnic humor, laughter to some extent at the teller's expense. It is sharp wit with a barb on both ends.

Religion was another subject with distinctly class-related overtones. Secular and sacred life were and are very closely connected in Ireland, since the country was and is overwhelmingly Catholic. Thus the deficiencies of Irish society are easily identified with the deficiencies of Irish Catholicism—an Irish joke is often a Catholic joke, for instance. In addition, the social structure was more or less rigidly defined by religious affiliation: the well-to-do were most often Protestant (and usually descended from English families). Consequently, many economic and cultural benefits were tied to church membership. As a Catholic, for example, Joyce was expected to attend University College instead of Trinity College, the Protestant and preferred institution. And of course in Ireland as elsewhere, one of the requirements for social respectability was church membership, if not regular attendance. But Joyce managed to dismiss all three parts of the Irish call heard in *Finnegans Wake*: "O! Our island, Rome and duty!" (374.19).

Joyce spurned respectability along with the established order and tradition that the Church represented ("In some, lawanorder on lovinardor," according to *Finnegans Wake* [374.15–16]) to become an artist and create his own order. He probably switched loyalties from Christian faith to faith in art by the time he was fifteen or sixteen. It is interesting, however, that he never rejected the aristocratic Jesuits, who virtually raised him from the age of six until he graduated from Belvedere. He made sure that his friend Frank Budgen identified him correctly in his book *James Joyce and the Making of "Ulysses"*: "You allude to me as a Catholic. Now for the sake of precision and to get the correct contour on me, you ought to allude to me as a Jesuit" (reported by RE, 27). Kevin Sullivan has mentioned the close link between Joyce's repudiation of Church and homeland and his family's social and economic decline. Indeed the link seems so strong that Sullivan "cannot escape the impression . . . that had Joyce's—or more properly, his father's—fortunes taken a different turn, had the young man not seemed destined to the corrosive and contemptible milieu of Dublin's lower-middle class, there would have been no deterioration in his relations with the Jesuits, no rejection of Catholicism, no abandonment of home and country, and possibly no *Portrait of the Artist as a Young Man*."[18] Joyce, like Stephen, received from his family's ruin the need to align himself with an elite whose position was higher than the one either Ireland or the Jesuits could provide.

At any rate, a brief period of piety, like Stephen's, soon gave way to Joyce's artistic vocation. Stanislaus Joyce records the change "when the reaction set in" and Joyce discovered Ibsen. But he does not dwell on it: the bigger mystery to him is not why his brother left the Church but how he could manage to devote himself to beauty under their domestic circumstances. "It seems to me little short of a miracle," he relates, "that anyone should have striven to cultivate poetry or cared to get in touch with the current of European thought while living in a household such as ours, typical as it was of the squalor of a drunken generation. Some inner purpose transfigured him."[19]

18. Kevin Sullivan, *Joyce Among the Jesuits* (New York, 1958), 11–12.
19. Stanislaus Joyce, *My Brother's Keeper*, 84.

Devote himself to beauty Joyce did. Finding little order or elegance at home, imagining himself assaulted with the stigma of social and cultural inferiority because he was Irish in Europe, Catholic in Ireland, and a member of the Joyce family in Dublin, he tackled the European world of letters with all the energy that desperate egotism could provide. As can be anticipated of his hero Stephen Dedalus, however, Joyce's method of attack was neither straightforward nor orthodox. He displayed an unusual antipathy for cleanliness, tact, and prudence (for example, in matters where money was concerned—especially when the money belonged to other people, such as his brother). He refused to join the Irish or English literary elite on its own terms: he wrote about vulgarity, flouted aesthetic as well as social conventions, and declined as many literary friendships and opportunities as he accepted.

The texts from Joyce's artistic apprenticeship bear stylistic evidence of the urge to prove artistic nobility. The "Epiphanies," for example, the brief descriptions of moments of spiritual meaning that Joyce wrote and gathered into a collection from 1900 to 1903, fall into two groups—those that reflect the superior mind of the artist and those that represent the vulgarity of the life around him. The first group depicts anything but anxiety over the influence of a noble literary past (in one a dog, "recumbent," howls, and passersby are "arrested, it may be, by that lamentation in which they seem to hear the utterance of their own sorrow that had once its voice but is now voiceless, a servant of laborious days"). In the other group a narrator's voice is effaced so that the voices of characters can unknowingly reveal moral or intellectual obtuseness in their own recorded speech (as when a "Tobin" remarks, "O there's nothing like marriage for making a fellow steady").[20]

The issue of narrative distance, implicit even in the "Epiphanies," surfaces plainly in Joyce's first extended piece of prose that followed an outline of his own life. In one day in early January, 1904, he drafted a curious essay, which he titled "A Portrait of the Artist." This first "Portrait," an odd little work that is part disqui-

20. James Joyce, "Epiphanies," in Robert Scholes and Richard M. Kain (eds.), *The Workshop of Daedalus: James Joyce and the Raw Materials for "A Portrait of the Artist as a Young Man"* (Evanston, Ill., 1965), 18, 19.

sition and part fiction, is an elaborately mannered account of a young man's life written (in the words of the essay) in order "to liberate from the personalised lumps of matter that which is their individuating rhythm, the first or formal relation of their parts."[21] Stanislaus Joyce described another early essay in terms that apply well to the style of the first "Portrait." As he saw it, his brother's work was "ornate, involved, highly stylized, and sometimes deliberately obscure" and "bore witness to a determined struggle to impose an elegance of thought on the hopeless distortion of the life that surrounded him."[22] It is ironic that in this product of the chaotic months following the death of Joyce's mother in 1903, both style and subject imply that art is characterized by superior distance from the world's disarray. We see little positive evidence of what must have been the disordered and distinctly ungenteel personal life of a young writer in John Joyce's ravaged household. That life, however, is revealed by its absence: the deliberate rehearsal of autobiographical events, emphasizing a steady rhythm beneath the surface cacophony, is a highly rhetorical demonstration that its author is indeed "the artist." This works in two ways. First, the story shows how such a condition came about: it proves the artistic status by cause and effect. Second, the style and form demonstrate the same status by performance: the artist proves himself by creating such order in a narrative that is obviously autobiographical.

Joyce also assumes in this first "Portrait" a more openly rhetorical stance from which to tell a story about himself than he allowed himself later when he was rewriting the material as a novel. The narrator is omniscient and intrusive, giving opinions about the young man that might be expected to reflect the attitudes of the writer of the essay. The overall tone is clearly admiring of the nameless hero. But even here anyone who has read *A Portrait of the Artist as a Young Man* may find it difficult to discern whether the voice of the essayist who tells the story has some reservations about the young man. The reason for this ambiguity is a stylistic device

21. James Joyce, "A Portrait of the Artist," in Scholes and Kain (eds.), *The Workshop of Daedalus*, 60.

22. Stanislaus Joyce, *My Brother's Keeper*, 163.

that anticipates many of the ways Joyce manipulated narration in his later works. There is more than a hint of the character of the young man in the style of the essay. For example, the "extravagance" that the narrator attributes to the young man is echoed in the prose itself. His artistic calling is described in the following language: "And was it any wonder that out of this marvellous life, wherein he had annihilated and rebuilt experience, laboured and despaired, he came forth at last with a simple purpose—to reunite the children of the spirit, jealous and long-divided, to reunite them against fraud and principality. A thousand eternities were to be reaffirmed, divine knowledge was to be re-established. Alas for fatuity! as easily might he have summoned a regiment of the winds."[23]

Even in his first attempt to frame an autobiographical narrative, Joyce seems to be working with the problems and possibilities inherent in autobiographical fiction. In linking the young man's personality stylistically with that of the narrating voice's—so that the essay is as "extravagant," as prideful, and as full of "lofty diagnosis" as its hero—he seems already to be manipulating narrative distance.[24] A careful reader thus will ask how closely "the artist" of the essay's title is related to the "Jas. A. Joyce" who signed it. (Interestingly, it is not even clear who recognizes the "fatuity" of the young man's sentiments about his vocation in the passage above.) Already we begin to see narration that represents stylistically the perspective of a principal actor, one of the trademarks of Joyce's style.[25]

By February 2, 1904, one month after "A Portrait of the Artist" was written, submitted to a journal, and quickly rejected, Joyce had decided to recast his material as a novel. Stanislaus recorded in a journal entry for that day (Joyce's twenty-second birthday) that "this evening, sitting in the kitchen, Jim told me his idea for the novel. It is to be almost autobiographical, and naturally as it comes from Jim, satirical." It is also interesting for us to note, regarding the fate of the essay, that according to Stanislaus "Jim thinks that

23. James Joyce, "A Portrait of the Artist," in Scholes and Kain (eds.), *The Workshop of Daedalus*, 64.

24. *Ibid.*, 63, 61.

25. This stylistic device, as it appears in *A Portrait*, was dubbed "the Uncle Charles Principle" by Hugh Kenner in *Joyce's Voices* (Berkeley, 1978), 15–38.

they rejected it because it is all about himself, though they professed great admiration for the style of the paper" (RE, 147). Joyce was well aware that editors, reflecting the tastes of readers, often dislike autobiographical works: it is common to expect such works to be flawed by their authors' lack of emotional detachment. With typical aplomb, however, Joyce seems to have been confident about keeping his novel "all about himself." Instead of abandoning autobiographical fiction, he would negotiate with the problem of authorial distance that lies at the heart of the form. His brother's remark that the new novel would "naturally" be "satirical" tells us that Joyce had for some time been given to assuming an ironic or satiric stance, separate from and judgmental of the world around him. He would now explore the extent to which his authorial voice should be separate from the story of Stephen Dedalus, while maintaining the obvious relationship between the character and the writer of the novel. (According to Stanislaus, Joyce intended to affix the signature *Stephanus Daedalus Pinxit* to the end of the book to make the relationship impossible for readers to miss.)[26]

The ten or so chapters of *Stephen Hero* that have been preserved are only a segment of the long manuscript that Joyce abandoned unfinished in 1907 to rewrite the material into *A Portrait of the Artist as a Young Man*. The earlier version of the book was much longer, much less tightly organized, and more discursively written than *A Portrait*. Unlike the extremely limited focus through Stephen's consciousness in the finished novel, much more of the world around Stephen appears in *Stephen Hero*. The external environment is much more fully realized and has a greater role to play in the action of the earlier work. Stephen's family, for instance, affects him far more obviously. His mother's opinions are important to him, and he has lengthy discussions with her about the Church and Ibsen. Stephen's brother Maurice (modeled after Stanislaus) is a foil to the older son in the family and shares Stephen's discontent with their life, and two climactic scenes concern the death and funeral of Stephen's sister Isabel.

A more important difference between the two versions of the

26. Stanislaus Joyce, *My Brother's Keeper*, 244.

novel (and between *Stephen Hero* and the earlier "Portrait" essay) involves Joyce's representation of authorial distance. A novel gives more opportunity than an essay, even a narrative one, for the voice of the storyteller to avoid stating authorial opinions explicitly. In *Stephen Hero* the narrator often hesitates to reveal directly how we should view the young hero. Unlike the meticulously circumscribed narrative of *A Portrait,* in which almost nothing is presented except as it occurs to Stephen's mind and senses, *Stephen Hero* does include passages in which the narrator's voice intrudes. But even in such passages the narrator is unusually reticent, for the most part, so that the opinions of the writer are more deliberately withheld than they were in the earlier "Portrait." For example, in the following excerpt the narrating voice describes Stephen's unusual career at the university indirectly, not from an omniscient perspective but by describing what others think of him.

> Though he was still in his first year he was considered a personality and there were even many who thought that though his theories were a trifle ardent they were not without meaning. Stephen came seldom to lectures, prepared nothing and absented himself from term examinations and not merely was no remark passed on these extravagances but it was supposed probable that he represented really the artistic type and that he was, after the fashion of that little known tribe, educating himself. . . . Stephen may be said to have occupied the position of notable-extraordinary: very few had ever heard of the writers he was reported to read and those who had knew them to be mad fellows. At the same time as Stephen's manner was so unbending to all it was supposed that he had preserved his sanity entire and safely braved temptations. People began to defer to him, to invite him to their houses and to present serious faces to him. (*SH*, 38–39)

We do not know what the voice that is presumably Joyce's thinks about Stephen, but we do know what the consensus of Stephen's contemporaries was—what the anonymous "many" supposed.

At times the narrator's voice does intrude, telling us a page later, for instance, how perfect Stephen's apprehension of Ibsen was: "The minds of the old Norse poet and of the perturbed young Celt met in a moment of radiant simultaneity" (40). But often the narrator presents a dialogue or a scene without comment, or with comments only from Stephen's perspective. Joyce had mastered the former technique by the time he finished *Dubliners*, whose "style of scrupulous meanness," as he described it (RE, 210), is effected by a narrator who prefers not to reveal his or her opinions about the pitiful, paralyzed city the stories reveal. Instead, the narration of most of the stories is limited so that we see through the eyes of a character, such as Maria in "Clay" or Little Chandler in "A Little Cloud," whose moral or intellectual purblindness is obvious but unstated by a narrator. The difference between these stories and *Stephen Hero* is that in the novel Joyce applied his mastery of such third-person narration to a fully developed autobiographical narrative for the first time (a task made easier since the creation of Gabriel Conroy, a character drawn from the material of Joyce's personal life, although he is not called upon to live in a *Bildungsroman*). In *Stephen Hero* the confessional form of the first three stories in *Dubliners*—"The Sisters," "An Encounter," and "Araby"—is extended backward from a first-person to a third-person narrative and forward in time to a period in the near past of the narrating voice. This change represents a watershed in Joyce's writing—the discovery of a form appropriate to contain, and be contained by, many of his most distinctive preoccupations.

The final version of the novel was finished after Joyce had published a volume of poetry and completed *Dubliners*, thus certainly proving to himself his own ability (in 1904, before Joyce had published anything of note, imputing literary talent to Stephen Dedalus was interestingly premature). Joyce's mature confidence makes itself felt in the distance to which the authorial voice has retreated. *Stephen Hero*'s narrative has been replaced by an extremely limited point of view from Stephen's perspective. The narrating voice almost never explicitly comments on the action, so that even though we have a much greater sense of a controlled authorial attitude than we did in the earlier version of the novel, it is extremely difficult to determine just what that attitude is. In general we are led to feel that the conclusions we reach about Stephen are not so much the narrator's as our own. Joyce has moved his narrator a step back, as it were, to let his story and his protagonist move more independently, seeming to prove or disprove meanings without intrusion from a storyteller. Much like the ballad "Turpin Hero" that fascinated him because it began in the first person and ended in the third, the change from *Stephen Hero* to *A Portrait of the Artist as a Young Man* is a movement away from personal involvement to detached objectivity.

However, as we have seen, as the narrative distance increases, so also does the portrayal of Stephen's budding awareness of how badly he needs distance. We see not only Stephen's belief in his superiority but also the necessity of that belief: how imperative it is to him that he occupy an exalted position in the abstract world of art to compensate for an utter lack of position in the material world. The most important difference between "A Portrait of the Artist" or *Stephen Hero* and *A Portrait of the Artist as a Young Man* is that in the finished novel the paradigm of artistic potential has become more complex to allow it to operate more consistently on the levels of both content and expression. Stephen must learn a lesson his author has mastered: it will be impossible to create genuine art by eradicating the personal, even the humiliating. One must not fly past nets.

After all, Stephen is a good observer in spite of himself. His impressions of the life around him are very perceptive—the sensation of wetting the bed as a small child, the wet ring of porter froth on a whore's bare table, crusts of tea-soddened bread lying haphazardly after his family's teatime, the feel of a louse, "tender yet brittle as a grain of rice" (*P*, 233). Of course he is also capable of heightened, abstract language remarkably like that of the early "Portrait." When he recognizes his artistic calling at the end of Chapter 4, "his heart trembled; his breath came faster and a wild spirit passed over his limbs as though he were soaring sunward. His heart trembled in an ecstasy of fear and his soul was in flight. His soul was soaring in an air beyond the world and the body he knew was purified in a breath and delivered of incertitude and made radiant and commingled with the element of the spirit. An ecstasy of flight made radiant his eyes and wild his breath and wild and radiant his windswept limbs" (*P*, 169).

But he is a better potential artist in his unconsciously perceptive intelligence of the world around him than he is when he waxes "artistic" about himself. Luckily, his self-absorption does not completely overtake his ability to see outside himself, even when he is most intensely preoccupied with artistic pretentiousness.

This inability to achieve emotional distance is one of the important distinctions between an artist and an aesthete. As long as he cannot escape successfully from his world, Stephen will at least avoid the predicament of James Duffy, from the *Dubliners* story "A Painful Case." Duffy, who "lived in Chapelizod because he wished to live as far as possible from the city of which he was a citizen," also studiously avoids his surroundings: "He lived at a little distance from his body, regarding his own acts with doubtful side-glances. He had an odd autobiographical habit which led him to compose in his mind from time to time a short sentence about himself containing a subject in the third person and a predicate in the past tense."[27]

The autobiographical compositions that Stephen may one day write are likely to be of much greater interest than Duffy's could possibly be, because Stephen cannot escape his world. Neither could Joyce, who had clearly realized by the time he finished *A Portrait* that art should be both escape and entry. It is a way to discover what it means to be human, and therefore to redeem that condition, as well as a way to avoid personal problems. In fact, in order for art to be honest, the artist must deny neither side of this equation. Even though he is still interested in running away, by the end of *A Portrait* Stephen has formulated the idea of transcending ugliness and pain only by returning to it and rejoining it as an artist. His creator also wrote into the novel what he had learned of this lesson himself by the experience of writing and rewriting his autobiographical fiction. By the time Joyce wrote *A Portrait,* he had long relinquished the rhetorical imposition of formality and elegance that characterizes the stiff "Portrait" essay in favor of a style that attempts to show elegance as well as the inelegant life from which it must come, to maintain a novelistic distance as well as autobiographical fidelity to life in a radically new fictional experi-

27. James Joyce, *Dubliners,* 107–108.

ment. *A Portrait of the Artist as a Young Man* shows the tension produced by Joyce's attempt. Just as the autobiographical hero takes off with a wing and a prayer at the end of the novel, at the same time confident and unsure of himself, so the autobiographical novelist's "determined struggle" with the opposing forces at work in autobiographical fiction is essential to this difficult and dynamic work.

2

The Personal and Special Sense

James Joyce almost stumbled onto the idea of creating fiction from his own past for his first novel. Hearing that two acquaintances were starting a new intellectual journal, he dashed off "A Portrait of the Artist" in great speed, hoping to seize the opportunity of the personal connection with the editors to help him establish his career as a writer. The immediate motive for writing the essay was to get his name in print. Furthermore, when he began planning *Stephen Hero* a month later, he was acting to some extent out of spite for the editors who rejected his essay. Stanislaus' diary for the day records that his brother "has decided to turn his paper into a novel, and having come to that decision is just as glad, he says, that it was rejected. . . . Jim is beginning his novel, as he usually begins things, half in anger, to show that in writing about himself he has a subject of more interest than their aimless discussion" (RE, 147). Little did either brother realize that Jim had found a subject of such interest that it would occupy the rest of his life and work.

Like Joyce, Thomas Wolfe happened onto the fictional form that would dominate his literary career practically by accident. Wolfe apparently chose to base his first novel on his own childhood and adolescence at the suggestion of Aline Bernstein, his lover, patron, and mentor. He had been trying his hand at prose fiction since his first trip to Europe in the autumn of 1924 (the trip he later dramatized in *Of Time and the River*). He spent some time the following year drafting sketches about his childhood along with other fragmentary pieces of prose narrative while he struggled with depression over his failure at writing plays. These sketches were admittedly "random." He "did not know what to do or how to go about it," he said later (*LTW*, 211). But he met Mrs. Bernstein on the voyage back to New York in August, and during the course of the winter of 1925–1926, as the two learned about each other in the early months of their affair, their long conversations provided the spark that ignited the idea for *Look Homeward, Angel.* According to Richard S. Kennedy, Wolfe and Mrs. Bernstein, spending many hours in a room they rented together, "poured out detailed accounts of their lives to each other, recalling forgotten years in their childhood. In this way . . . Wolfe began to reassemble the accumulated moments of his life, along with the flood of feeling that surrounded them. His mind was filled with memories which he now viewed afresh; from his new position of clarity and certainty, he saw his past as a whole" (RSK, 113). He began to make notes for a novel and, given encouragement and financial backing by Mrs. Bernstein (she offered to pay for a year in Europe while he wrote the novel), sailed to Europe in June, 1926. There, as he recalled later, "how, why, or in what manner I have never exactly been able to determine, I began to write my first book."[1]

Interestingly, these accounts of how both Joyce and Wolfe began to write autobiographical fiction are colored by what are usually interpreted as dominant traits in each man's personality. The beginnings of Wolfe's novel reflect his often-remarked and admitted sense of uncertainty about his work, while *A Portrait*'s inception, as Stanislaus reports it, is shot through with Joyce's equally characteristic self-confidence and bravado. Despite what were probably vast differences in temperament, however, Joyce and Wolfe shared an impulse to fictionalize their own lives that, once established, absorbed their whole careers.

1. Thomas Wolfe, *The Story of a Novel*, in Leslie Field (ed.), *The Autobiography of an American Novelist* (Cambridge, Mass., 1983), 7.

Wolfe had nagging doubts about his ability as a writer, and he was also plagued with considerable misfortune, during his lifetime and afterward, with editors. Indeed his work was so extensively altered by badly handled editing that no serious reader can afford to ignore the silent parts played by Maxwell Evart Perkins, Wolfe's editor at Scribner's, or Edward C. Aswell, his editor at Harper and Brothers, in the creating of the books that bear his name, particularly the novels that followed *Look Homeward, Angel.* Lack of self-confidence and overreliance on editors are egregious tactical errors for a writer to make, and critics of Wolfe's work have been harsh on him for being guilty of these sins. But *Look Homeward, Angel* is Wolfe's own book (to a far greater extent than his later work), and its integrity as a work of autobiographical fiction was relatively undamaged by the heavy editing the manuscript received.

Architectonics does not figure among the achievements of *Look Homeward, Angel.* Indeed, if it did, thanks would be due to Perkins as well as to Wolfe: large blocks of material were cut from the original manuscript, reducing the book by nearly a third, from 1,114 manuscript pages to 800 (some 90,000 words), and of course changing its larger structure.[2] But Wolfe was not primarily interested in a tightly controlled structure. Unlike most of his American contemporaries as well as Joyce, he followed a romantic, organic model for his art. In fact, the unusual phenomenon of a book being edited to this extent and yet remaining more or less imaginatively and formally intact is revealing of the kind of novel Wolfe was writing, in which the action is that of the remembered self growing toward the authorial self. The excision of a scene or a character does not materially affect the plan of the book, since that plan depends primarily on the autobiographical equation rather than on other novelistic elements such as symbolic or thematic patterns and the pacing of the plot. Perkins recognized the critical importance of Eugene Gant as a focusing intelligence and thus did not tamper

2. In addition to the biographies of Kennedy and Donald, see Francis Edward Skipp, "Thomas Wolfe and His Scribner's Editors" (Ph.D. dissertation, Duke University, 1962), for information about the editing of Wolfe's first two novels. Also useful are A. Scott Berg, *Max Perkins: Editor of Genius* (New York, 1978), and John Hall Wheelock (ed.), *Editor to Author: The Letters of Maxwell Perkins* (New York, 1950), for Perkins' point of view about the problem of editing Wolfe.

with Wolfe's major concern in his book, which was not so much what happens but to whom it happens—and the rhetorical drama taking place in Eugene's relationship to the voice telling us about him.

Perkins did not change many of Wolfe's words: he either left the writing alone or removed large pieces of it.[3] Most of the editing consisted of cutting whole paragraphs, pages, and scenes. The sections that Perkins removed most often were lengthy descriptions of minor characters; historical passages about Eugene's father, W. O. Gant, or his mother's relatives, the Pentlands; direct addresses to the reader on various subjects; parodic or satirical passages; and several scenes set in places other than the town of Altamont (RSK, 175). With one exception (Gant's interior monologue as he walks through the town, which was moved from Part 2 to Part 1 of the novel), Perkins did not alter the order of any passages. The vast majority of the material focusing on Eugene, particularly the sections describing his childhood and youth in his hometown, was not touched.

Thus, while the editing certainly altered the text as a whole, changing the relative weight of certain component elements, it left intact the central story of Eugene Gant and the way in which that story is told. The autobiographical material and the narrating voice through which the material is unfolded remained as Wolfe intended them. Indeed Perkins' editorial suggestions and changes made the book focus more closely on that central story than it did in the first draft. David Herbert Donald reports that such focus was in fact the editor's main concern: Perkins later remarked that he had tried to limit the book to events "all virtually within the experience and memory of this boy Eugene" (DD, 203). Thus the edited novel bears more resemblance to *A Portrait* and less to an encyclopedic work like *Ulysses* than did the first version Wolfe gave to his publisher. It is more narrowly concentrated on the character Eugene and his growth toward his calling to be a writer.

Wolfe was greatly enamored of Joyce when he wrote the work

3. Interestingly, several of the few changes in wording that Perkins made were slips of Wolfe's pen that gave away the narrator's sense of social inferiority. Skipp lists descriptions emphasizing monetary worth as a sign of glamour or prestige and errors showing ignorance of social felicities. Skipp, "Thomas Wolfe and His Scribner's Editors," 205, 274.

he eventually named *Look Homeward, Angel.* He readily admitted Joyce's influence, saying that he was "a great deal under his spell" while he wrote his novel.[4] It was in fact *Ulysses* and not *A Portrait* that he admired. Wolfe probably had not read Joyce's earlier novel, but he kept a well-marked copy of *Ulysses* with him from the early spring of 1927 onward and referred to it frequently. The results of this referral are easily seen in *Look Homeward, Angel,* most obviously in verbal experiments with neologisms, onomatopoetic imitations of sounds, and fragments of literary allusions inserted into the narrative. One lengthy sequence also borrows a technique in exposition from the "Wandering Rocks" chapter of *Ulysses*: in almost cinematic fashion, random fragments of scenes appear one after another to represent a cross-section of daily life in the town of Altamont, much as Joyce had done to evoke Dublin.[5]

But in essential form, *Look Homeward, Angel* is of course similar to *A Portrait.* Both novels exhibit similar strengths and weaknesses (although they are as different in conception and execution as they are in many other respects). Wolfe commented on the relationship between his novel and Joyce's, as well as on the broader issue of autobiographical fiction, in one of his last pieces, a speech called "Writing and Living" delivered at Purdue University in May, 1938. Discussing what he had learned in the seven years since writing *Look Homeward, Angel,* Wolfe mentions that his first book

> still showed unmistakably the evidence of the stages I had gone through, the periods of development, the special aesthetic faiths and creeds of the time. It is what is called an autobiographical novel . . . in the personal and special sense: it was possible, for example, to identify the life of the hero with the life of the author—to suspect that a great many of the characters

4. Wolfe, *The Story of a Novel,* in Field (ed.), *The Autobiography of an American Novelist,* 8.

5. Nathan L. Rothman, in "Thomas Wolfe and James Joyce: A Study in Literary Influence," in Richard Walser (ed.), *The Enigma of Thomas Wolfe: Biographical and Critical Selections* (Cambridge, Mass., 1953), 263–89, demonstrates a number of parallels between *Look Homeward, Angel* and both *Ulysses* and *A Portrait,* as does Jimmie Carol Still Durr in "*Look Homeward, Angel,* Thomas Wolfe's *Ulysses,*" *Southern Studies,* XXIV (1985), 54–68. See also RSK, 156, and DD, 160–63, for discussions of Wolfe's indebtedness to *Ulysses.* Donald speculates that Wolfe first read *A Portrait* sometime during his Guggenheim year in Europe (May, 1930–February, 1931), when he bought a copy of the book in France.

and incidents in the book were drawn pretty closely and directly from the writer's own experience. And, although I have not read the book for years, I believe that in this sense of the word—in this special autobiographical sense—was the book's greatest weakness: I believe the character of the hero was the weakest and least convincing one in the whole book, because he had been derived not only from experience but colored a good deal by the romantic aestheticism of the period. He was, in short, "the artist" in pretty much the Harvard Forty-seven Workshop sense of the word—the wounded sensitive, the extraordinary creature in conflict with his environment, with the Babbitt, the Philistine, the small town, the family. I know that I was not satisfied with this character even at the time: he seemed to me to be uneasy and self-conscious, probably because I was myself uneasy and self-conscious about him. In this sense, therefore, the book followed a familiar pattern—a pattern made familiar by Joyce in *A Portrait of the Artist as a Young Man*, and later in *Ulysses*.[6]

The book, in other words, reveals the lack of definitive distance between its author and its protagonist. The character Eugene, in his romantic quest for identity as an artist, reveals not only who the author was in his past but also who the author is at the time of writing. He does the first through the story, and he does the second through the rhetoric of the discourse in description, narration, and commentary by the authorial voice. That voice's uneasiness and self-consciousness and the emotions of the fictional personage it creates are often very close to each other. This dilemma is, as Wolfe notes, the result of fiction that is autobiographical "in the personal and special sense" of *Look Homeward, Angel.*

Thus the practical problem facing any writer of such fiction is how to tell the story of a highly talented character based on oneself without being fatuous. The implied author must not give the impression of overinvolvement with the action: he or she must stand far enough above and away from the fiction to allow it to perform its particular kind of persuasive task properly. This is the

6. Thomas Wolfe, "Writing and Living," in Field (ed.), *The Autobiography of an American Novelist*, 120–21. The "Forty-seven Workshop" was a group of students, faculty members, and interested others who staged performances of the best plays written for Professor George Pierce Baker's famous graduate courses at Harvard, English 47 and 47a, "The Techniques of the Drama." Wolfe was a member of the "Baker's Dozen," the ten or twelve students accepted in the courses, for three years. See DD, 65–102, for an account of Wolfe's years at Harvard.

charge Wolfe lays on his own novel in the passage cited above: Eugene Gant is unconvincing because his emotions were too much Wolfe's own.

Look Homeward, Angel frequently embodies a dangerous closeness between author and fiction. I disagree with Wolfe's assessment only in that I do not necessarily see this difficulty as a fault: it is inevitable in a novel like *Look Homeward, Angel* but can be a source of unusual strength as well as weakness. Joyce used a greatly distanced, ambiguous stance and fictional techniques that emphasize the artistry of the authorial voice in *A Portrait* to counterbalance the tendency toward identification of author and character that he also took pains to make prominent. Consequently his novel flirts with this danger while it explores what it means to create autobiographical art.

Irony and technical wizardry also play a part in Wolfe's novel, but they do not serve the consistent function that they do in Joyce's work: Wolfe's narrating voice moves in and out of close sympathetic identification with Eugene through most of the book. Instead, *Look Homeward, Angel* undergoes an unusual change in point of view late in the novel to reconcile the competing measures of authorial distance. Wolfe attempted by this experiment in focus to make art out of autobiographical material without sacrificing either artistic integrity or factual truth. As *Look Homeward, Angel* nears its conclusion, the distance between Eugene and the authorial voice decreases until art and reality become nearly fused in a visionary state. In the final scene of the novel, the author's perspective and the character's imagination are nearly identical for a climactic moment as Eugene's future as an artist is predicted dramatically as well as stylistically.

Wolfe's drive to eliminate the rigid boundary between art and life in this novel, like Joyce's working and reworking of his autobiographical portrait, was intimately bound up with the personal history he relates in his fiction. Eugene Gant devotes himself to finding a way to separate from a family, a community, and a region to which he feels that he does not belong. He chafes under the burden of the most basic of tasks undertaken in childhood, self-definition, and he searches for an identity that will carry him safely away from the uncivilized Gants, provincial Altamont, and the stifling South. Like Stephen, Eugene needs first to escape his actual surroundings in order to find symmetry and beauty in being an artist. To make the life of an artist his own, however, he will need also to return artistically to his childhood and youth, to reclaim his origins and redefine art in such a way that it can encompass an uncompromising view of his past. He needs to look homeward, in other words. As Eugene moves upward and outward, growing physically and venturing beyond Altamont intellectually and spiritually, the novel also recounts his gradual discovery and appropriation of a specific version of "the artist" as a self-image that shows fair promise of satisfying both counterimpulses, his need to transcend and his need to return to the world of his childhood. We can see a definite pattern of escape and return in *Look Homeward, Angel*, as we could in *A Portrait of the Artist as a Young Man*.

We can also read in several aspects of Wolfe's young life, especially as they relate to social class, an explanation for this urge of Eugene's. Unlike the Joyces, Thomas Wolfe's large family suffered no economic decline. Far from it: although a tombstone business provided W. O. Wolfe and Julia Elizabeth Westall with a better income than 90 percent of the families in the small town of Asheville, North Carolina, they did not begin their married life with extensive resources (DD, 9). But the skill of Wolfe's mother in the real estate market swelled the family fortunes considerably during the boy's childhood. According to Andrew Turnbull, by Wolfe's twelfth year his family was in the top 2 percent of Asheville society in terms of income.[7] But the Wolfes did not belong to the social class to which their money might otherwise have entitled them.

One reason for this state of affairs was that the family exhibited anything but respectable behavior. W. O. was a wild character, given at regular intervals to loud rhetorical declamations and drunken rampages through the streets of the town. On several occasions his wife had to run from his violent alcoholic temper to temporary refuge at neighbors' houses. Nor was W. O. the only Wolfe with a temper or a flair for the dramatic: fighting was com-

7. Andrew Turnbull, *Thomas Wolfe* (New York, 1967), 13. The Wolfes' statistical standing does not indicate a relationship to any well-defined upper class. Despite the presence of a few millionaires, such as E. W. Grove and George W. Vanderbilt, Asheville could not support genuine Brahminism.

mon and chaos was a way of life for the household. After Wolfe was five, the family no longer lived together even nominally. Julia Wolfe moved out of her husband's house in 1906 to the boardinghouse she owned and operated, and the family lost whatever regularity and cohesion it had had. The children lived in one house or the other according to their preference or the exigencies of the moment (although Wolfe stayed more or less permanently with his mother). The old family home, presided over by daughter Mabel, and Mrs. Wolfe's household at the "Old Kentucky Home" were irregular: the boardinghouse in particular lacked both peace and privacy, and tensions within the family were increased by the varying temperaments of the many boarders.

The family's idiosyncrasies, outlandish as they were at times, cannot be entirely blamed for the Wolfes' exclusion from the genteel element of Asheville society. Even in small-town America, where class is heavily dependent upon money, the "almighty dollar" has not been the only standard by which social position is established and maintained. The Wolfes would have been suspect because of their social, economic, and regional derivation even if they had lived an orderly life. The mountain people of Julia Wolfe's background and her rather graceless, open interest in moneymaking, manifested both in her boardinghouse business and in her real estate dealings, would probably have been enough to keep her from the ranks of polite society. Even though the "Old Kentucky Home" was profitable, its reputation, as one of her relatives remembered, was of "an untidy, dirty, squalid, down at the heels, second class boarding house. Drab as to furniture, meager in food."[8] Kennedy tells us that Wolfe's father, a northerner and a Republican (even if he were not also an alcoholic and an intimate acquaintance of the local brothel) was "looked on as somewhat of an outsider" in Asheville (RSK, 24). Despite their financial resources, the Wolfe family probably belonged to the middle class if they could be labeled by class status at all.[9] Wolfe's father was a

8. Reported in DD, 12.

9. See Walter Fuller Taylor, "Thomas Wolfe and the Middle-Class Tradition," in C. Hugh Holman (ed.), *The World of Thomas Wolfe* (New York, 1962), 141–48. Taylor argues convincingly that Wolfe's world view reflects the attitudes of the American middle class of the late nineteenth century. His case for Wolfe's "typical

stonecutter, his brother Fred was a salesman, and his brother Ben left high school before he graduated to work in the circulation department of the local newspaper.

But the Wolfes, like the Joyces, had no secure social standing. According to Kennedy, the family experienced significant "insecurity . . . about its class position" throughout the children's childhoods (RSK, 37). Like Joyce, Wolfe grew up in a home characterized by general disorder that was tied to the unsettled position of the family in the community. Wolfe also made the psychological association of ugliness and chaos with undesirable social status, later recalling his youth as that of "a poor boy who grew up in anarchy" (*LTW*, 184).

Wolfe left his confused and unlovely background to become a writer, and he found the mode best suited to that writer in autobiographical fiction. Like Joyce, he began his career by escaping his family and the place where he was raised. He left Asheville first to go to college in Chapel Hill, North Carolina, then to pursue graduate studies at Harvard, and then to live and work in New York, journeying to Europe whenever he could afford it. But he too began his best work only when he wrote from and about memory, exorcising his past by re-creating it from voluntary exile.

The social aspects of the protagonist's childhood are stressed almost from the opening pages of *Look Homeward, Angel.* After the first chapter, which describes the history of the Gant family, we are told of the birth of their youngest child. The naming of the baby boy foreshadows the important question of his position in life: his mother, "with a full, if inexact, sense of what portended . . . gave to Luck's Lad the title of Eugene, a name which, beautifully, means 'well born,' but which, as any one will be able to testify, does not mean, has never meant, 'well bred'" (34–35). Despite innate qualities that should find a home in a refined environment, then, Eugene Gant is born into a family singularly lacking in what is called "good breeding."

The first episode from Eugene's early life that takes place outside the immediate circle of his family involves the issue of social

---

middle class biography" (142), however, is less convincing. The Wolfes, like their fictional counterparts, were an atypical family in many ways. See also RSK, 37–38.

class. One spring morning the two-year-old child escapes from the hired woman who is temporarily taking care of him and wanders into the drive leading to the home of the Hilliards, a neighboring family who "were among the highest aristocracy of the town." It is his first taste of freedom, and he heads directly for the "forbidden and enhaloed region" of the "lords of the castle who descended into the village, but did not mix with its people." The serious accident that follows provokes the Hilliards merely to put up a "No Trespassing" sign. Eugene later broods that "the people and the life next door were crudely and symbolically above him." And "when he was older, he wondered sometimes if the Hilliards had issued from their high place when he had so impiously disturbed the order of the manor. He never asked, but he thought not: he imagined them, at the most, as standing superbly by a drawn curtain, not quite certain what had happened, but feeling that it was something unpleasant, with blood in it" (41–44).

In his first encounter with aristocracy, we see its allure for him but also his disgust at the lack of sympathy for the rest of humanity that the favored people display. The Hilliards have retreated into bloodlessness and therefore lifelessness. As he re-creates it in his imagination later, this incident provides Eugene with an early, deep impression about the upper class that corresponds to Stephen's perception of magistrates: they are the favored ones, to be envied, but they have only disdain toward his family. He feels both longing and personal rejection.

The sarcasm in Eugene's memory of this incident is not simply jealousy of a higher class, however, for the Gants do not fit easily into any class of Altamont society. Like the Dedaluses, they have a place neither in the working class nor the gentry. They do not have money troubles, but they have even fewer temperamental or hereditary qualifications than the Dedaluses to recommend them to a place among the upper classes of the town. We might suppose them to fall into the category of middle class, but we are told that their eccentricities keep them from their bourgeois neighbors.

They were a life unto themselves—how lonely they were they did not know, but they were known to every one and friended by almost no one. Their status was singular—if they could have been distinguished by caste, they would probably have been called middle-class, but the Duncans, the Tarkintons, all their neighbors, and all their acquaintances throughout the town, never drew in to them, never came into the strange rich color of their lives, because they had twisted the design of all orderly life, because there was in them a mad, original, disturbing quality which they did not suspect. And companionship with the elect—those like the Hilliards—was equally impossible, even if they had had the gift or the desire for it. But they hadn't. (64)

There is an emphasis on the other members of the protagonist's family in *Look Homeward, Angel* and a warmth expressed toward them that is for the most part absent from *A Portrait* (these characteristics are more reminiscent of *Stephen Hero*). W. O. and Eliza Gant are more fully realized characters than Mr. and Mrs. Dedalus. In fact, parts of Wolfe's narrative are presented through the eyes and voices of Eugene's parents. Stephen has no relationship with his siblings to parallel Eugene's with his brother Ben or even with his sister Helen. Eugene's eventual exile from his family will never be as complete a break as Stephen's, in part because Wolfe never distanced himself from his first, heavily autobiographical version of his novel as Joyce did by redesigning *Stephen Hero* into a more rigid structure. Nor will Eugene's conception of the artist include as rigid an enforced solitude. Nevertheless he is to some extent isolated not only from the community but also from the Gants. "Pent in his dark soul," he is "a stranger in a noisy inn" even at home as a small child; the older children think him "queer" because of his solitary dreaming and his violent temper when disturbed (82–83).

Like Stephen, Eugene begins to seek art and to construct artistic fantasies soon after he can read. He runs from the painful realities of school, where "he was a desperate and hunted little animal" (89), and of the neighborhood after school (where he half-joins in the petty prejudices against blacks, Jews, and poor whites, hating himself and the others even as he participates in their cruel games [95–97]) to his father's shop and the world of novelistic romance and adventure. Gant's monument shop is itself a means of escape from the restlessness and ugliness of life outside it. The stonecutter's artisanship comes to symbolize the changelessness of art, since his work "would never, as men reckon years, be extinguished." Men such as Gant have "scored their name upon a rock, blasted their mark upon a cliff, sought out the most imperishable objects of the world and graven there some token, some emblem that utterly they might not be forgotten" (101).

Cheap novels, which Eugene reads "with a tearing hunger," are another respite from life's imperfections. He likes to imagine himself as the heroes of these books, foiling villains, rescuing beautiful, pure women, and landing huge fortunes in the process. In the novelistic scenes inserted into the narrative, we can see the boy's desire for the kind of life a stonecutter's son from a mountain town in the American South will probably never lead. The components of these novels and his dreams, as the narrating voice tells us, are "rigidly conventionalized" (104): fortune, fame, love of beautiful women. Interestingly, it is fortune—the American dream of happiness achieved through limitless wealth—that holds the greatest instant appeal. He learns how to transcend the Gant household and Altamont by "going unweariedly through the infinite monotony of the Algers": the narrator tells us that "all the details of money—the value of the estate usurped by the scoundrelly guardian and his caddish son, he feasted upon, reckoning up the amount of income, if it were not given, or if it were, dividing the annual sum into monthly and weekly portions, and dreaming on its purchasing power. His desires were not modest—no fortune under $250,000 satisfied him: the income of $100,000 at six per cent would pinch one, he felt, from lavishness" (103).

Later, when "the erotic gropings became more intelligible, he turned passionately to all romantic legendry" in his reading material (104). Beneath it all, the narrator explains: "Eugene wanted the two things all men want: he wanted to be loved, and he wanted to be famous" (108).

This section of the narrative, with its parodies of climactic scenes from penny novels and descriptions of Eugene's sentimental reactions to them, puts the boy at a clear comic distance. The narrator stands apart with us to make a linguistic identification of heart with nose that ensures our opinion of the boy's emotional response when he finishes the story of Bruce Glendenning, international vagabond: "He pulled his clotted handkerchief from his pocket and blew the contents of his loaded heart into it in one mighty, triumphant and ecstatic blast of glory and sentiment. Ah, me! Good old Bruce-Eugene" (108).

Hence we cannot take too seriously Eugene's first attachment to fiction. He must find another way to ease the painful tension of his life in Altamont, of belonging and not belonging to his family or community. As in the episode with the Hilliards, we are assured by the tone of this section that Eugene's brush with an outside world is not the discovery of a satisfying direction for him to take.

But the novels do work for a time. Eugene finds that, "lifted, by his fantasy, into a high interior world, he scored off briefly and entirely all the grimy smudges of life: he existed nobly in a heroic world with lovely and virtuous creatures" (108). But he is soon sent into the town to earn money by selling the *Saturday Evening Post*, and the reality of Altamont invades his private imaginings, much as the move to Dublin overpowers Stephen Dedalus' vision of Mercedes in *A Portrait*. Immediately following the chapter devoted to the young boy's novelistic reveries, we are informed that "this freedom, this isolation in print, this dreaming and unlimited time of fantasy, was not to last unbroken" (112): Eugene's parents insist on his getting a job.

The Gants believe unreservedly in the clichés of the work ethic. They tell themselves that employment after school and during the holidays will promote their children's independence and self-discipline. But their real reason for requiring their boys to have jobs is the value they attach to money, however acquired: "Unhappily, neither Eliza nor Gant were at any pains to examine the kind of work their children did, contenting themselves vaguely with the comfortable assurance that all work which earned money was honest, commendable, and formative of character" (112). The "base of worth" to them is money: "It was not enough that a man work, though work was fundamental; it was even more important that he make money—a great deal if he was to be a great success—but at least enough to 'support himself'" (114).

The narrator's sarcasm about this unthinking confidence in money gives way to open denunciation when recalling the effect it had on Ben. By the time Eugene starts working, his favorite brother is so seldom home that he is "like a phantom" in the house.

Ben is sleep-starved and undernourished, walking "evidence" of his parents' "tragic fault" (112). That fault is more tragic, of course, because the Gants do not actually need money.

Eugene instinctively shrinks from his parents' ethic, even though he feels guilty when they or his older brother Luke berate him for spending idle time alone, reading or daydreaming. Thus "his shame, his distaste for his employment was obvious, although he tried to conceal it: he was accused of false pride, told that he was 'afraid of a little honest work,' and reminded of the rich benefits he had received from his big-hearted parents" (123). He is tortured by conflicting emotions. On the one hand, he tries earnestly to please his parents; on the other, everything in him recoils from the values they try to inculcate. For *earning* money is a very different thing from simply *having* it, which he has often dreamed about. The act of earning money does not decrease the discomfort of being without it—if anything, Eugene learns, it is more openly shameful.

Eugene's beloved older brother Ben is his only ally against the money-centered ethic that his parents preach. Ben seems to have resolved for himself the tensions that torment Eugene by leaving the family in all but the physical sense, sullenly aloof from all the money-making schemes. Structurally, Ben's life and death provide a counterplot to Eugene's growth, showing the fate of a kindred spirit who chose pure withdrawal as a mode of coping with existential anxieties similar to Eugene's. Ben too is "a stranger" in the Gant household, even though he loves that from which he is unrelievedly alienated: "His passion for home was fundamental" (113). His way out of his own internal conflict, which amounts to denial of life, leads ultimately to his death. Eugene will recognize Ben's failure and find another way for himself, but the problem he faces and will solve by his art is much the same as his doomed brother's.

Significantly, that problem is first identified in social terms. An interesting passage begins with the observation that the brothers are ill at ease in the Gant household because

> Both Ben and Eugene were by nature aristocrats. Eugene had just begun to feel his social status—or rather his lack of one; Ben had felt it for years. The feeling at bottom might have resolved itself simply into a desire for

the companionship of elegant and lovely women: neither was able, nor would have dared, to confess this, and Eugene was unable to confess that he was susceptible to the social snub, or the pain of caste inferiority: any suggestion that the companionship of elegant people was preferable to the fellowship of a world of Tarkintons, and its blousy daughters, would have been hailed with heavy ridicule by the family, as another indication of false and undemocratic pride. He would have been called "Mr. Vanderbilt" or "the Prince of Wales." (123–24)

The Gants' attitude toward their social superiors is a curious mixture of emulation and denunciation. They are perfectly willing to deny their considerable property, professing a life of near-poverty while they make disparaging remarks about snobbish aristocrats. At the same time, they (in particular, Eliza) are unceasingly acquisitive and eager to instill their materialistic morality in their children. This materialism has at its core a desire to ascend the social scale, to prove that the Gants are as respectable as anyone in town.

The attitudes of the family in general, however, are less complex than those of Eugene and Ben. Both boys link elegance with sexuality (as Stephen Dedalus does when he fantasizes about Mercedes) and successful escape from the Gants' "jangled and clamorous household" into peace and order (113). But their refined sensibilities clash with the inescapable influence of family and community. Ben hides his sensitivity under a callous exterior. He cannot rid himself of the small-town distrust of elegance enough to escape Altamont, so he stagnates, killing time with the newspapermen with whom he works and voicing his bitterness with "a brief nod upwards and to the side to the companion to whom he communicated all his contemptuous observation—his dark satiric angel: 'Oh, my God! Listen to that, won't you?'" (124). Eugene also cannot avoid confusing discrimination in taste with un-American hauteur. We expect the man to become his own author and find his way as Wolfe himself did, locating a successful avenue of escape in being an artist who returns to his roots in his art. He will be able to counter charges of "undemocratic pride" and satisfy his own need for aristocratic elegance simultaneously by celebrating the people and the country he comes from, writing fiction based on his own life that fuses the figures of aristocratic artist and democratic everyman.

For Eugene and Ben, the issue of money is also closely associated with insincerity. Ben sees more clearly than his younger brother the falseness of their parents' insistence that they are poverty-stricken, and he does not hesitate to confront them. He tells Eliza, "You and the Old Man like to make out you're paupers, but you've a sock full of money" (125). Not only does the family's supposed need of money reek of untruth, but the act of making it does as well. Eugene's brother Luke, the salesman of the family, considered "the generous and unselfish one," is motivated by a need for praise rather than any genuine impulse of selflessness. His false front, as well as the act of selling in which he is always engaged, throws Eugene "against the torturing paradox of the ungenerous-generous, the selfish-unselfish, the noble-base, and unable to fathom or define those deep springs of desire in the human spirit that seek public gratification by virtuous pretension, he was made wretched by the conviction of his own sinfulness" (116). He will eventually run from the falseness that sickens him in middle-class life, believing that he can live in a truer as well as a nobler world as an artist. In fact, we may easily believe of this artist that he might—as Wolfe did—risk and lose the approbation of many people in his hometown because he insists on writing what he considers the truth about them in his fiction. Eugene's intolerance of commercial dishonesty presages and becomes a part of his urge toward factual art.

The feeling of homelessness is another important ingredient in Eugene's development. The Gants do not move with the frequency of the Dedaluses, but Eugene, like Stephen, experiences the loss of a sense of home at an early age. In his eighth year, his mother opens a boardinghouse and moves into it. She takes her youngest son with her away from the rest of the family, causing the "complete disruption of their life together, the rooting up of their clamorous home." The move is intimately connected with economic motives: from the first, the purchase of the boardinghouse, called "Dixieland," is spoken of "evasively as 'a good investment'" (129). The "great chill tomb of Dixieland," associated with loss and cold, is a symbol of the "pain of caste inferiority" of which Eugene has been increasingly aware. His mother has become a servant to her boarders as well as a penny-pinching landlady. Dixieland is less a home than a place of business where the customers are always the first priority.

Like Stephen, who is shuffled from house to house in and around Dublin as his family's fortunes decline, Eugene is shuffled from room to room as his mother's prosperity increases: he stays in whatever room is unoccupied by a paying guest. His sense of home is permanently displaced: "Before he was eight, Eugene gained another roof and lost forever the tumultuous, unhappy, warm centre of his home. He had from day to day no clear idea where the day's food, shelter, lodging was to come from, although he was reasonably sure it would be given: he ate wherever he happened to hang his hat, either at Gant's or at his mother's" (130).

In the move to Dixieland, he loses not only his home but also one of his parents. W. O. refuses to leave the house he built on Woodson Street. He has always had "a particular revulsion against lodgers: to earn one's living by accepting the contempt, the scorn, and the money of what he called 'cheap boarders' was an almost unendurable ignominy" for him (51). So he appears at Dixieland for meals or company, to rail at Eliza or to declaim on politics or current events for the benefit of the guests. But he is a guest there himself; his central role in the household has been taken over by his wife. The motif of searching for a father, especially prominent in *Of Time and the River* and Wolfe's posthumously published books, begins here with Eugene's loss as his mother takes him away from his father's house because of her greed.

Eugene soon begins to realize what the move to Dixieland means: "He saw plainly by this time that their poverty, the threat of the poorhouse, the lurid references to the pauper's grave, belonged to the insensate mythology of hoarding; anger smouldered like a brand in him at their sorry greed. There was no place sacred unto themselves, no place fixed for their own inhabitation, no place proof against the invasion of the boarders" (137).

Insincerity, greed, and loss of home are all symbolized by the boardinghouse. The lowering of status it represents is also associated with a lack of order that Eugene becomes convinced is evil. In an important passage we are informed that

> Eugene was ashamed of Dixieland. And he was again afraid to express his shame. As with *The Post,* he felt thwarted, netted, trapped. He hated the indecency of his life, the loss of dignity and seclusion, the surrender to the tumultuous rabble of the four walls which shield us from them. He felt, rather than understood, the waste, the confusion, the blind cruelty of their lives—his spirit was stretched out on the rack of despair and bafflement as there came to him more and more the conviction that their lives could not be more hopelessly distorted, wrenched, mutilated, and perverted away from all simple comfort, repose, happiness, if they set themselves deliberately to tangle the skein, twist the pattern. He choked with fury. (136–37)

This "rage for order" is another urge that art will satisfy for Eugene. He will return to his youth by way of art, finding (or making) an order by remembering what was not apparent while he lived through these years.

Immediately following the passage quoted above, we learn that Eugene turns again toward the idea of an elite as he struggles to identify and remedy the trouble into which his family has fallen. He yearns for privacy and comfort and equates physical surroundings that supply these needs with spiritual good: we are told that "he had even then an intense faith in food, in housing, in comfort—he felt that a civilized man must begin with them; he knew that wherever the spirit had withered, it had not withered because of food and plumbing" (137). He is intensely aware during this period of the "petty cruelty of village caste," although he exaggerates the rigidity of class lines in a town whose "caste system was liquidly variable, depending chiefly upon wealth, ambition, and boldness" (137–39).

The manifestation of social strata in the church membership of Altamont is the context for Eugene's newest attraction to an aristocratic group. The Gants attend the Presbyterian church, although they do not quite fit into the upper-middle-class niche of the rest of the congregation. Eugene is drawn to Presbyterianism, even though most of his neighborhood friends are Baptists, because of "its sober decency, its sense of restraint, its suggestion of quiet wealth, solid position, ordered ritual, seclusive establishment" (139–40). Religion has social overtones in Altamont no less than in Stephen Dedalus' Dublin, and Eugene is no less quick to notice and be affected by them than is Joyce's young artist—although Eugene is never attracted to a spiritual life as Stephen is. Later in the novel, Eugene's friend George Graves explains the social importance of religion. It is vital to be a church member, he says, because "'it helps you in a business way. . . . You won't get far in this town, 'Gene, without them. It pays,' he added devoutly, 'to be a Christian'" (330). Incidentally, a note Wolfe jotted down in his Harvard years shows how closely these sentiments reflected the gospel he learned at home: "My family could not be termed a religious family. . . . Attendance at church was advocated mainly because it gave one business and social 'standing' in a small community, such as ours. The best people belonged to the church. If one was to live here one simply couldn't afford not to belong. . . . It is a good club to belong to especially if one wants to go into business."[10]

The pattern of Eugene escaping from a situation that he finds particularly shameful by dreaming about wealth and elegance is repeated throughout Part 1 of *Look Homeward, Angel*, until Eugene is twelve years old. For example, when Eliza takes him with her to Hot Springs, immediately sending him out to sell the *Saturday Evening Post* and to distribute cards advertising Dixieland, he spends his days thinking about the high-society people who patronize the curative waters: "He gazed for hours into the entrances of the fashionable hotels, staring at the ladies' legs upon the verandas, watching the great ones of the land at their recreations, thinking, with a pang of wonder, that here were the people of Chambers, of Phillips, of all the society novelists, leading their godlike lives in flesh, recording their fiction" (160). Here, interestingly, the idea of aristocracy is aligned in the boy's mind with the writing of novels.

Near the end of Part 1 of *Look Homeward, Angel* we are introduced to another aspect of Eugene's emotional makeup that will play a significant role in his development as an artist—his feelings about the South. We are told, in a metaphor that Wolfe repeated throughout his works, that the South "burned like Dark Helen in Eugene's blood." He is fascinated by the legends of the Old South, the "romantic halo that his school history cast over the region," but the narrator gives us a glimpse of the future to tell us that his emo-

10. Richard S. Kennedy and Paschal Reeves (eds.), *The Notebooks of Thomas Wolfe* (2 vols.; Chapel Hill, 1970), I, 10–11.

tions will not always be this simple. He will hate southerners' "cheap mythology, their legend of the charm of their manner, the aristocratic culture of their lives, the quaint sweetness of their drawl," but later he will be so unable to shake their influence "that he still pretended the most fanatic devotion to them, excusing his Northern residence on grounds of necessity rather than desire" (154–55).

In Eugene's regional identity we can see elements of the same sense of inferiority that he feels about his class status, although it is complicated by the double image of the South—at once the land of chivalric antebellum gentility and the cultural backwater of the United States. Eugene's feelings are complicated even further by the ambiguous relationship that the Gants and the town in which they live have to the American South as a whole. Altamont, the mountain resort town, is a far cry from the mythic plantation culture of the Deep South, and the Gant family is only one generation away from being Pennsylvanian Yankees. But there are many Souths and Eugene is raised in one of them. Like Stephen, he has at once a deep attachment and a powerful aversion to his native region (to the South and, in *Of Time and the River* especially, to America as a whole). If Ireland was to the young Joyce "an afterthought of Europe" (RE, 67), the poor relation who served the Continent and Mother England primarily as the butt of jokes, surely the South was to a young American in the early years of the twentieth century an "afterthought" of the United States—and the Appalachian region, just as surely, might be called an "afterthought" of the South.

The passage about the South ends with a curious statement of what is presumably Eugene's most recent stance on this issue. The emotional distance between narrator and character suddenly disappears as we hear what Eugene resolves in order to free himself from the grip of his southern roots: "Finally, it occurred to him that these people had given him nothing, that neither their love nor their hatred could injure him, that he owed them nothing, and he determined that he would say so, and repay their insolence with a curse. And he did" (155).

The anger in this passage is in the narrator's rhetoric as well as the reported feelings of the character; the distinction between the two is momentarily erased. The next logical step for the reader is to ask if we are meant to infer that Eugene's "curse" is to be found in the pages of the novel we are reading. The wording of the passage certainly seems to encourage such an inference. We are being shown the character Eugene growing closer to the position of the author of the novel as he grows up in its pages. Such vacillations in distance proliferate as the narrative continues into Eugene's adolescence and young adulthood.

In Part 2 of *Look Homeward, Angel*, as Eugene passes from childhood, his urge to become an artist is more clearly defined. Vague longings for elegance and fantastic wealth are replaced by a growing awareness of the power of words over the chaos of his life. The narrative changes as well: portions of it seem almost to have been written by the youth. At times the distinctive narrating voice fades into a voice that resembles Eugene's, but it is Eugene consciously ordering his thoughts into literary form. We seem to overhear not the random stream of his subconscious mind but his characteristic shaping of impressions into patterns that might be included in a journal or worked into a poem—or an autobiographical novel.

The opening section of Part 2 contains such a passage. The narrator's voice is heard first, musing poetically on the seasons of winter and spring. In the paragraph immediately following, we are given a poetic description of Ben that is almost identical to the preceding one tonally but is identified by the parenthetical phrase "thought Eugene" as the character's language, not the narrator's. The next paragraph continues the description of Ben, again with no noticeable break in style, but again it is the narrator who speaks (165).

This dissolution of boundaries between the voices we attribute to the author and the main character occurs earlier in the novel as well. For instance, Eugene's passionate but indistinct yearnings as a small child are recorded in a passage that begins as a description in the third person ("and when the bells broke through the drowning winds at night, his demon rushed into his heart") but ends as direct address ("to crouch against a lonely storm-swept house, to gaze obliquely through the streaming glass upon a woman, or your enemy" [91]). As in the description of the football as "a greasy leather orb" flying "like a bird through the grey light" in *A Portrait*, in this passage we are seeing with Eugene's eyes, but we are not hearing a six-year-old's language. The words are those of the authorial voice who is recalling what the boy felt as he for the moment travels back in time to relive the experience he is relating. As the novel progresses, the narrative is often interrupted by present-tense rhapsodic passages, but the words now belong not to the narrator alone but to the protagonist as well. Eugene is forming his thoughts into a linguistic pattern as if he plans to write down his thoughts. These passages lessen the formal distance between the protagonist and the authorial voice as the temporal distance between the two diminishes. As Eugene nears the time when he will write his story, we begin to hear in his voice the voice of our author: we are meant increasingly to listen for and recognize his growing ability to verbalize his experience.

The middle sections of the novel contain considerable mimicry of literary language, which also serves a formal function by representing stylistically Eugene's stage of development. The young man is growing into a writer, but he is by no means ready to become one yet. His ideas about art, especially about its relation to the real world, are not fully formulated. By awkward (often humorous) insertions of literary language into the story, the text reflects his still-immature efforts at articulation. Following Eugene's enrollment at the Leonards' Altamont Fitting School, where his love of literature is encouraged, quotations from his favorite authors begin to be sprinkled into the text. These appear with greater frequency as he reads voraciously and his perceptions are filtered through newly digested literary phrases.[11] Thus he declines a ride on "Pap" Rheinhart's horse, and we hear a line from Virgil, "*Quadrupedante putrem sonitu quatit ungula campum,*" as the horse gallops away (326). Eugene also makes a sarcastic reference to a Chaucerian pilgrim as old Colonel Pettigrew rides by: "He was a very parfit gentil knight" (347).

The irony that results from making this kind of literary creation

11. Wolfe borrowed the technique of inserting allusions or quotations directly into the text for ironic effect from *Ulysses*, as Durr and Donald have remarked. See Durr, "*Look Homeward, Angel,* Thomas Wolfe's *Ulysses,*" 59–60; and DD, 162. Donald notes that Wolfe kept long lists of such passages in his working notes so that he could work them into his text at opportune places.

out of the everyday events of Eugene's life indicates, first, the considerable distance between the narrator and the town that the narrator is mocking. Second, the irony portrays the still-considerable distance between the narrator and the boy, whose love of literature cannot eradicate the inelegance of the life around him. The absurdity of applying stylized phrases from the great poets to the citizenry of Altamont pokes fun at Eugene's nascent learning as well as at the townspeople. Eugene continues to think of art as an aristocratic phenomenon, and the narrator uses the boy's idea of art for comic effect throughout this part of the novel. For example, the language of high culture, such as he might employ, is often used to describe small-town life. In the description of a retired English teacher's patriotic fervor at the beginning of World War I, Eugene's own "delirium of promised glory" is mocked as well as the old spinster's exaltation as we hear that "of all the English, none can show a loftier or more inspired love for Albion's Isle than American ladies who teach its noble tongue" (349).

Probably the clearest illustration of this kind of irony, coming from the incongruity between Eugene's exalted ideas about art and actual life, may be found in the treatment of his adolescent bardolatry on the tercentenary of Shakespeare's death. His family discovers the portrait he has nailed to the wall while he composes his entry for an essay competition, and they tease him mercilessly with the quotation from "the great echoing paean of Ben Jonson's" that Eugene has attached to the picture.

> Thereafter, he was called poetically to table, to the telephone, to go an errand.
>
> "My Shakespeare, rise!"
>
> With red resentful face, he rose.
>
> "Will My Shakespeare pass the biscuit?" or, "Could I trouble My Shakespeare for the butter?" said Ben, scowling at him.
>
> "My Shakespeare! My Shakespeare! Do you want another piece of pie?" said Helen. (371)

Eugene is not the only target of the humor in this section. The town is also satirized for its pageant in honor of the occasion, which features Shakespearean advertisements for local businesses, the pompous Dr. George B. Rockham as "the Voice of History," and "the innocent children of Altamont's schools" as "the mute illustrations of that voice" (372). Eugene is meant mutely to illustrate Prince Hal, but he appears dressed in a green linen clown suit so wildly inappropriate that it puts a halt to the proceedings and the pageant dissolves in laughter.

Eugene's appreciation of Shakespeare is presented seriously as well, as we might expect: an artist such as he will become is likely to have the good taste in literature that a love of Shakespeare implies. In fact, the narrator appears to admire the same works that the boy does. We hear of Eugene's high regard for Heine, Xenophon, Burns, Wordsworth, "the great song from *Cymbeline*: 'Fear no more the heat o' the sun,'" and "the greatest of all" the sonnets, "That time of year thou mayest in me behold" (308–309). It is not Eugene alone who regards these as great: the adjectives are the narrator's. Likewise it is the narrator who calls Edmund's monologue on bastardy in *King Lear* "terrible and epic" and "drenched in evil," and we may believe that its "call to the unclassed" and its "cry for those beyond the fence"—especially for "all of the men who are too tall"—are still audible to the authorial voice (310).[12] The boy's relationship with Shakespeare, the universal artist, functions to some extent as a touchstone of his artistic development (as does Stephen Dedalus' intricate theorizing about Shakespeare in *Ulysses*).

Indeed both Stephen and Eugene do much more than appreciate the Bard: they appropriate him, literally putting on a writerly identity. Eugene *is* "My Shakespeare," his embarrassment notwithstanding. Similarly, later in the novel he is called "Hegel Gant" in his college philosophy class and enjoys registering in hotels in surrounding towns under the names of famous poets—Robert Her-

12. Wolfe, of course, was unusually tall (six feet four and one-half inches, according to Donald). The idea of a man alienated from his environment because of height had a certain continuing appeal for him. One of his first attempts at writing publishable prose, which he later developed in the sketch "Gulliver" (included in *From Death to Morning*, a collection of stories), treated this theme. See Kennedy and Reeves (eds.), *The Notebooks of Thomas Wolfe*, I, 37–40; Thomas Wolfe, *From Death to Morning* (New York, 1935), 134–49. The idea was of sufficient interest to cause a revealing misreading of Shakespeare's character, one of whose chief arguments in the bastardy speech rests upon the fact that he is as well-proportioned as a man of legitimate parentage (*King Lear*, act 1, sc. 2, lines 7–8).

rick, John Donne, William Blake, and the like. He is discovered by a desk clerk when he registers as Henry W. Longfellow: "'You can't fool me,'" says the clerk. "'That's the name of a writer'" (594–96). Ironically, of course, the clerk is right: he is indeed not fooled because Eugene's name is, or will be, that of a writer.

Eugene's longing to find the aristocracy for which he is innately suited continues through the third and final part of the novel. The pattern of frustrated attempts to escape his family and Altamont continues as well, as does his movement toward the moment when he will embrace an artistic way of looking at his life in order to make sense of it. As Part 3 opens, the fifteen-year-old boy is entering college. In keeping with his dreams of aristocratic achievement, he and Margaret Leonard have dreamed of the best schools: Vanderbilt or Virginia, Harvard, then Oxford "to top things off" (388). But Gant interposes his own ideas about Eugene's future, and his son is sent to the more plebeian State University in Pulpit Hill. The Gants, with their usual interest in instilling guilt, carefully remind Eugene of the financial strains his college education will allegedly cause them, and Ben, just as characteristically, exposes their false motives. He tells Eugene to "take every damn cent you can get out of them," since they are using Eugene to improve their status in the community. If his brother will "get all you can," Ben says, perhaps he can undo some of the shame of both brothers' unclassed upbringing: "When you get down there, if you find you need more to hold your own with the other boys, make the old man give it to you. You've never had a chance to hold your head up in your own home town, so make the most of your chances when you get away" (394).

Eugene expects to be able to hold his head high by virtue of his romantic ideas. We are told that he "remained a fantasist of the Ideal" even though "he was a child who had looked much on pain and evil." "He belonged with the Mythmakers" among men; he believes that he can live by imagining, by creating a world that corresponds to his dreams. He knows that "he believed in beauty and in order, and that he would wreak out their mighty forms upon the distressful chaos of his life" (391).

His college years disabuse him of some of this fantasy. Hopelessly out of place among his classmates because of his lack of experience and his awkward adolescent appearance, Eugene finds that his freshman year is "filled for him with loneliness, pain, and failure" (394). He begins "to dislike and envy" successful men on campus whose dress and behavior are easy and perfect (395). His mixed emotions are traceable in part to the same unsatisfied desire for status that has been present throughout the book: he looks at the "happy and idle" fraternity men and sees in them "the highest reach of urbane and aristocratic life." They are "the lords of the village and county"; they are "the flower of chivalry, the sons of the mansion-house" (420–21). Eugene cannot sustain himself by his imagination; he still regards himself as an unhappy outsider, and "he wanted to get in. He wanted to be urbane and careless. He wanted to wear well-cut clothes. He wanted to be a gentleman" (421).

Notable failures in his encounters with the opposite sex contribute to the pain of his college years. His first visit to a prostitute in Exeter, a neighboring town, ends in fruitless embarrassment; later trips there result in his going home for Christmas diseased and desperate with remorse. The summer following his first year at the university, he meets Laura James and falls in love, then undergoes his first heartbreak when she leaves him to marry the fiancé she has had all along. A year later he spends a mad summer in Norfolk, Virginia, working or going hungry, wandering through the streets and wharves both looking for her and hoping not to find her.

The greatest blow to Eugene's idealism, the death of Ben, also occurs in this section of the book. Ben's death precipitates the awakening of the artist in Eugene, since it severs his closest personal tie with his family and enables him to replace it with an imaginative relationship.[13] Henceforth he must see Ben through his mind and his memory. The loss of their closeness allows Eugene the distance he needs to find or create meaning out of their lives and thus to rejoin his brother, and the rest of the family, emotionally. Through the isolation of art he is granted kinship with his world. Thus, in the last hours before Ben's death, Eugene watches the event seem to transform his family: "And as they looked and saw his bright eyes already blurred with death, and saw the feeble beating flutter

13. See A. Carl Bredahl, Jr., "*Look Homeward, Angel*: Individuation and Articulation," *Southern Literary Journal,* VI (Fall, 1973), 47–58, for a discussion of the importance of Ben's death to Eugene's artistic development.

of his poor thin breast, the strange wonder, the dark miracle of his life surged over them its enormous loveliness. They grew quiet and calm, they plunged below all the splintered wreckage of their lives, they drew together in a superb communion of love and valiance, beyond horror and confusion, beyond death" (552). Eugene is also transformed, first blinded and deafened "with love and wonder," then imaginatively becoming "a part of their loveliness" (522). He "soar[s]" above the immediate event and is simultaneously "a part" of it in a new and beauty-filled way.

Throughout the preceding chapters, the gap between the authorial voice and the character has been gradually narrowing. Descriptions of Eugene's reading reveal the author's tastes, as occurred earlier in the novel with his love of Shakespeare. Eugene "liked the fabulous," for instance, because "the best fabulists have often been the greatest satirists: satire (as with Aristophanes, Voltaire, and Swift) is a high and subtle art, quite beyond the barnyard snipings and wholesale geese-slaughterings of the present degenerate age. Great satire needs the sustenance of great fable. Swift's power of invention is incomparable: there's no better fabulist in the world" (422). It is clearly the author whose opinion we are hearing here, as he uses Eugene as his own mouthpiece.

The Laura James section includes a revealing apostrophe spoken directly by the author but expressing Eugene's emotions. At the ecstatic climax of the chapter in which they fall in love, the third-person narrative breaks into a rhapsodic passage addressed to "my young love" that ends with a clear enunciation of the aesthetic relationship their affair has become for the artist: "Ghost, ghost, come back from that marriage that we did not foresee, return not into life, but into magic, where we have never died, into the enchanted wood, where we still lie, strewn on the grass" (456).

Three more apostrophes—to Dixieland, to the sea, and to women—appear in the next few chapters. They are obviously Eugene's: the phrase "he thought" introduces the first two (494, 522), and the third is presented ironically as his self-pitying tirade against "my sweet bitches! My fine cheap sluts!" (522–23). Eugene is using the same kind of rhetorical flourish that we have seen the narrator use throughout the book. The rigid distinction between the two is relaxing, and it will temporarily disappear altogether in the last lengthy apostrophe of the novel, at the end of the chapters about Ben's death. The change that Eugene is undergoing occurs as expression as well as event.[14]

Eugene has gone to the cemetery to grieve for Ben. In his "numbed mind, which for days now had fumbled curiously with little things, with little things alone, as a child fumbles with blocks or with little things, a light was growing" (581). Following this narration is a descriptive paragraph that grows in repetition, assonance, and a chantlike rhythm until it becomes the broken phrases running through Eugene's mind. Then the text breaks into first-person plural: "We shall not come again. We never shall come back again. But over us all, over us all, over us all is—something" (582). Is this Eugene speaking of himself and Ben? The author speaking of himself and us? The author and Eugene speaking together? The ambiguity serves Wolfe's rhetorical purpose well, for Eugene's revelation, the "light" that is growing in him of a new aesthetic relation to the world, joins him to Ben and will make an artist of him. The passage ends with a paragraph that can only be spoken by both the author and Eugene, in which artist and brother assure themselves that "Ben will come again, he will not die again, in flower and leaf, in wind and music far, he will come back again," then repeat the phrase that functions as a refrain for the novel, "O lost, and by the wind grieved, ghost, come back again!" (583).

The newfound artistic vision that allows Eugene to escape familial and social shackles and yet retain his past has indeed transformed him, as the final chapter of the novel shows. There he sees himself from the perspective of the artist he is becoming. The "thousand forms of himself . . . that came, that passed, that wove and shifted in unending change, and that remained unchanging Him" are perceivable only to the artist's view. Eugene remembers and thus re-creates himself, calling the child in the vision "My son! My child!" (622). He is the creator of all that he recalls and a part

14. For two readings of the last scene in the novel that stress its significance for Eugene's artistic vocation, see Richard Walser, "The Angel and the Ghost," in Paschal Reeves (ed.), *Thomas Wolfe and the Glass of Time* (Athens, Ga., 1971), 45–67, and John Hagan, "Structure, Theme, and Metaphor in Thomas Wolfe's *Look Homeward, Angel*," in John S. Phillipson (ed.), *Critical Essays on Thomas Wolfe* (Boston, 1985), 32–47.

of it through the act of creating. Thus the ghost Ben tells him at the scene's climax, "*You* are your world" (624).

The final chapter of *Look Homeward, Angel* in essence attempts to create a truer, more noble reality from the junction of art and life. The rhetoric functions as incantation, the weaving of a spell that is meant to turn a young man into a figure of the artist that is essentially mythical in orientation. As something like myth, the autobiographical story of Eugene Gant can become art, a structured form, while remaining as close to amorphous fact as memory can be. The experiment is a dangerous one, as the fortunes of the book have proved: if the spell does not work, the book's climactic ending falls flat and Wolfe is guilty of overwriting, as some readers have charged. Whether or not it succeeds, however, it does illustrate some of the peculiar challenges of autobiographical fiction. It shows also that the idea of the artist as aristocrat played a significant role in how and why Wolfe, like Joyce, undertook such challenges.

3

The Problem of Authority

Of Time and the River, Thomas Wolfe's second book, is in some ways the unfortunate victim of the success of *Look Homeward, Angel*. Wolfe was an instant celebrity after the reviews started to appear and the sales figures began to be tallied for his first book, which received some generous critical comments and sold respectably (no mean feat for a book published the week of the stock market crash of 1929, entering the market at the start of the worst economic depression in the nation's history). With this success came the pressure to follow with a second novel. The public wanted to know if Wolfe was "more than a one-book man," in the words of an early reviewer, and Scribner's wanted to capitalize on its investment in *Look Homeward, Angel* by continuing to bring out works by the novel's author.[1] Wolfe found himself in the uncomfortable position of having to prove himself, quickly, by producing a second, preferably nonautobiographical, novel. (Unfortunately, critical opinion tended to confuse autobiographical fiction with autobiography and

1. Harry Hansen, Review of Thomas Wolfe's *Look Homeward, Angel,* in the New York *World,* October 26, 1929, reprinted in Paschal Reeves (ed.), *Thomas Wolfe: The Critical Reception* (New York, 1974), 6. See also DD, 220.

to distrust the latter as serious art, as Mark Van Doren's contemporary comment in the *Nation* reveals: "Thomas Wolfe's one novel to date, 'Look Homeward, Angel,' needs to be followed by others before anybody can know whether Mr. Wolfe is an artist in anything beyond autobiography" [cited in DD, 306].) Wolfe worked determinedly, even desperately, without taking the time he needed to discover how to proceed. He never found a form to contain his second book. In fact, the book was published before he felt it was finished. In good part, as we shall see, his difficulties in shaping and finishing it arose because he could not abandon the autobiographical character of his fiction and did not, in his haste, allow his work to evolve formally to reflect the demands of a second autobiographical novel. *Of Time and the River* illustrates well that fiction about a subsequent stage of the life of a Eugene Gant (or a Stephen Dedalus) requires a rethinking of authorial stance that Wolfe, for many reasons, never mastered.

Wolfe was not even certain that his second novel would be a continuation of the story of Eugene during the first three years that he worked on it. The first-person narrative of David Hawke, an autobiographical character who differed from Wolfe (and Eugene) in few respects other than his physical appearance, was only one of several projects to which Wolfe devoted his energies from 1930 to 1933. In a letter to Perkins written in late 1930, Wolfe described the plan for Hawke's story: it was to be based on the myth of the giant Antaeus, who could not be defeated in battle since his strength was renewed whenever he touched his mother, Gaea, the goddess of the earth. Wolfe wrote:

> Now don't get alarmed at all this and think I'm writing a Greek myth. All of this is never mentioned once the story gets under way, but it is a magnificent fable, and I have soaked myself in it over a year now: it says what I want to say, and it gives the most magnificent plot and unity to my book. . . . Antaeus of course, is a real person; he is in me but he is *not* me as the fellow in the first book was supposed to be; he is to me what Hamlet or Faust may have been to their authors. Thank God, I have begun to create in the way I want to—it is more completely *autobiographic* than anything I have ever thought of, much *more* than the first one, but it is also completely *fictitious*. Nobody can identify me with Antaeus—whose real name is David Hawke . . . except to say, "He has put himself into this char-

acter." It is a magnificent story, it makes use of all the things I have seen and known about, and it is like a fable. (*LTW*, 279)

In this projection for the new novel, we can recognize a successor to the experiment of enlarging life into myth with which *Look Homeward, Angel* concludes. It is tantalizing to imagine what such a book would have been like if Wolfe had written it (especially in a study of both Wolfe and Joyce, whose second novel is saturated with Greek myth and in whose last work, *Finnegans Wake*, "Time and the river and the mountain are the real heroes").[2] But he did not. Although his plans for "The October Fair," as the second novel was to be titled, were constantly changing, its episodes did not form a consistent mythological pattern. Because of its projected length Wolfe tended to work on it in a piecemeal fashion, writing on whatever part of the huge whole inspired him at the time.[3] This writing technique kept him from shaping the novel as he went along, and he later found it nearly impossible to organize the stacks of manuscript he had accumulated into an orderly work. Finally he and Max Perkins worked together to edit the material into *Of Time and the River*, with Wolfe rewriting Hawke's story as a continuation of Eugene's, from his departure from North Carolina to his meeting with Esther Jack, the fictional counterpart of Aline Bernstein. Only traces of the early plan remained after the book was finished. For example, the eight sections of the published book have allusive titles such as "Telemachus," "Young Faustus," "Antaeus: Earth Again," and "Kronos and Rhea: The Dream of Time," which reflect Wolfe's early mythological orientation for his story. The title of the book itself, interestingly, was originally chosen to represent Wolfe's plan to use the ideas of time and change ("the river") to give unity and structure to his work. It indicates that he was thinking seriously about the implications of memory and growth—two

2. The description of *Finnegans Wake* is from a remark that Joyce made to his friend Eugene Jolas in 1931 that Jolas recalls in "My Friend James Joyce," in Seon Givens (ed.), *James Joyce: Two Decades of Criticism* (2d ed.; New York, 1963), 11–12.

3. Francis Edward Skipp describes the change in method from the chronological one Wolfe had used in writing "O Lost" (the manuscript of *Look Homeward, Angel*) to the new style. See Skipp, "Thomas Wolfe and His Scribner's Editors" (Ph.D. dissertation, Duke University, 1962), 107.

concepts that have great bearing on authorial distance—for his autobiographical fiction as he worked on his second novel.

As published, *Of Time and the River* follows the protagonist of the first book from Altamont to Boston, New York, and Europe as he exiles himself from home, region, and native country in his search for art. The novel ends when his search is complete, after 912 pages of episodes describing his school years at Harvard, his brief career teaching English in Greenwich Village, and his journey to England and France. Eugene discovers his vocation as he realizes that he will be an autobiographical artist, and he returns home to begin his work in earnest, meeting a woman on shipboard who will change his life in the future beyond the pages of the novel. The published text thus records the story of a young man's attempt to escape his background and become an aristocratic artist. He learns, however, that he cannot find what he is looking for even in the "best" society—at a great university in New England; in New York City, at the hub of contemporary American culture; with the wealthiest or most refined of friends; at an ancient university in England; among the Parisian avant garde; or even in the company of the titled nobility of France. In this process of elimination, he is left with nothing but memories of his home. He realizes, however, that by remembering and re-creating his past he can finally answer the questions posed in the proem to the book: "*Where shall the weary rest? When shall the lonely of heart come home? What doors are open for the wanderer?*" (2).

Because of the chaotic manner in which the book was written and prepared for publication, when *Of Time and the River* finally appeared, it was a messy, flawed book. It was regarded as such almost from the long-delayed date of its publication. Typically, Wolfe provoked some of the criticism levied against the book without realizing that he was doing so, by candidly admitting how difficult it had been for him to follow up the promise of *Look Homeward, Angel* with a second novel and telling how much help he had received in getting *Of Time and the River* to press.[4] In *The Story of a*

4. In "Thomas Wolfe and his Scribner's Editors," Chapters 3 and 4, Skipp discusses the complicated editing of the novel. See Skipp's article "*Of Time and the River*: The Final Editing," *Papers of the Bibliographical Society of America*, LXIV (1970),

Novel he gave a fascinating if perhaps ill-advised confession of how he spent years writing without a plan, swept in the "rolling and ungovernable tide" of a "floodtide river of creation" but producing at first "no ordered narrative, no planned design."[5] His struggle to shape and finish the book ended, he recalled, when Maxwell Perkins literally took the manuscript from him:

> In the middle of December of that year [1933] the great editor, of whom I have spoken, and who, during all this tormented period of struggle and frustration, had kept a quiet but vigilant watch upon me, called me to his home and quietly informed me that my book was finished. I could not believe him. I could not credit my own hearing. I could only look at him with stunned surprise, and finally I could only tell him out of that bottomless depth of my own hopelessness, that he was mistaken, that the book was not finished, that it could never be completed, that I was unequal to the task, that I could write no more. He answered with the same quiet finality that the book was finished whether I knew it or not, and he told me then to go to my room and spend the next week in collecting in its proper order the manuscript which had accumulated during the last two years.[6]

The Story of a Novel incited Bernard DeVoto to launch a scathing attack on Wolfe in the *Saturday Review of Literature*.[7] Wolfe, DeVoto claimed, needed less raging genius and more careful craftsmanship if he were to be a great novelist. He needed to learn to write his

---

313–22, which also analyzes Perkins' cuts from the final typescript and the literary tastes of both the editor and author that are revealed by those cuts. Richard S. Kennedy suggests that Wolfe had more control over the editing process than has been commonly assumed: see Kennedy, "What the Galley Proofs of *Of Time and the River* Tell Us," *Thomas Wolfe Review*, IX (Fall, 1985), 1–8. Nonetheless, Donald's account of the entire process of revising *Of Time and the River* into publishable form (DD, 278–82, 292–306) is that of a tremendous exercise in artistic folly. Wolfe finally surrendered the task of editing and proofing almost completely to Maxwell Perkins and John Hall Wheelock, the copy editor, leaving for the Chicago World's Fair when the galleys were only partly finished. His later resentment toward Scribner's over the whole affair seems well founded.

5. Thomas Wolfe, *The Story of a Novel*, in Leslie Field (ed.), *The Autobiography of an American Novelist* (Cambridge, Mass., 1983), 36.

6. *Ibid.*, 69.

7. Bernard DeVoto, "Genius Is Not Enough," reprinted in Louis D. Rubin, Jr. (ed.), *Thomas Wolfe: A Collection of Critical Essays* (Englewood Cliffs, N.J., 1973), 72–79.

own books without the kind of help he had received from Perkins in the editing of his manuscript. Entitled "Genius Is Not Enough," DeVoto's essay seriously influenced Wolfe's career by precipitating the writer's break with his "great editor" to affiliate himself with another publishing firm, and the essay has had similar importance for Wolfe's literary reputation by foreshadowing the now-standard indictments of Wolfe's prose as juvenile and overblown.[8] The main points of attack are worth restating here, for several of the weaknesses DeVoto found in *Of Time and the River* are traceable to problems inherent in autobiographical fiction, the form with which Wolfe was still absorbed.

Besides the charge of "shocking contempt of the medium," by which DeVoto meant inconsistencies within the text from one scene to another (copy-editing errors that were found throughout the book, resulting from the haste with which it was rushed to press), DeVoto's primary accusations were against what he saw as "infantilism" and the "logorrhea" of Wolfe's "blank verse, bombast, and apocalyptic delirium."[9] The first problem was Eugene's emotional responses: the character tended to imagine that other people were bigger than life and to inflate the importance of all his experiences. Second, the rhythmic, heightened prose in the many chanted or declaimed passages offended DeVoto's sense of the kind of language proper to fiction: a novelist should not interrupt his story to give his opinions directly to his readers.

Both of these charges point to Wolfe's insufficient control of narrative distance in *Of Time and the River*. Eugene *is* less believable in this novel than he was in *Look Homeward, Angel*. The reasons for this phenomenon lie not so much in the author's "infantile regression," however, as in the uncertain distance at which the authorial voice stands from the character. Following the climax of *Look Homeward, Angel*, when Eugene embraces what is essentially an ar-

8. DeVoto's article was not by any means the only reason for the highly emotional split between Perkins and Wolfe, who were both professional associates and good friends. See Skipp, "Thomas Wolfe and His Scribner's Editors," Chapter 1, for a bibliography of works that analyze the split (through 1961); and Skipp's own analysis, "Thomas Wolfe, Maxwell Perkins, and Politics," *Modern Fiction Studies*, XIII (1967), 503–11. See also RSK, DD, and A. Scott Berg, *Max Perkins: Editor of Genius* (New York, 1978), for more recent discussions of this complex series of events.

9. DeVoto, "Genius Is Not Enough," in Rubin (ed.), *Thomas Wolfe*, 74, 77.

tistic way of viewing his world in order to be able to live with it, his relation to his experiences—to the action in *Of Time and the River*—has changed. His emotions and actions and his ordering of them into words are now intimately joined, and the words of the novel's text must reflect Eugene's own growing ability thus to articulate his experience. In this ability (as well as by his age, older and therefore nearer Wolfe's own) he is increasingly close to the author. Wolfe needed in his second novel to portray the continued growth of Eugene into the writer of a book such as *Of Time and the River*. He needed also to find narrative techniques that would reflect the new relation between his character and the voice that tells the story.[10]

As Kennedy notes, *Of Time and the River* displays "an abundance of verbal experiments" such as "a great potpourri of dithyrambic chants, catalogues, exercises in word play, declamations, meditations, parodies, satiric sketches, short stories, essays, fantasies, and even journal notes."[11] These rhetorical displays were some of the extensive stylistic experiments with which Wolfe attempted to create a new kind of self-conscious fiction for his second book. As they appear in the published version of that book, they perform the same function as the poetic sections of the earlier book, drawing attention to the authorial voice and decreasing the distance be-

10. Several critics have also pointed to the question of the narrator in *Of Time and the River* as a key element in the novel's success or failure. Daniel R. Fruit, in "Of Time and the Rhetoric: The Narrator in Thomas Wolfe's Second Novel," *Thomas Wolfe Review*, IX (Fall, 1985), 31–40, disagrees ultimately with Louis D. Rubin, Jr., "The Sense of Being Young," introduction to Rubin (ed.), *Thomas Wolfe*, 1–30, that the narrator undermines the effectiveness of the fiction. As is apparent here, I agree with Rubin and with C. Hugh Holman, *The Loneliness at the Core: Studies in Thomas Wolfe* (Baton Rouge, 1975), that the novel is badly damaged by mismanaged point of view.

11. RSK, 271. *Dithyramb* was the word that Perkins often wrote in the margins of Wolfe's manuscript to identify a passage of lushly poetic style that he recommended cutting. The word's slightly derogatory tone indicates one of the basic differences of opinion between editor and author about the style, and hence also about the meaning and purpose, of Wolfe's prose. See Skipp, "Thomas Wolfe and His Scribner's Editors," 178–83. Perkins tended to value prose that impelled the story along or dramatized characters, while Wolfe often worked for rhythmic, Whitmanesque creation of mood. The excision of such passages obviously changed the formal nature of the text and therefore should be noted.

tween that voice and the character Eugene.[12] Their proliferation, however, together with the almost complete lack of irony in the depiction of Eugene, often creates the impression not of the character transcending his experiences but of the author descending to the character's level, relinquishing his position above and apart from the action. Rather than seeming highly sensitive and likely to develop into an artist, Eugene seems overcome by his emotions, and the authorial voice seems overly intrusive.

The central flaws in *Of Time and the River* may be traced to a failure of rhetoric: parts of this novel are not convincing in the way that Wolfe seems to have intended. The problems result not from the author's infantilism or unrestrained prolixity but from stylistic misjudgment undermining the authority within the novel of the voice representing the author. This question of authority (the basic issue of rhetoric) leads to the further question of rhetorical purposes in *Of Time and the River*. Why did Wolfe press certain points in the novel? Interestingly, the text reveals a definite correlation between rhetorical intensity and the sensitive subject so prominent in *A Portrait* and *Look Homeward, Angel*—the social circumstances of the young artist.

The perceived authority of the authorial voice is, of course, one of the basic conventions of novel-writing and novel-reading, the unspoken rules of the game that are either followed or broken for a purpose in well-written fiction. The perceived author should be our trustworthy guide to the book. If we are presented with action or discourse, we generally assume that the action occurred or that the discourse is reliable commentary. Likewise, if something is omitted, we are usually meant to assume either that it is not significant or that part of the book's meaning resides in our ignorance of it.

A novelistic problem occurs if this convention is broken. We begin to doubt that the writer knows what he or she is writing about if we sense that his or her narration or evaluation is not in an artistic sense *true*, if we have trouble believing the voice that represents

12. For an early examination of Wolfe's rhetoric from a phenomenological point of view see Maurice Natanson, "The Privileged Moment: A Study in the Rhetoric of Thomas Wolfe," in C. Hugh Holman, *The World of Thomas Wolfe* (New York, 1962), 78–84.

him or her. Authority is threatened or damaged or (in some very bad novels) lost entirely. This problem plagues *Of Time and the River*, as Louis D. Rubin, Jr., has noted.[13] It lies at the heart of DeVoto's and many other critics' censure of the book and its author for such "faults" as its rhapsodic interludes, its philosophical ideas, the emotionalism of Eugene Gant, and even the narrative "honesty," the fidelity to actual event, of Wolfe's obsessively autobiographical form. Obviously, the flaws do not lie in the rhapsody, rhetoric, or intellectual underpinning per se. The poetic has its place in many prose works, and all fiction is rhetorical in one sense or another. Wolfe did not have a structured metaphysical system uniting his intellectual assumptions, but many other novels have substructures of organic, unschematized, or relatively simple ideas.[14] And, of course, autobiography is often (if not always, as some assert) an inextricable part of fictional form. A novel is not necessarily second-rate because it is autobiographical.

The question we must ask is whether or not the poetic passages, the declamations, the metaphysics, the autobiographical material, or any other part of this novel serve their intended function. Do they convince us of Thomas Wolfe's authority? Do they provide his authorial second self with fictional integrity?

The novel is very uneven in quality. Some sections are sadly unsuccessful, while others are among the best pieces that Wolfe wrote (in this novel or in any other work). Even the worst parts, however unimpressive they are as fiction, clearly reveal the undermining of authority that has caused the damage to them, and they allow us to isolate a central reason why the authorial presence fails in these instances to gain credibility. In addition, ironically, Wolfe's mastery of the same impulse that foils his authorial voice in some parts of the novel intensifies that voice's power in other parts. As Faulkner and others recognized, Wolfe's weaknesses and his strengths have

13. Rubin, "The Sense of Being Young," in Rubin (ed.), *Thomas Wolfe*, 13.

14. For studies of Wolfe's metaphysical suppositions see Louis D. Rubin, Jr., *The Weather of His Youth* (Baton Rouge, 1955), Chapter 3; Monroe M. Stearns, "The Metaphysics of Thomas Wolfe," in Richard Walser (ed.), *The Enigma of Thomas Wolfe: Biographical and Critical Selections* (Cambridge, Mass., 1953), 195–205; and Larry Rubin, "Thomas Wolfe and the Lost Paradise," in Paschal Reeves (ed.), *The Merrill Studies in "Look Homeward, Angel"* (Columbus, Ohio, 1970), 107–116.

similar origins. Faulkner's famous comment about the writers of his generation, that "we had all failed, but Wolfe had made the best failure because he tried hardest to say the most," is worth repeating. Wolfe would, Faulkner continues, "throw away style, coherence, all the rules of preciseness" so that he could "try to put all the experience of the human heart on the head of a pin, as it were."[15] Wolfe's unflagging attempt to wrest every shred of truth from his work is both his greatest achievement and his most serious failure. As he had done in the ecstatic conclusion of *Look Homeward, Angel*, Wolfe tried in *Of Time and the River* to yoke artistic and literal truth by creating a fictional world that would also do justice to reality as he had lived it. When his work succeeds at this ambitious undertaking, the result is fiction of the highest quality; when it fails, the price paid is poor writing that reflects badly on its author as only autobiographical fiction can.

Among the successes in *Of Time and the River* are the story of Bascom Pentland, reworked from the short novel "A Portrait of Bascom Hawke";[16] the nearly flawless series of episodes leading up to and including the death of W. O. Gant; most of the scenes on trains, especially the race at the beginning of Book 4; and the brief chapter near the end of the book in which Eugene sits in Dijon, France, remembering his home—the scene in which he finally begins to be a writer after all and that tells us what he will write about in his first novel. Among the failures are certainly the account of Eugene's brief teaching career in New York, with the disturbing anti-Semitism that runs through it and Eugene's relationship with Abe Jones and his family; several scenes with Robert Weaver, Eugene's wealthy, dissipated friend; the remnant of a book that Wolfe could never write about Eugene's friendship with the aristocratic

15. Quoted by Richard Walser in the preface to Walser (ed.), *The Enigma of Thomas Wolfe*, vii.

16. The character Bascom Pentland was based on Wolfe's maternal uncle Henry Westall. The earliest version of the story was originally developed for "O Lost." When the length of that book precluded the use of the story, Wolfe set it aside, but he later revised it for "The October Fair" manuscript. It appeared as a novelette in *Scribner's Magazine* in 1932 and finally was edited into *Of Time and the River*, first as a whole, by Wolfe, and then in segments interspersed by Perkins with other episodes of Eugene's experiences at Harvard.

Joel Pierce and his family, the Hudson "River People"; the description of the Rhodes scholars Eugene encounters at Oxford; and particularly the wild scenes in France with his Cambridge friend Starwick and Starwick's friends Elinor and Ann, the "big, dumb, beautiful Boston bitch" (757) who fails to return Eugene's amorous attention.

The latter sections of the novel have several things in common. One of them is extratextual: the worst sections are often among the last that Wolfe wrote. In the last months before publication, when he was in a desperate hurry to finish the manuscript, Wolfe dashed off, among other segments, the descriptions of life at the Hotel Leopold, Eugene's lodgings in New York (though not the climactic scene with Robert Weaver, his mistress, and her dying husband), part of the "River People" episode, and many of the adventures with Starwick, Elinor, and Ann (RSK, 266–68).

There are significant internal similarities between these sequences as well. The better ones tend to show Eugene either alone or in familiar company, with his family or with a kind or class of people he knows well, although individually they may be strangers to him. The less successful scenes, correspondingly, show him among people he knows slightly and feels either threatened by or slightly inferior to. Of course, it is a truism that all writers write best about what they know best. But the problems these scenes present is deeper than the vagueness or oversimplicity we associate with an author's lack of familiarity with a subject. The narrator of the scenes in the unsuccessful sections, without clearly departing from the limited third-person narrative pattern that is the norm for the novel, utters with an unusual degree of certainty opinions and judgments of the situation or the way of life being depicted, as if to convince us that he knows it and all that it implies intimately. And if he does, then the character Eugene Gant, who will be this writer in the future and through whose eyes we view the book's actions, must have intuitive "insider's" knowledge, too. Yet we can see that Eugene lacks such understanding.

The section that introduces us to Eugene's student and friend Abe Jones, for instance, begins with an oracular passage about "man's youth" that ends in first-person plural, so that Eugene and the narrator are linked in "finally remembering with tenderness and joy the good bleak visage of the pavement cipher who was the first friend we ever knew in the great city—in whose gray face its million strange and secret mysteries were all compact—and who was our friend, our brother, and this earth's nameless man" (455). As Eugene becomes familiar with Abe and his family, several general pronouncements by the narrating voice are interjected into the text, seeming to indicate retrospective artistic understanding of the Joneses. For instance, a highly stylized panegyric precedes the introduction of Abe's family:

> What earth had nourished him? Had he been born and grown there among the asphalt lilies and the pavement wheat? What corn was growing from the cobblestones? Or was there never a cry of earth up through the beaten and unyielding cement of the streets? Had he forgotten the immortal and attentive earth still waiting at the roots of steel?
>
> No. (458)

Although Abe is an interesting minor character, these explicit assurances that he is somehow symbolic of the city's mysteries are not reinforced on a dramatic level in the scenes devoted to him. Thus, as DeVoto charged, Wolfe is "telling" and not "showing" here. The fault, however, is not the presence of rhetorical intensity, but the unsatisfactory correspondence between the narrator's rhetoric and the action in this section.

Most bothersome in the Abe Jones material is the racial stereotyping and obvious anti-Semitism that appears throughout the section. The formal problem that this stereotyping causes comes from the same lack of convincing knowledge on the part of the narrator that plagues the section generally. We do not easily believe that the music Abe's sister plays on the piano "awakened a thousand subtle echoes in his Jewish soul," for example, or that he reads over an invective-filled letter before he sends it, "grinning widely with Kike delight" (464, 465). The offense to our sensibilities that occurs when we read that Abe, "with a million other dreary Hebrew yearners, [was] convinced that he was the messiah for which the earth was groaning" or that "the Jewish women were as old as nature, and as round as the earth," strikes a blow to our opinion of both the narrator and Eugene, since both character and authorial voice have formed opinions and found words to describe, for instance, Jewish women as "female, fertile, yolky, fruitful as the earth, and ready for the plow" (468, 480). The artist may think he understands Abe and his people, but his vision of the artistic truth about New York and Jews living there rings false. It is more likely that we will perceive in the author an unresolved conflict of emotions on this issue—admiration for an alien culture mixed with xenophobia.

The story of Robert Weaver is also damaged by weakness attributable to rhetorical failure. Like Abe Jones, Robert Weaver, Eugene's wealthy and charming but utterly unstable friend from Altamont, represents a way of life about which Eugene knows little and about which we might imagine him to have mixed feelings. We are introduced to Robert in the first scene of the novel, as he boards the same train that Eugene is taking on his way north. Our attention is first drawn to a characteristic, involuntary action: he "thrust one hand quickly and nervously into his trouser's pocket in such a way that his fine brown coat came back, and the large diamond-shaped pin of the Delta Kappa Epsilon fraternity was revealed" (16). This is the fraternity, we know from *Look Homeward, Angel*, of the social elite. The "fraternity men" who seem to Eugene in his first year at Pulpit Hill to "represent . . . the highest reach of urbane and aristocratic life" as he watches them from a distance are "Dekes" (*LHA*, 421).

Robert is carelessly superior to Eugene in social position, and Eugene responds to him as he did to the fraternity men in *Look Homeward, Angel*, with envy that manifests itself both in respect and hostility. Robert's rank, we learn, is high enough to allow him to be on speaking terms (but not genuinely intimate) with Altamont's one representative of English aristocracy, who is also aboard the train. (John Hugh William Macpherson Marriott, the aristocrat, is clearly based on John Francis Amherst Cecil, the English nobleman who married Cornelia Vanderbilt). Late in the night Robert and Marriott enter the car where Eugene is sitting. The Englishman soon dismisses the young man, and Eugene marks the clear signs of relative status in the scene: Robert speaks to "Hugh" with "almost fawning eagerness," then comes over to stand above Eugene, assuming the same distinctive pose, "thrust[ing] one hand quickly and impatiently into the trousers' pocket of his well-cut clothes in such a way that his Delta Kappa Epsilon pin was for a moment visible" (62, 64).

Eugene's hidden resentment surfaces soon after he joins Robert and another youth and, standing on the rocking platform between two of the traincars, becomes "wild and dark and jubilant" on illicit corn whiskey (68). The *veritas* the liquor prompts reveals a slight from Eugene's and Robert's boyhood, when Robert, with the same servile attitude we have just witnessed in his interaction with the Englishman, called Eugene a "tomb-stone cutter's son" in front of some socially superior boys. The insult has rankled Eugene for years: he calls Robert a "'cheap Deke son-of-a-bitch—Too good to talk to us on the street when you were sucking around after Bruce Martin or Steve Patton or Jack Marriott—but a life-long brother—oh! couldn't see enough of us, could you, when you were alone?'" And he tries to reverse the snub: "'Who do you think you are with your big airs and big Deke pin!—My people were better people than your crowd ever hoped to be—we've been here longer and we're better people'" (74).

The social inequality of the two friends is stressed throughout the sections of the novel that tell Robert's story. His mistress, Martha Upshaw, is a social luminary, an heiress to the fortune of the Westermans, who made their wealth in "vacuum cleaners and electric refrigerators" and whose name is a transparent pseudonym for the Westinghouses (307). His friends include Emmett Blake, "a nephew of George Blake, the great Middle-western manufacturer of cheap motor cars," obviously a fictional counterpart to a member of the Ford family (363). Eugene's importance to and innate superiority over Robert is equally stressed: almost every encounter between them ends with the "tomb-stone cutter's son" (or, in one instance, a member of his family) serving as a source of strength or agent of rescue for the other. Eugene listens to Robert's drunken recitations of his troubles, acts as arbitrator between Robert and the landlord at the Hotel Leopold (after helping him to get a room there), and is the only sane presence in the violent final scene with Robert, Martha, and Martha's husband, Upshaw. Luke Gant bails his brother along with Robert and Emmett Blake out of jail in Blackstone, South Carolina, the loud protests of influential connections proving less effective than Luke's plebeian but immediately available wallet.

A great deal of space in *Of Time and the River* is devoted to Robert Weaver and the odd friendship between him and Eugene. In fact, readers are likely to be baffled by the amount of attention given to this story. Eugene sees Robert only a few times during the course of the narrative and does not seem to have been a good friend of his during their childhood. Despite the narrator's lengthy descriptions of Robert, Eugene does not actually know him well. The narrator seems more fascinated by than familiar with Robert.

The balance between novelistic depiction and the subject matter being depicted is upset, in part, because Wolfe was surely dwelling on the suicide of his friend Henry Stevens, on whom the character Robert Weaver is based (RSK, 257n). Moreover, this section of the text was probably dictated, since Wolfe injured his right arm early in 1932 and experimented with this method of composition, which lends itself to expansiveness, out of necessity (RSK, 248). It was an unhappy coincidence that Wolfe had to dictate a section of his narrative that contained material over which he seems to have previously struggled to gain artistic control. The author does not seem in this section to be completely aware of his own motives for exploring Robert's impending suicide, the self-destruction of an acquaintance whose social and material advantages he has envied. And thus we probably are not convinced by the Robert Weaver sequence as a whole: after the first scene on the train, the narrator does not present Eugene's ambivalence toward Robert but seems to fabricate a rather forced picture of Eugene's kindness to and superiority over his friend. The point seems to be that Eugene will succeed and Robert will not, yet we feel that the complex relationship between them is simplified and to some extent falsified during the course of the story.

The problem of narrative authority reappears, in a slightly different form, in the "River People" episode. This long section, which was adapted from a novel Wolfe planned to write as early as 1928 (before the manuscript of *Look Homeward, Angel* had even found a publisher), fictionalizes Wolfe's friendship with a young acquaintance from Harvard, Olin Dows. Dows initiated the close friendship in 1924, after Wolfe had moved to Manhattan, by asking for help in finding an apartment in the cheap hotel where Wolfe was living. Dows was younger than Wolfe and engagingly modest—so unpretentious, in fact, that when he first invited Wolfe home for a vacation, Wolfe was astonished to discover Dows's enormously wealthy background. The Dowses were genuine plutocrats, the first Wolfe had met at close range, and he was very taken with them and with Rhinebeck, their two-thousand-acre estate on the Hudson River near the estates of the Vincent Astors and the Franklin D. Roosevelts. He remained close to Olin and spent a good deal of time at Rhinebeck intermittently over a five-year period.

The "River People" section of *Of Time and the River* is one of the most fascinating in the book for what it reveals about Eugene's search for his vocation and the narrator's perceptions about that search. The progress it represents toward Eugene's goal of becoming an artist lies not so much in what the narrator or the young protagonist assert to be true about the aristocratic culture as in what is revealed about their own class consciousness and the role that this sensitivity plays in the artist's development. For not only Eugene thinks that Joel Pierce (the character drawn from Olin Dows) and his family live in an earthly paradise and is shattered when he realizes that he cannot live there. The authorial voice clearly assures us at the beginning of the episode that for us, too, as well as for Eugene, the house at Far Field Farm would be "a dream house, a house such as one sees only in a dream," if we were fortunate enough to visit it (515).

Seen from the window of a train, the Pierces' great house captures Eugene's imagination before he actually visits it. Preoccupied by a desire he cannot define, but which we recognize as his need for art, he rides trains for escape from his immediate surroundings and for a way to view life from a vantage point out of time. From the still interior of his berth, he looks out at the countryside and is arrested by a vision of a life that he is subconsciously drawn toward.

> And his memory of these journeys of the night, and these wonderful returns at morning, was haunted always by the vision of a single house. It was a great white house, set delicate and gleaming in frail morning light upon a noble hill that swept back from the river, and it was shaded by the

silent stature of great trees, and vast swards of velvet lawn swept round it, and morning was always there and the tender purity of light.

That house haunted his memory like a dream: he could not forget it. (476)

Eugene responds initially to the wealth and elegance of his Harvard friend Joel Pierce and the Pierce family with sheer delight, and the narrator's voice gives no hint of qualification of these feelings. When Mr. Pierce takes the two young men to dinner and the theater, the atmosphere of grace and assurance inspires in Eugene a rapturous sense of fulfillment of his desires, and the narrative assumes a corresponding tone. Dinner in a fine restaurant with its "huge nameless thrill and prophecy of oncoming night touched him with a feeling of joy and nameless anticipation." Under its spell,

suddenly, all the horror, heat and desolation of the day was forgotten. He forgot the blind horror of the man-swarm thrusting through the mazes of the furious streets. He forgot the drowning flood of humid flesh, the pale, wet, suffering faces that thrust from nowhere out of sweltering heat, that were engulfed again into the heat-hazed distances of swarming streets in which man's life seemed more unaccountable than the sands of the sea, and more blind, lost and horribly forsaken than the lives of those eyeless crawls and gropes that scuttle blindly and forever through murky ooze upon the sea's vast floor. (501)

Using this kind of language, the narrating voice goes on to describe the youth's "wild prophecy, its huge and secret joy," the revival of "his childhood dreams of the enchanted city, the city of great men and glorious women, the city of unceasing joy, of power, triumph and success, and of the fortunate, good, and happy life," and his "indescribable sense of wealth and power and prosperous ease" during the evening (501).

Unmixed approval of Joel Pierce's life continues as Eugene visits the family at their wonderful home on the Hudson River. Joel Pierce's pleasant manner with a servant at the train station prompts Eugene to notice that his friend's "warm, instinctive humanity was evident in all he did, it came out somehow in the most casual words and relationships with people," although Joel's words seem more the product of easy familiarity with the role of master than an "enormous decency and radiance in his soul and character" coupled with a "curious impersonality" (512–13). Almost everything about Joel's family is colored for Eugene by an aura of beauty and goodness that we can see is largely the result of the insulation from ugliness or temptation that wealth can provide.

Eugene realizes gradually that shelter from unpleasantness is impossible without a willingness to not see a part of reality, to pretend that it does not exist. His need for beauty is also a need for truth as it is found in the world beyond the boundaries of Far Field Farm. But he does not arrive at this opinion until after we have heard voiced (by the narrator, through Eugene's mind) a countering argument for the value of an aristocratic way of life.

> It was not merely the wealth, the luxury and the comfort of the scene that filled his heart with a sense of joy and victory. Far more than this, it was the feeling that this life of wealth, and luxury and comfort was so beautiful and right and good. . . . It seemed to him to be the most wonderful and beautiful life on earth, not only because it existed for the comfort and the soul-enrichment of its choice few, but because it stood there as a beacon and a legend in the hearts of all men living—a symbol of what all life on earth should be, a promise of what every man on earth should have. (539)

The rhetoric here is so unreserved in its approbation, without a perceivable touch of irony or doubt to qualify Eugene's enthusiasm, that we believe that our author shares in it. When the bubble bursts and the young man discovers that he must search elsewhere to satisfy his yearning for what is "beautiful and right and good," the author seems to share his agonizing disappointment: "It was a desolating loss, a hideous acknowledgment, a cruel discovery—to know that all the haunted glory of this enchanted world . . . was gone for him forever. It was a bitter pill to know that what had seemed so grand, so strong, so right, and so inevitable at the moment of discovery was now lost to him—that some blind chemistry of man's common earth, and of his father's clay, and of genial nature, had taken from him what he seemed to possess, and that he could never make this enchanted life his own again" (571). As Eugene makes up his mind to leave Joel and all that the Pierce family represents, we are meant to assume that our own initial wonder and delight at their way of life, and our ultimate disappointment and painful loss, would be the same.

We would not respond as Eugene does if we happen not to have the same sense of social and cultural inferiority that our narrator seems to possess. His attitudes convince us that he is far from an authority on the Jewish race or the moneyed life of a Robert Weaver or a Joel Pierce—or on such subjects as New England and the bitches that live there, the culture of a group of Rhodes scholars in England, or his own repressed resentment of his friend Starwick. (The sections with Starwick and Starwick's two friends Elinor and Ann in France are particularly plagued by this flaw. They are based on an equally pointless adventure with Wolfe's Harvard friend Kenneth Raisbeck and two women, which lasted for several weeks in January, 1925. Raisbeck, like Starwick, hid his homosexuality beneath a refined, "artistic" manner. Wolfe, like Eugene, came to feel betrayed both by Raisbeck's attractiveness to his female companions and the unspoken threat to the masculinity of art that he represented. In the novel, Eugene is made to seem a true artist rather than an impotent dilettante, innocent of Starwick's empty worldliness, but he is obviously unaware of his own, less disinterested motives for distrusting his three companions.) On the contrary, if we listen as we read, we can hear plainly the traces of an ordinary, middle-class, southern American accent. And we can hear it wanting to be other than that. Thus we are not completely convinced of the accuracy of our narrator's report when he speaks as if he has mastered the inner truth of matters in which we suspect him of having an unmasterable bias.

On the other hand, however, we can easily believe that Eugene Gant does not find what he is looking for in the search that unifies this sprawling novel until he discovers his vocation.[17] He does not belong in Altamont (as *Look Homeward, Angel*, the first part of his quest, proved to him and to us). The door he looks for will not open into fulfillment while he is at home, nor can it open into a culture or a class other than the one from which he came. It only opens back into his memories of home through the art of remembering and writing.

17. See John Hagan, "Thomas Wolfe's *Of Time and the River*: The Quest for Transcendence," in Richard S. Kennedy (ed.), *Thomas Wolfe: A Harvard Perspective*

In the best sections of *Of Time and the River*, as in *Look Homeward, Angel*, the relationship between the narrating voice and the narrative material parallels the relationship that Eugene is groping toward with his family, his community, and his past. This relationship will be an aesthetic one, and so the artistic understanding that the narrator demonstrates, however it is manifested (in straightforward dialogue or narration, intrusive rhetoric or poetic musing) foreshadows Eugene's own future understanding.

Eugene struggles with the tension of being out of place in familiar surroundings, being temperamentally unlike his own people. The narrator re-creates the experience of tension, then points the way to resolution through Eugene's discovery of the same kind of artistic vision that characterizes the narrative. Thus the events within the text illuminate the novel's characteristic style, and both join to produce the complex entity that is coherent autobiographical fiction. For example, when the young man goes to visit his dying father in Baltimore on his way to Cambridge, in Book 1, he is lost in hatred of "the great engine of the hospital, with all its secret, sinister, and inhuman perfections, together with its clean and sterile smells which seemed to blot out the smell of rotting death around one" (84). The awful knowledge of his father's impending death is transcended for us, though, by the beauty of the prose in Chapter 6 (77–86). We are shown the image of the old man's "powerful and living" hands, which symbolize W. O. Gant's indomitable spirit by their stark contrast to the rest of his dying frame and which mirror his own artistic nature as a stonecutter who dreamed of being a sculptor.

Nothing was left but his hands. The rest of the man was dead. But the great hands of the stonecutter . . . had lost none of their character of power and massive shapeliness.

In the huge shapely knuckles, in the length and sinewy thickness of the great fingers—which were twice the size of an ordinary man's—and in the whole length and sinewy contour of the hand, there was a quality of sculptural design which was as solid and proportionate as any of the marble

(Athens, Ohio, 1983), 3–20, for a persuasive analysis of Eugene's search and the mythic, cyclical pattern it follows.

hands of love and grace which the stonecutter had so often carved upon the surface of a grave-yard monument. (78)

The narrator then recounts, from Gant's point of view, memories of his youth during the Civil War, which nearly redeem the subsequent misspent years by the vision of timeless unity they prompt in him. The vision, given in a poetic segment with the refrain "all of it was his," dissipates in the realization (it is not clear whose: the point of view is simultaneously Gant's and the narrator's) that Eugene's father did not find the artistic ordering that could have saved him. He felt "something wild and secret" that "had been weaving through the generations, a dark terrific weaving of the threads of time and destiny," but he could not finally make out the pattern of the fabric: "But it had come to this: an old man dying on a porch, staring through the sun-hazed vistas of October towards the lost country of his youth. This was the end of man, then. . . . This was the end, and the end was horrible in ugliness. At the end it was not well" (83). These literary devices immediately precede the final meeting of Gant and his son, as if to show us what Eugene will need to recognize or create in order to achieve his own victory, by artistic understanding, over the fact of death. Eugene is his father's son in his predisposition to look for an essentially artistic understanding of this greatest of human mysteries, but, as this successful scene proves to us, he will succeed where Gant has failed.

We do not have to reconstruct Eugene's accomplishment from the narrator's alone. We can see in the character as well the impulse to create art in order to distance himself from an immediate situation and thus to understand it more fully. At Gant's funeral back in Altamont, his son is "haunted" by his father's hands. They evoke for him "in an instant searing flash of memory and recognition the lost world of his father's life of manual power, hunger, fury, savage abundance and wild joy, the whole enchanted structure of that lost life of magic he had made for them" (271). He is repelled by the rest of the scene—the artificiality of the prepared corpse, the "oily swollen faces" of the mourning women, and the mingled smells from the coffin, the flowers, and the food being prepared in the kitchen—but he conquers the "weird disbelief" into which his disgust has driven him by looking again at his father's hands. Eugene can grasp the mystery of life and death that is occurring around him only by an image of the hands that "seemed to rest there upon the groomed, bereft and vacant horror of the corpse with a kind of terrible reality as if there really is, in death, some energy of life that will not die, some element of man's life that must persist and that resumes into a single feature of his life the core and essence of his character" (273).

The explanation of the importance of this image for Eugene is redundant, since the earlier scene contained such a lengthy description of the hands, and the treatment of the funeral might have profited by the editing Wolfe never had time to give the manuscript. (Almost verbatim repetition of phrases is found throughout *Of Time and the River*, an easily recognizable result of its piecemeal writing and hurried editing. It is interesting, however, to note ideas or motifs that were of recurring importance to Wolfe in the perhaps inadvertent repetitions.) Nevertheless, the reappearance of the image of the hands is not useless. Like the recurring images of birds in *A Portrait*, it depicts the habits of thought of a would-be artist, for whose vocation imaging is a vital prerequisite.

As I mentioned earlier, some of the many stylistic experiments in *Of Time and the River* fail in their attempt to close the distance between narrator and protagonist because they, in effect, lower the author to the character's level rather than raise the character momentarily to the author's level by granting him a foretaste of authorial vision. But others succeed, illustrating beautifully the narrowing gap in time and experience between Eugene and the writer of an autobiographical novel about his life. From the beginning of the book we find lengthy reveries that shift between an origin in the mind of Eugene and an origin in the mouth of the narrating voice, a pattern reminiscent of *Look Homeward, Angel.* For example, *Of Time and the River* begins as a generally external, omniscient narrative with the main character called "the boy." Then, when the train ride north from Altamont to Boston begins, the boy is everyman: now he is called "the traveller" and is referred to by a generalizing pronoun. It is not Eugene but "one" who "gets on the train and with a sense of disbelief and wonder sees the familiar faces, shapes, and structures of his native town recede out of the last fierce clasp of life and vision" (25). A rhetorical passage that begins "Who has seen fury riding in the mountains?" follows, shifting from third- to first-person plural: now the fury that Eugene feels "is a strange and subtle worm that will be forever feeding at our heart . . . a madness working in our brain . . . a devil moving in the conduits of our blood . . . a spirit . . . swelling in our soul" (28). As the chapter ends we realize abruptly that it may have been not the omniscient narrator but the boy who felt and perhaps formed the words to express this fury. The section following the rhetorical passage answers the last question the passage poses: "Was he then, on such a night, betrayed to fury—was it then, on such a night, that fury came?" The section begins "He never knew" (29), continuing the stream of ideas in a different style. Now we witness almost an interior monologue that moves from thought to thought, from memory to memory, in the boy's mind, although the third-person convention is maintained.[18]

In this section and in many of the sections that revolve around memory, such a dangerous technique can work well indeed. We witness the process of artistic creation in both an early and a late stage: we look at where the impulse to be a writer comes from, and we see that impulse still alive in the words of the narrator of the book we read. This doubling of point of view makes splendid reading. But when the narrator pictures Eugene as moved by an emotion or influenced by a set of circumstances that we recognize as a motive for the creation of Wolfe's art, he must not intimate that Eugene will conquer or transform it so that it ceases to be important to him (implying that the narrator has already done this). For then the book belies the narrator, and his authority is, for the moment, lost.

Of Time and the River is a novel about needing to write, about raw and painful experiences of familial, social, regional, and national

18. A troublesome critical question about *Of Time and the River* is the shift from first- to third-person narrative, a convention that was altered in the editing of the novel. Wolfe's varying distance from his character, and the distinctive narration of his fiction, are clearly illustrated by the fact that such a change could be made at all. See Richard S. Kennedy, "Thomas Wolfe's Fiction: The Question of Genre," in Paschal Reeves (ed.), *Thomas Wolfe and the Glass of Time* (Athens, Ga., 1971), 33–39; Holman, *The Loneliness at the Core*, Chapter 4; and DD, 280–81, for discussions of this problem.

self-consciousness that Eugene can conquer only by recording them in art. Hence, his record, the book itself, must not assume any other control over the ugliness, confusion, and shame of his background. The narrator is at his most authoritative when he assumes the least power over his past, except for the power that he commands by the act of writing about his weaknesses. We know that important contributing causes for Eugene's coming to be the writer he struggles to be are his roots in a chaotic, badly flawed home, the middle class, the southern Appalachians, and the United States. When these themes appear with this emphasis in *Of Time and the River*, the book accomplishes its difficult task of continuing *Look Homeward, Angel*.

Eugene comes to realize during the course of the novel that he has been running from the very wellspring of his art. The narrator comments on this irony long before it occurs to the character, in the difficult period when Eugene, fresh out of Harvard, has gone back to Altamont to wait to hear if his play will be chosen for production in New York. Everyone knows that Eugene does not have the aristocratic mystique of an artist, but this is not the disadvantage that they believe it is:

> The reason, in fact, which argued in Eugene's family's mind against his succeeding in the work he wished to do, was the very thing that should have been all in his favor. But neither he nor his family thought so. It was this: a writer, they thought, should be a wonderful, mysterious, and remote sort of person—some one they had never known. . . . But none of them could see this. . . . And none of them could see that his greatest asset, his greatest advantage, if he had any, was that he was made out of the same earth—the same blood, bone, character, and fury—as the rest of them. (358–59)

The young artist must make his order and beauty out of what Yeats called "the foul rag-and-bone shop of the heart." His deficiencies, like those of Stephen Dedalus, are the sources of his strengths. And so in the last scene in Dijon, the young man ends his search by finding his way to art made from memory. Suddenly a small town in France is infused with his recollection of another small town. Under the spell of the same kind of instant, involuntary memory that marks Proust's artistic reentry into his childhood, Eugene begins the action that marks the inception of his autobiographical novel.[19] Time, his albatross, is conquered, and the America he has been looking for is found as he returns to Altamont through art.

> From a distance there came suddenly a woman's low, rich burst of sensual laughter, the receding hoof-beats of a horse, and then all around there was silence, the overpowering fragrance of the earth, the huge thrill and mystery of night, and the sense of an intolerable desire, close and palpable and lovely, and never to be grasped or found: and from the huge and haunting familiarity of all these things, a thousand receding and unuttered memories of time arose, a feeling of bitter loss, wild joy and pain—of a door that closed, a cloud-shadow that had gone forever. He thought of home. (892)

A bell strikes, he recaptures his college days by a spontaneous memory of another bell, and the refrain sounds: "He thought of home" (896). The everyday sounds of the village square awaken the memory of the sounds of his childhood, and "suddenly he was a child, and it was noon, and he was waiting in his father's house to hear the slam of the iron gate, the great body stride up the high porch steps, knowing his father had come home again" (897). He is pierced by "a suddenly living and intolerable memory, instant and familiar as all this life around him, of a life that he had lost, and that could never die" (898). We know, although we did not learn it from this novel but from another one, that this moment will ultimately lead to the union of the narrator and his character. Both are remembering and making words. Both are the Eugene Gant who will be the writer of *Look Homeward, Angel* (and the George Webber who will write *Home to Our Mountains* in Wolfe's later fiction). Like Buck Mulligan joking on a fictional day in June, 1904, in a novel by the writer of *A Portrait*, about his friend Stephen Dedalus writing something in ten years, the daring closeness of a writer to his narrating voice and his fictional representative at this climactic moment of his novel is a risk well taken.

19. For discussions of Proust and Wolfe see Louis D. Rubin, Jr., *The Teller in the Tale* (Seattle, 1967), Chapter 5 (esp. 122–29); and Margaret Church, "Thomas Wolfe: Dark Time," *PMLA*, LXIV (1949), 629–38. *Cf.* Samuel Beckett's analysis of "involuntary memory" in *Proust* (see Beckett, *Proust and Three Dialogues Between Samuel Beckett and Georges Duthuit* [London, 1965], 32–35).

4

The Son Consubstantial with the Father

The Stephen Dedalus who emerges from "dark winding stairs" into the June morning at the beginning of *Ulysses* may be only a few months older than the Stephen we last saw in *A Portrait of the Artist as a Young Man*, but he is also the product of seven years of artistic maturing on the part of his creator. In the years between 1915 and 1922, Joyce's art had undergone a series of changes that resulted in radical transformations of style and theme from the earlier book. Whereas *A Portrait* is tightly limited in scope and focus, presenting the story of one character mostly from his own point of view, *Ulysses* more nearly represents the broad range of characters and actions of an epic, the genre of the Homeric poem that Joyce used to provide a mythic parallel and substructure for his story. *Ulysses* also employs many, often flamboyantly undependable points of view to present a day in the lives of two citizens of Dublin. Nor was *Ulysses* a departure only from Joyce's previous work: it was also a novel that practically redefined prose fiction for its time—after it was finally published, that is, amid numerous squabbles (including two court cases in the United States) over its alleged obscenity and considerable trouble because of its supposed obscurity. Joyce had almost as much trouble getting his second novel privately published under the imprint of a small French bookshop as Wolfe had keeping *Of Time and the River* from being printed prematurely by a major American publishing house.[1] But *Ulysses,* of course, ultimately repaid its author's emotional investment in the woes of publication as *Of Time and the River* never did. By it Joyce was assured of his preeminence in twentieth-century letters.

Joyce took Stephen Dedalus along with him into his masterwork but transformed him, too, in the process. We do not have to read much of *Ulysses* to see that the namesake of Daedalus, the "old artificer," has lost the first flush of artistic confidence that colored the ending of *A Portrait.* He has returned from Paris, with nothing to show for himself but a "Latin quarter hat" (*U*, 14, 35), to a family that is dissolving after the death of Mrs. Dedalus, and with no easily foreseeable future, as an artist or anything else. This is not to say that Stephen's bravado has been shattered along with his self-confidence. On the contrary, as we see during the day, his air of authority around Haines, with the crowd at the *Freeman's Journal,* or in the National Library (teaching his elders like the young Jesus in the temple in Jerusalem) is generally convincing to others. In fact, the "Ithaca" chapter reports that "confidence in himself" seems to Leopold Bloom to be one of "the predominant qualities of his guest" (*U*, 550). But to himself, the point of view we see at the beginning of the novel, his confidence has been badly undermined. He has surrendered to the inertia of depression and the mental sterility of obsessive intellectualizing. Passive, if resentful, he allows his arrogant roommate Buck Mulligan to use for satirical purposes intellectual conceits that are dear to him. In the first chapter, Mulligan mocks Stephen's idea of the priesthood of art, trivializes his grief and remorse over his mother's death, wins the symbolic service and favor of Ireland in the figure of the old milkwoman, and takes the key to the tower they are living in, leaving Stephen metonymically homeless. Daedalus, the great artist of flight, has been traded for Icarus, the drowned failure, as a personal myth. The

1. This is not to say that Joyce was not under considerable pressure during the writing of the book to finish each chapter by the deadlines imposed by serial publication in the *Little Review.* See RE, 441–42, for a table of the dates of completion and publication of each chapter.

artistic vocation with which Stephen supposed he could arm himself against his sea of troubles does not seem to have succeeded: he looks as though he is drowning in them.

Some of his trouble stems from his striving to be a certain kind of artist, a problem that harks back to *A Portrait* and also points to a central concern in *Ulysses*. We may imagine that it was easier for him to imagine a priestlike artist "transmuting the daily bread of experience into the radiant body of everliving life" (*P*, 220) than it has been since to put this idea into practice. It is all very well to posit an artist distancing himself from his art and at the same time transforming his own life in order to make it, whether the subject is the "disorder, the misrule and confusion of his father's house" or an unsympathetic girl turned "temptress" in an abstract villanelle (*P*, 162, 223). It is quite a different matter to create a significant work of objectified art out of one's own life: the reality of personal stresses and social influences is not easily eradicated. Of course, Stephen's failure at the beginning of *Ulysses* to be the artist he was so sure of being at the end of *A Portrait* does not completely invalidate either his theory or his resolve to be an artist (or the much-debated victorious tone of the conclusion of the earlier novel, despite its irony). Both theory and resolve need adjusting, but they are not unredeemable. As S. L. Goldberg asserted, "the difficulty with Stephen's theories, indeed, is that they are not wrong in any simple, black-and-white sense at all; he is always at least partly right."[2]

Stephen's notion of art in *A Portrait* falls short in precisely the area with which we find him struggling at the beginning of Joyce's second novel. Stephen cannot solve his personal problems by distancing himself from them through his art, even if that art returns to his life for its subject matter and theme. The young man has learned in the time that has passed since the end of the earlier novel that art cannot be made unless the whole self of the artist is brought to bear upon his or her work. Although in *A Portrait* Ste-

2. S. L. Goldberg, *The Classical Temper: A Study of James Joyce's "Ulysses"* (London, 1961), 45. See also A. Walton Litz's criticism of Goldberg in "The Genre of *Ulysses*," in John Halperin (ed.), *The Theory of the Novel: New Essays* (New York, 1974), 109–120.

phen does realize that art must begin in "the daily bread of experience," he certainly stresses there the "radiant body of everliving life" rather than the common elements—including, most notably, the personal elements—from which it is made. The Stephen of *A Portrait* is convinced that art and life must be kept rigidly separate in practice, if not in theory. Thus he attempts in *A Portrait* to use artistic detachment first to escape, then to return with new immunity to the life he finds intolerable without some mediating distance. But in neither the theory he proposes to Lynch nor his actions does he do very much returning.

Setting aside the question of its value as a working model for creating art, a theory such as Stephen presents in *A Portrait* of a godlike artist who is disengaged from his or her work conveniently dismisses a more basic concern—the relationship between art and the way the artist as a person copes with life. But when we see him again in *Ulysses*, Stephen is beginning to understand that his raw needs, although they fall under the category of what he termed "emotion which is kinetic," both precede and inform the creating of the "esthetic stasis" he expounded to Lynch in the earlier novel (*P*, 204–209). This understanding is a crucial ingredient of autobiographical art, just as it is a central component of self-awareness.

A Portrait shows that its author has such self-understanding and hints that its protagonist will find it. *Ulysses* shows the protagonist unable to proceed further toward becoming an artist without achieving this knowledge. This novel tells us that Stephen will eventually work out the problems preventing him from creating significant art, although it does so convincingly only if we keep in view, in addition to the "plot" (such as it is), the unusually prominent relationship between the authorial presence and the fictional world of the novel. Joyce, who later refused to discuss world events with his brother Stanislaus by announcing that "the only thing that interests me is style" (RE, 697), wrote in *Ulysses* a book in which style is as much a part of the action as are the incidents in the fictional time and place it represents.

And so Stephen, with all his troubles, may also be in the middle of making a discovery on this day in the middle of June. He is a bundle of raw nerves in the "Telemachus" chapters that open the book, with his psychological wounds gaping. Besides being a "usurper," Mulligan the medical student probes these wounds easily (19). He is an appropriately perceptive, if singularly insensitive, candidate for his profession (his bedside manner is perhaps more suitable for a coroner than a general practitioner). His operation reveals that part of Stephen's hypersensitivity is his lingering sense of social inferiority, which he sought to banish in the name of art but which still surfaces in his consciousness.

One of our first impressions of Mulligan is of his social standing. He is well dressed and well fed, and his "plump shadowed face and sullen oval jowl recalled a prelate, patron of arts in the middle ages" (3). Stephen's dislike of him seems even at this first glimpse to include an element of recoil against the social superiority such "patronage" implies. The negative adjectives "shadowed" and "sullen" adumbrate the strained relationship between the stately, plump Buck and the defiant, ragged Stephen. The perception of social inequality is not only Stephen's, however. We note that Mulligan emits the shadows and sullenness in the description above. Likewise it is Mulligan who feels it interesting enough to tell Stephen twice that Haines, the Englishman who is staying with them temporarily, "thinks you're not a gentleman" (4, 6). The "patron of arts" also takes advantage of Stephen's sensitivity to their relative status, while maintaining the illusion of friendly generosity, by giving Stephen hand-me-down clothing (a gesture not lost on Stephen, who mimics Buck's voice to himself a few pages later and again in "Proteus": "God, we'll simply have to dress the character" [14, 35]).

The resentment of an Irish Catholic toward Protestant Great Britain still smolders in Stephen's attitude toward Haines. We never hear from the Englishman whether he thinks Stephen a gentleman or not, but his clumsy patronizing certainly rankles, especially as Mulligan manipulates the oblivious Haines into mocking Stephen unconsciously while he collects Stephen's sayings like folklore and reduces Stephen's theory of Shakespeare to intellectual cliché: "'I read a theological interpretation of it somewhere,' he said bemused. 'The Father and the Son idea'" (16). This pedestrian condensation of an idea that has vital implications for Stephen hurts, as Mulligan knew it would. Thus Stephen's bitterness at not being taken seriously by his roommate goes hand in hand with resentment over his subordinate station. As an Irishman raised a Roman Catholic, he is "the servant of two masters," as he says, "an English and an Italian" (to which Haines thoughtlessly responds with a typical British understatement: "We feel in England that we have treated you rather unfairly. It seems history is to blame" [17]).

The same conviction of his servitude to the English returns to Stephen's mind an hour later, when we see him in the "Nestor" chapter at his job teaching at a Protestant school. He is ashamed to be working there, so such ideas occur in the context of his general attitude. In the evening Stephen will lie about the source of the money he will spend on drink, if we can believe the narrator of "Oxen of the Sun," telling his companions that his salary from Deasy is actually payment "for a song which he writ" (320). Now, though, he thinks of Haines and Ireland after coining what he thinks is a witty definition of a pier as a disappointed bridge: "For Haines's chapbook. No-one here to hear. Tonight deftly amid wild drink and talk, to pierce the polished mail of his mind. What then? A jester at the court of his master, indulged and disesteemed, winning a clement master's praise. Why had they chosen all that part? Not wholly for the smooth caress. For them too history was a tale like any other too often heard, their land a pawnshop" (21).

It does indeed seem that history is to blame, although not in the sense that Haines intended. Ireland is trapped in the myths it spawns, as its young son is trapped in his mythic kinship with his fatherland. Stephen here is a bit wiser than when, as "Stevie," he declared to Davin that he would "try to fly by those nets" of "nationality, language, religion" (*P*, 203). He has to grapple with the nets themselves, to face his ineluctable personal and cultural history. Nonetheless, as he reveals in his conversation with his employer (a good Orangeman), he is still far from being reconciled with this fact: he regards history, he says, as "a nightmare from which I am trying to awake" (*U*, 28).

The "Proteus" chapter, which follows the scene with Deasy, gives us more specific information about Stephen's personal nightmare. As Stephen walks on the beach, lost in thought, we hear (among other things) how much his distrust of Mulligan in the first scene was related to his discomfort at his family's debased social position. His avowed detachment from their dismal circumstances only adds to his depression, although he does not realize, again, that his failure to soar over them does not necessarily indicate his lack of artistic ability. It may be a sign (for him to read, along with the less personal "signatures" he tries to decipher throughout the chapter) of an integral aspect of art that he has not been including sufficiently in his plans. He asks himself whether he intends to visit his maternal aunt's house, which is nearby (presumably to ask for a place to stay, since he does not intend to go back to the tower and Mulligan), and he imaginatively re-creates his father's opinionated voice ridiculing his artist son and imitating the stuttering speech of Simon Dedalus' brother-in-law: "Here. Am I going to aunt Sara's or not? My consubstantial father's voice. Did you see anything of your artist brother Stephen lately? No? Sure he's not down in Strasburg terrace with his aunt Sally? Couldn't he fly a bit higher than that, eh? And and and and tell us Stephen, how is uncle Si? O, weeping God, the things I married into!" (32).

He can hear his "nuncle Richie" Goulding's friendly but common voice: "Would you like a bite of something? None of your damned lawdeedaw airs here. The rich of a rasher fried with a herring? Sure? So much the better. We have nothing in the house but backache pills" (32–33). Stephen decides to shun the visit, although traffic with people such as Goulding (who is a friend of Leopold Bloom's, we discover later) is exactly the kind of experience he needs in order to escape his sterile abstractions and to become able to create his art. The brief imagined scene with his relatives shows us that this is so by exposing one of Stephen's latent artistic strengths: as he did in *A Portrait*, Stephen has a talent he does not perceive for re-creating the familiar. Here, in other words, we must read the style as we usually read the action, to find the dramatic meaning of the episode. Only thus can we see the irony of Stephen's refusal, on supposedly artistic grounds, to carry out the hypothetical visit: "Houses of decay, mine, his and all. You told the Clongowes gentry you had an uncle a judge and an uncle a general in the army. Come out of them, Stephen. Beauty is not there" (33). Here too is a clear example of the close connection in Stephen's mind between social status and the pursuit of art. The lie he told as a child to hide his family's lack of social prominence and his disinclination to face truth now (in the name of beauty) are two manifestations of the same impulse, although he does not realize it. He is still very much the victim of that insecurity, and his attempt to deny it by means of what Zack Bowen calls a "conscious rationalization of art as a way of coping with the world," even in the face of the obvious insufficiency of that rationalization, is part of what is making his first failure as an artist into a major psychological crisis.[3]

The first three chapters of the novel, devoted more or less exclusively to Stephen's consciousness, constitute the exposition of that crisis. The deep need Stephen has had for his aesthetic credo, a need that reflects his troubled economic and social background, has contributed directly to his current predicament. He has denied his mother's dying request to pray for her, remaining true to his ideas that have become so crucial to his fabricated identity that he could not relax them even for her. But the guilt over his act that now envelops him comes in part because he suspects that he was being faithful to a creed not worthy of such devotion. His self-accusatory thoughts about his art also reflect the extent to which his sense of his own worth is wrapped up in the image of the Daedalean artist. He satirizes his flight to Paris, his fantasies of popular acclaim ("You bowed to yourself in the mirror, stepping forward to applause earnestly, striking face. Hurray for the Goddamned idiot!"), and his dreams of future glory ("Remember your epiphanies written on green oval leaves, deeply deep, copies to be sent if you died to all the great libraries of the world, including Alexandria?" [34]) with obsessive venom. He allows Mulligan to torment him, in a relationship that is the first of many implicit or explicit references to Sacher-Masoch in this novel, from a conviction of inferiority that runs deeper than his confidence in his artistic project. Thus he extends his idea of Mulligan's usurpation to absurd lengths, backward in history, for instance, to the landing of the Vikings in Ireland: "Galleys of the Lochlanns ran here to beach, in quest of prey, their bloodbeaked prows riding low on a molten pewter surf. Dane vikings, torcs of tomahawks aglitter on their breasts when Malachi wore the collar of gold. A school of turlehide

3. Zack Bowen, "*Ulysses*," in Zack Bowen and James F. Carens (eds.), *A Companion to Joyce Studies* (Westport, Conn., 1984), 430.

whales stranded in hot noon, spouting, hobbling in the shallows. Then from the starving cagework city a horde of jerkined dwarfs, my people, with flayers' knives, running, scaling, hacking in green blubbery whalemeat. Famine, plague and slaughters. Their blood is in me, their lusts my waves" (37–38).

"Proteus" ends with Stephen looking over his shoulder at the ship *Rosevean* coming back into harbor without the use of its sails, paralleling his return to Dublin with the wind knocked out of him after his journey away in the "black arms of tall ships" at the end of *A Portrait* (*P*, 252). The mysterious figure of the ship manages to sail upstream, but the question of whether Stephen will succeed at his difficult journey to his homeland of art remains unanswered. A dramatic tension whose resolution we expect in the rest of the novel is established as the "Telemachiad," the first three chapters of the novel, closes.

But the second part of *Ulysses* gives us something—and someone—new, whose importance to Stephen, and how that importance is demonstrated, are the unusual matter of the rest of *Ulysses*. Our introduction to Mr. Leopold Bloom contains a surprising tonal shift. With his entry into the novel, the hyperintellectual, almost neurotically self-absorbed consciousness of Stephen, through whom the first chapters are filtered, gives way to a voice unlike anything in *A Portrait* or in the first chapters of *Ulysses*. Stephen's ever-present sense of shame of his family and their continually sinking circumstances, of his racial and cultural heritage, and of the sensual side of human existence, is completely absent. Bloom does not have the creative potential that Stephen does, although he is a sensitive man with "a touch of the artist" about him, in Lenehan's often-quoted remark from "Wandering Rocks" (193). He has a touch of the artist of *Ulysses* about him as well, as we know—in his married state, his parenthood (of a girl and a boy, even though the latter died in infancy), in his concern over the fidelity of his wife, and in many small details such as his good ear for music and his dalliance with a woman named Martha.[4] Bloom has a body with

4. See RE for specific instances of how Joyce reproduced his own characteristics and concerns in the details of Bloom's life. RE, 448–53, gives an account of Joyce's passing interest in Marthe Fleishmann.

which he is comfortable, a home he loves, a nationality of which he is proud: in short, he knows who he is. And such self-definition is what Stephen lacks, for all of his elaborate attempts to create himself as an artist.

By introducing Bloom, Joyce also adds something new to a book that up to this point has been recognizably similar to his first novel. The "Telemachiad" is the kind of beginning we might expect of a sequel to *A Portrait*, but *Ulysses* is far from a simple continuation of the autobiographical story of Stephen Dedalus. In fact, Bloom rescued Joyce from being labeled by critics as an autobiographical writer, the charge that would later so disturb Wolfe. Ezra Pound, for instance, was noticeably relieved to find Bloom as he read *Ulysses* chapter by chapter for its serial publication in the American journal *Little Review*, even though he did not believe that autobiographical work was necessarily second-rate. Pound wrote Joyce in 1918 that in Bloom "you have almightily answered the critics who asked me whether having made Stephen, more or less autobiography, you could ever go on and create a second character. 'Second character is the test' etc. etc., jab jab jobber-jabble."[5]

This new character does indeed change the personality of the book. For some readers, indeed, *Ulysses* is Bloom's book and not fundamentally Stephen's. We know that Joyce was more interested in Bloom than in Stephen as a character by the time he wrote the later chapters of the novel, or so he declared to Frank Budgen.[6] Bloom is also the character equivalent to Odysseus in this modern-day *Odyssey*, which surely argues for his centrality to the work. But *Ulysses*, like *A Portrait*, reveals in basic formal and thematic ways that it is intimately connected with the life of its author. It is indeed a different kind of book than the earlier novel, but the difference lies primarily in the increased complexity of the relationship between its central characters, both of whom are autobiographical in important, though distinctly different, ways, and between them

5. Ezra Pound, *Pound/Joyce: The Letters of Ezra Pound to James Joyce, with Pound's Essays on Joyce*, ed. Forrest Read (New York, 1967), 145.

6. Frank Budgen, *James Joyce and the Making of "Ulysses"* (1934; rpr. Bloomington, 1960), 107; see also Thomas F. Staley, "Stephen Dedalus and the Temper of the Modern Hero," in Thomas F. Staley and Bernard Benstock (eds.), *Approaches to "Ulysses": Ten Essays* (Pittsburgh, 1970), 7.

and its author—not in the fact of its autobiographical nature.[7] Thus the continuing drama of Stephen's growth is crucial. Bloom is the vehicle through whom the authorial voice most often enters and commands the action and is therefore the most fully realized character, but Stephen, as the closest representative of the writer in the story itself, continues to receive our especial attention. Stephen may genuinely change because of the events of the day on which *Ulysses* takes place. And as in *A Portrait*, we are interested in whether or not he does, even though the change will take place in the future outside the book if it occurs at all, because the book stresses the intimacy of its author with its story. Ellmann notes that "*Ulysses* divulges more than an impersonal and detached picture of Dublin life; it hints at what is, in fact, true: that nothing has been admitted into the book which is not in some way personal and attached" (RE, 364). Thomas F. Staley also describes how such personal attachment ensures the importance of the fictional representation of the young Joyce: "*Ulysses* itself provides the world in which Stephen finds definition. The total structure—the purposeful design—of *Ulysses* is what qualifies the attention we give to Stephen."[8]

Bloom, the middle-aged Jewish businessman and father, exists formally as the counterpart or opposite of Stephen, the immature artist and son with the Greek-sounding surname. Through the older man, our impressions of the younger will be put into better perspective than they could be if the novel focused on Stephen alone, just as Stephen also shows us Bloom in a chiaroscurolike pattern. Their opposition, which is vital to their meeting later in the novel, extends to their attitudes toward the social stations that claim them. Bloom is thoroughly middle-class, even in his most outlandish fantasies of success, which, according to the list in "Ith-

7. Ellmann calls Stephen "Joyce's immature *persona*" and Bloom his "mature *persona*" (RE, 359). For a persuasive interpretation of the radically autobiographical nature of both Bloom and Stephen, see Ralph W. Rader, "Exodus and Return: Joyce's *Ulysses* and the Fiction of the Actual," *University of Toronto Quarterly*, XLVIII (1978–79), 149–71. See also Rader's essay "Defoe, Richardson, Joyce, and the Concept of Form in the Novel," in William Matthews and Ralph W. Rader, *Autobiography, Biography, and the Novel* (Los Angeles, 1973), 31–72.

8. Staley, "Stephen Dedalus and the Temper of the Modern Hero," in Staley and Benstock (eds.), *Approaches to "Ulysses,"* 7.

aca," bear the unmistakable stamp of bourgeois dreaming. His "ultimate ambition" is said to be "to purchase by private treaty in fee simple a thatched bungalowshaped 2 storey dwellinghouse of southerly aspect, surmounted by vane and lightning conductor," every furnishing and ornament already selected to the minutest detail, plans for home improvement in place, and a "syllabus of intellectual pursuits" and "lighter recreations" also already outlined (585–87).

Dissatisfaction with his lot seldom occurs to Bloom, although he works steadily and muses often about what he could buy with the money he might or might not make. Indeed the many critical interpretations of Bloom as everyman or antihero point to just this aspect of his character. In the twentieth century, everyman is bound to be a member of the bourgeoisie; the antithesis of a classical hero surely would lead the kind of life that most readers of his story would consider ordinary, in the class to which most readers of novels belong. But Bloom is not only a parody of a hero like Odysseus or a representative of generalized humanity. He is also a necessary other whom an artist such as Stephen wishes to become must take into account.

Unlike Wolfe, who in *Of Time and the River* tried to continue Eugene's growth up to the time when he begins to write his first significant work, Joyce chose a way of presenting the rest of Stephen's history that does not take the artistic risk of actually evolving him into an artist within the story of his development. The potential for rhetorical failure, which haunts the ending of *Look Homeward, Angel* for some readers and certainly damages *Of Time and the River*, seems either unavoidable or nearly so in such novels. Nor is *A Portrait* immune from the problems created by the formal closeness of an authorial voice to the events in an autobiographical novel: Joyce's irony there avoids a dangerously close identification of author with character but must consequently also skirt issues of writerly involvement with the text. *Ulysses* attempts to engage these using Bloom and an increasingly dominant authorial presence to join the planes of story and expression, first by setting before us a novelistic situation in which discovery of Bloom is necessary for Stephen, and second by showing within the language and structure of the novel that such a discovery has already taken place. The plot does not contain such a discovery in any conclusive sense, although suggestive acts by Bloom and Stephen do occur (like mutual cocoa-drinking and micturition in the back garden). Rather, their reconciliation occurs in their symbolic import, their relative positions in structural schemata, and other such arenas. Thus Stephen is not required to solve his problems on Bloomsday in order for *Ulysses* to be successful in its presentation of his artistic growth.

Bloom's thoroughly middle-class character is significant for several reasons. First, his ordinariness is an integral part of his relationship with the narrating presence. Like Stephen's resolution to transcend his chaotic environment but to return to it through his art, the stance that the authorial voice assumes toward Bloom suggests that the writer of the novel stands apart, at a static distance, but simultaneously reenters the life of the city and its citizens primarily through this character. Bloom can be seen as the "conscience of my race," which an author who bears a great resemblance to Stephen Dedalus has created in his soul's smithy. Joyce hinted at the important intimacy between authorial view and conscientious character when he told Frank Budgen that Bloom was "a complete man" both in the sense that "I see him from all sides" and in that "he is . . . a good man. At any rate, that is what I intend that he shall be."[9]

Second, marking a clear departure from *Dubliners*, we recognize that Bloom is irregular as well as typical. His position in Dublin society is roughly equivalent to that of the group of his peers with whom he has contact during the day, but he is fundamentally different from them in moral character. He should be at home among the men who attend Dignam's funeral, work at the *Freeman's Journal*, eat at the Burton restaurant, drink at Barney Kiernan's pub, and generally participate in the life of the city. But he is not: although he knows nearly everyone and is known by them, we are hard pressed to name a genuine friend among the number of his acquaintances. In fact, he is the target of almost universal suspicion and mockery during the course of his day. He is far from perfect, but the criticism leveled at him (generally not in his hearing) usually points to his relative innocence and the petty viciousness of his

9. Budgen, *James Joyce and the Making of "Ulysses,"* 17; see also RE, 436.

detractors. Often, indeed, their animosity goes to absurd lengths. For example, John Henry Menton resents Bloom mentioning to him that his hat needs adjusting as they leave the funeral together, because of an imagined slight received once on the bowling green—"Why he took such a rooted dislike to me. Hate at first sight," Bloom remembers (94). Or there is the whole matter of the racing tip he is unaware of giving to Bantam Lyons: having mentioned the words "throw it away" while offering to give Lyons his newspaper in the morning, Lyons bet on the winning horse, named Throwaway (70, 552). Later, in "Cyclops," this incident precipitates an unpleasant scene in Barney Kiernan's pub, when the belligerent group gathered there realizes that Bloom, who is completely ignorant of his supposed windfall, does not intend to buy drinks all around with the money he has presumably won (274, 279–83).

Bloom escapes the lancet of Joyce's satiric art, unlike the rest of the citizens of Dublin—many of whom are the same characters at whom Joyce aimed his satire in *Dubliners*—because Bloom does not share their small-mindedness. The qualities that allow Bloom's escape—basic generosity, an ability to forgive, relative honesty and humility, and realistic understanding of love (the "word known to all men" [161, 474], which few of Joyce's men or women genuinely know)—are the qualities that Stephen needs from Bloom if he is to accomplish a successful journey from sterility to art.

Stephen must absorb the ordinariness as well as the extraordinariness of Bloom if he is to enter into kinship with him. The issue of Bloom's class status is thus a part of the larger issue of sonship and fatherhood in the novel. As the day progresses, Stephen and Bloom move closer together in a number of ways—in their physical proximity and mental processes on one level, in thematic parallels and structural positions on another. Finally, after "Oxen of the Sun," in which, as Joyce explained in a letter to his friend Frank Budgen, "Bloom is the spermatozoon . . . Stephen the embryo" (*LJJ*, I, 140), a process is begun that will result in the figurative birth of a son to a father. Bloom will pass on his humanity, as he needs to, and Stephen will receive it in a procreative event much like the one Stephen describes in his theory of Shakespeare. Mulligan is an unwitting prophet of this event early in the novel, paraphrasing Stephen's theory in which "he proves by algebra that

Hamlet's grandson is Shakespeare's grandfather and that he himself is the ghost of his own father" (15). Stephen, to the extent that he is Joyce, will create and relive a part of himself in Bloom (a semiautobiographical character) and will thus indeed become the spiritual or "ghostly" father of himself.

This is not to say that Stephen projects this solution to the dilemma that lies behind his Shakespeare theory. His views on the consubstantiality of fathers and sons are less specifically referential, even as his need for his theory is more immediate than this equation expresses. He argues especially vigorously when he advocates the corollary that involves fatherhood and sonship, despite its somewhat tangential connection with the main burden of the theory, indicating its importance to his trouble over a father figure. By his own admission, however, his vehemence is greater than his belief.[10] He does not finally, at the finish of the argument he sets forth for his listeners' and his own benefit in the "Scylla and Charybdis" chapter, seem to see any way out of his predicament.[11] Nonetheless, the hypothesis about the imprint of Shakespeare's biography upon his works represents a definite advance over Stephen's earlier notions of a godlike, indifferent artist. The scene in the National Library, in which Stephen performs for a group of Dublin's literati, shows us how far he has come from the young man arguing with his college friends in *A Portrait*, even though he now must pass through dangerous waters if he is to proceed further.

The theorizing has direct application to Stephen's personal circumstances. This causes the swirling arguments to be so dangerous for him, as well as so potentially constructive. Throughout the scene, Stephen's comments to himself show us that he realizes how important the theory is to him, even though he knows that it is false to Shakespeare. He constantly urges himself on and guides his jesuitical maneuvering with reminders and excited prompting, in

10. According to Ellmann, Joyce took the Shakespeare theory more seriously than he presents Stephen as doing. But as Ellmann also notes, Stephen's denial of belief in his theory of Shakespeare's personal life may be susceptible to more than one interpretation (RE, 364).

11. He does, of course, make progress toward realizing his vocation. See Brian G. Caraher, "A Question of Genre: Generic Experimentation, Self-Composition, and the Problem of Egoism in *Ulysses*," *Journal of English Literary History*, LIV (1987), 183–214, for an interpretation of what Stephen learns in this chapter.

phrases such as "Folly. Persist," but even when the excitement of the challenge fades, he continues to argue (152). Thus neither his admission that "I am tired of my voice, the voice of Esau" (174), the voice of the outcast who has given up his birthright as one of Ireland's promising young writers, nor his own objections to the logic of the argument prevent his relentless disputation:

> What the hell are you driving at?
> I know. Shut up. Blast you! I have reasons.
> *Amplius. Adhuc. Iterum. Postea.*
> Are you condemned to do this? (170)

He is so condemned, of course, and in his "reasons," of which he is increasingly aware, we can see once more the shadow of his family's social status.

The crisis that this chapter represents for Stephen, which seems to be recognized only by "Sonmulligan" among his auditors, is traceable ultimately back to Stephen's inability to define himself as the artist he wishes to be because he cannot banish his identity as the son of Simon Dedalus, the man whom Mulligan calls his "unsubstantial father" (171, 164). In the theory of the influence that Shakespeare's life had upon his art, Stephen makes the crucial admission that even the most impersonal "universal" art is made by living human beings who infuse their personal needs into their creations—indeed, who undertake the creative act because of personal need. Artists do not live in a vacuum; art does not, contrary to the opinion of Æ, merely have to "reveal to us ideas, formless spiritual essences" (152).[12]

Interestingly, Stephen also knows that the easy formulations he is constructing about Shakespeare's biography from his works of art are, as Æ charges, "the speculation of schoolboys for schoolboys" (152). Stephen is showing off his skill at intellectual gymnastics in the actual details of the theory. He is probably even getting some enjoyment out of the exercise, egging himself on with sarcastic comments such as "Local colour. Work in all you know. Make them accomplices" (154); "They list. And in the porches of their

12. Æ was the pseudonym of George William Russell (1867–1935), a mystic poet, landscape painter, and Irish nationalist.

ears I pour" (161); or "I think you're getting on very nicely. Just mix up a mixture of theolologicophilolological. *Mingo, minxi, mictum, mingere*" (168). But the absence of literal truth does not materially affect his struggle with the artistic necessity that the theory presupposes. He remarks to himself, after telling John Eglinton that he does not believe his theory, echoing the New Testament, "I believe, O Lord, help my unbelief. That is, help me to believe or help me to unbelieve?" (176).[13]

As the phrasing of the biblical verse is ambiguous, so Stephen is unsure if he can accept the implications of his aesthetic ideas. Presupposing, as these ideas do, that human relationships are intimately involved in the creation of art, they may be untenable to a young man intent on denying his sonship by doing away with father, *patria*, and God. Thus, interestingly, Stephen tries to twist into his theory a corollary stating that Shakespeare was able to become "the father of all his race" precisely because his own father was dead. We can easily see how much this part of the discussion matters to Stephen (although of the group in the library only he and Mulligan are aware of its importance), both by its insertion into the main argument, even though it does not really advance the line of reasoning, and by the energetic and conscious sophistry Stephen employs in its service.

Eglinton precipitates the introduction of the issue by an apparent slip of the tongue. Even though Stephen's whole theory rests on the identification of Shakespeare with Hamlet *père*, Eglinton, while counterarguing that Falstaff (who has no family) is Shakespeare's "supreme creation," asks, "What do we care for his wife or father?" (170). It is not Shakespeare's *father* with which Stephen's theory is concerned, but the young man's obsession with fathers and sons immediately takes over his argument. He imagines Eglinton's peasant father, and then he remembers his own during the period of his mother's death: "Hurrying to her squalid deathlair from gay Paris on the quayside I touched his hand. The voice, new

13. John Eglinton was the pseudonym of William Kirkpatrick Magee (1868–1961), a member of the staff at the National Library in Dublin, with whom Joyce became acquainted in December, 1902 or January, 1903. Eglinton was one of the two editors of the intellectual journal *Dana*, to which Joyce submitted "A Portrait of the Artist" in 1904.

warmth, speaking. Dr Bob Kenny is attending her. The eyes that wish me well. But do not know me."[14]

Then Stephen resumes his discussion of *Hamlet*, ostensibly to prove that Shakespeare could not be the young prince. His reasoning is unnecessarily elaborate, however, and we are told that he is "battling against hopelessness" in constructing the convoluted logic here. He has already presented as strong a case as he needs to prove that Shakespeare is King Hamlet, but he does not stop after underscoring it now ("If you hold that he, a greying man with two marriageable daughters, with thirtyfive years of life, *nel mezzo del cammin di nostra vita*, with fifty of experience, is the beardless undergraduate from Wittenberg then you must hold that his seventyyear old mother is the lustful queen"). He follows his statement that "a father . . . is a necessary evil" with an assertion that "paternity may be a legal fiction" and is certainly a universal cause of suffering: "The son unborn mars beauty: born, he brings pain, divides affection, increases care" (170). Then he enlists fallacious logic based on the Sabellian heresy ("that the Father was Himself His Own Son") and Aquinas' refutation of it ("Well: if the father who has not a son be not a father can the son who has not a father be a son?") to prove that Shakespeare could not be a son at all, since his father had died by the time he wrote *Hamlet*.[15] And therefore he "was and felt himself the father of all his race" (171).

Clearly, questions of the evil of fatherhood and of whether or not one must do away with one's father in order to be able to create for one's race have little to do with which character represents the playwright in *Hamlet*. But they have a great deal to do with Stephen

14. *U*, 170. It may be a touch of malice that causes Stephen to visualize Eglinton's father as a peasant coming to visit his son at the library. According to Weldon Thornton, Eglinton's father was not a peasant (*Allusions in "Ulysses": An Annotated List* [Chapel Hill, 1968], 201); he was probably a Presbyterian minister. Perhaps Eglinton's change of name, from an obviously Irish to an English-sounding patronymic, irritates a young Catholic Dubliner who has serious trouble with fathers.

15. Sabellius (*fl.* 230) was one the most famous proponents of modalistic monarchianism, the belief that the Godhead was not a Trinity but a single being and that Christ was divine but indistinguishable from God the Father. Christ, or God the Son, was one mode or face (πρόσωπον) of the one God. According to Thornton (*Allusions in "Ulysses,"* 204), Aquinas refuted this belief in several places, including *Summa Theologica*, Pt. 1, ques. 31 ("Of What Belongs to the Unity or Plurality in God"), esp. art. 2 ("Whether the Son Is Other Than the Father?").

Dedalus, who finds the issue of escape from his paternal inheritance crucial to his art and his life. This inheritance, as we have seen in *A Portrait,* must include the squalid home life of the Dedalus family and their debased class status, both of which have resulted directly from Si's improvidence and alcoholism and have left Stephen touched by shame and longing. It extends, in Stephen's mind, to other claims on him as a son by Dublin, Ireland, and, ultimately, God—claims that he can escape no more easily than he can run from his family.[16]

His experience since the end of the earlier novel has brought him to an impasse between two truths that are equally unacceptable taken by themselves. First, he realizes that art derives from the artist's passionate or "kinetic" grappling with his own life and the reality of the world around him (what Stephen calls "ineluctable modality of the visible" [31] or "space: what you damn well have to see" [153]). Artistic creation is Aristotelian in that truth is only derived from direct contact with the visible, tangible world. Distance, however, is necessary as well. These two propositions sound together through "Scylla and Charybdis": *Hamlet* may indeed be "immortal," as Æ avers, but not because its author's life is immaterial to its own (155). On the other hand, Stephen's logic is not fallacious when he asserts that the perfect body, the "entelechy, form of forms," exists only because "memory" makes it by distinguishing it, separating it, from the "everchanging forms" of immediate reality, even though when he thinks these words he is trying to rationalize away debts incurred in the past (156). In fact, Stephen's difficulty in negotiating distance appears to prevent him from acting altogether. Unable to route an aesthetic course without geographical separation from Dublin, he connects his failure to play the part of Daedalus and fly successfully out of the maze of the city with the paralysis with which he is currently afflicted, which extends further than his inability to write. He calls himself "lapwing" as he blames

16. See Stanley Sultan's discussion of "Scylla and Charybdis" in *The Argument of "Ulysses"* (Columbus, Ohio, 1964), esp. 169–75. See also Hélène Cixous, *The Exile of James Joyce,* trans. Sally A. J. Purcell (London, 1976), esp. Chapter 20; and two books published since this study was written: Patrick McGee, *Paperspace: Style as Ideology in Joyce's "Ulysses"* (Lincoln, Neb., 1988), and Frances L. Restuccia, *Joyce and the Law of the Father* (New Haven, 1989).

himself for his dual failure at living as well as creating: "But act. Act speech. They mock to try you. Act. Be acted on" (173).

But he cannot simply fly a second time. The ties holding him to Dublin, which cannot be severed by running to Paris (and indeed must not be if he is ever to become an artist), hold him as tightly as he holds to his conviction that the artist must be in some sense detached from his environment in order to create. Immediately after he exhorts himself to act, we hear his regret at the exile he has imposed upon himself (as, significantly, he reveals a trait that links him to his father): "I am tired of my voice, the voice of Esau. My kingdom for a drink" (174). He reveals his own loneliness in asserting the loneliness of Shakespeare: "The note of banishment, banishment from the heart, banishment from home, sounds interruptedly from *The Two Gentlemen of Verona* onward till Prospero breaks his staff, buries it certain fathoms in the earth and drowns his book" (174). Then he confesses that the Bard is a son, after all.

> He laughed to free his mind from his mind's bondage.
>
> Judge Eglinton summed up.
>
> —The truth is midway, he affirmed. He is the ghost and the prince. He is all in all.
>
> —He is, Stephen said. (174)

Stephen finishes his presentation, "promptly" denies that he believes it, and soon leaves the library with Mulligan. By the time he departs, he has not convinced Eglinton to pay him to publish his theory in *Dana,* as he had hoped, but he has achieved something (176). By explaining it verbally, he has defined for himself the problem that is keeping him in Dublin and keeping him from writing, although he does not seem much closer to a solution than he was before. At this point, however, we perceive another kind of progress being made for Stephen, of which he is unaware but which we are meant to note. At the doorway Mulligan steps outside. As Stephen begins to follow, he pauses to allow someone to precede him, and Bloom (who has been at the library looking up an advertisement in the Kilkenny paper) exits between the two young men. In a reference to the Homeric parallel for the chapter, Stephen thinks of the workings of fate, and Bloom, like Odysseus, demonstrates the way out of a dilemma by steering carefully between two opposing forces:

> About to pass through the doorway, feeling one behind, he stood aside.
> Part. The moment is now. Where then? If Socrates leave his house today, if Judas go forth tonight. Why? That lies in space which I in time must come to, ineluctably.
> My will: his will that fronts me. Seas between.
> A man passed out between them, bowing, greeting. (178–79)

Like Bloom, whom Mulligan calls the "ancient mariner" after he is out of earshot and who will almost always find a way to avoid trouble, Stephen must learn how to compromise if he is to live and create with the paradox that frustrates him now. An artist must not ever achieve true detachment from his environment, for art cannot be devoid of "matter," of reference to the real world. On the other hand, he must withdraw from his circumstances in order to form them into the coherent pattern that art requires.

This encounter marks the first time that Stephen's and Bloom's paths actually cross during the day (Bloom saw Stephen earlier from the carriage window on his way to Dignam's funeral, and the two nearly met at the newspaper office, but they have not run into each other until now). They do not speak, but they do occupy the same space, so that Stephen's comment "That lies in space which I in time must come to, ineluctably" is accurate in a specific sense that he does not suspect. He will come to Bloom in time, ineluctably, first tonight, through the manipulation of his fate by the writer of *Ulysses*, and then in the future when a man who is related to Stephen through memory (the only relationship possible between self and former self anyway, since "molecules all change," as Stephen thought to himself [156]) comes to Bloom by coming to create him.

The final meeting occurring within the pages of the novel, as any reader finds, is anticlimactic in the extreme if only what happens in the story is considered. Bloom takes a drunken, exhausted Stephen home with him after midnight, but the young man declines Bloom's offer to stay the night. Stephen thereby refuses to be drawn into a real relationship with the Blooms, despite the hopes of both members of the couple, as we discover when we begin to hear Molly's thoughts on the matter in the final chapter. It is difficult to see that a change has taken place in either character, although Stephen mellows a bit under Bloom's solicitous care and Bloom recovers somewhat from the inner agitation he has felt all day because of his wife's infidelity.

But we do have a sense that something has happened, because of the careful preparation for the final scenes in ways other than by the action of the plot. Each succeeding chapter since "Sirens" has announced the presence of an increasingly flamboyant narrator, arranging the perambulations of Bloom and Stephen with such style that their eventual contact is nearly upstaged by the comic abandon of his virtuosity. The episodes grow longer: the first eight hours of the day are rendered in 209 pages in the Gabler edition, but approximately the same length of time, from 4 P.M. until a couple of hours after midnight, requires over twice that number. In these many pages we encounter lengthy parodies of one style after another and verbal displays that at times divert our attention altogether from what is happening by the sheer effects of the words.

Of course, we have encountered techniques that emphasize the narration before. The limited point of view of Stephen's interior monologue, which more or less dominates the "Telemachiad," suggests an authorial presence in addition to a character's. We have also seen in *A Portrait* that, in Hugh Kenner's words, "where we get only Stephen's version of everything, the careful limitations of style serve to remind us that there might be other versions."[17] In *Ulysses* there have been several limited points of view since Bloom appeared, and the addition of other perspectives defines even more clearly the impression of an omniscient authorial outlook. Moreover, chapters like "Æolus," with its parody of newspaper reportage, and "Wandering Rocks," with the deliberately overingenious and confusing artifice of its eighteen sections, have amply demonstrated that in this novel we must read the style as carefully as the plot for information about what is happening. In *Ulysses* we become increasingly aware that the drama this work offers and the meanings its author intends to convey are occurring to an extraordinary

17. Hugh Kenner, *Joyce's Voices* (Berkeley, 1978), 83.

extent in the *how* as well as the *what* of the narrative—in the manner of presentation as well as through the things presented. In fact, at times the expression overcomes the subject matter entirely: it is no easy task to see Bloom and Stephen through the linguistic amnion surrounding them in "Oxen of the Sun" or beneath the phantasmagoria of "Circe."

Part of the technical extravagance that overtakes the text of *Ulysses* is the proliferation of narrating styles. At least one new voice tells each chapter's segment of the story, in a style unlike any other, from "Sirens" on. Indeed, whether it is appropriate to speak of one narrator or many, one authorial presence behind many different masks, or any terminology suggesting a human source for the narration has been a matter of continuing critical discussion.[18] Clearly the chauvinistic narrator of "Cyclops" is unlike the cliché-prone voice relating the events in "Eumaeus," and it may not be appropriate to speak of "Circe" as "narrated" at all. Nonetheless, the text bears witness to brilliant verbal technique (a word that, like its Greek root, implies a human creator—even, perhaps, a τεκών or τεκοῦσα, a father or mother). Moreover, the novel is unified thematically and symbolically, and the conspicuous manipulation

18. David Hayman first suggested calling the narrator of *Ulysses* an "arranger" in *"Ulysses": The Mechanics of Meaning* (Englewood, Cliffs, N.J., 1970). Hugh Kenner discusses the "arranging presence" or "the Arranger," following Hayman, in *"Ulysses"* (Baltimore, 1987). See also Kenner's *Joyce's Voices*, which formulates the "Uncle Charles Principle" to explain how "the narrative idiom need not be the narrator's" in Joyce: the words used are often those that a character would have chosen, as when Uncle Charles in *A Portrait* is described as "repairing" to his outhouse (15–20). Bernard and Shari Benstock warn against any anthropocentric terminology such as *narrator, voice*, or any equivalent terms and suggest a refinement of the "Uncle Charles Principle." Their "Benstock Principle" states that not only characters but also "inanimate, mechanical, spontaneous, even organic processes" can influence a narrative such as *Ulysses*. See Benstock and Benstock, "The Benstock Principle," in Bernard Benstock (ed.), *The Seventh of Joyce* (Bloomington, Ind., 1982), 18. See also Hazard Adams, "Critical Constitution of the Literary Text: The Example of *Ulysses*," *New Literary History*, XVII (1986), 598–99. For other examinations of the narrative voice(s), see Goldberg, *The Classical Temper*, 280–90; Arnold Goldman, *The Joyce Paradox: Form and Freedom in His Fiction* (Evanston, Ill., 1966); Wolfgang Iser, *The Implied Reader* (Baltimore, 1974), 179–95; Marilyn French, *The Book as World: James Joyce's "Ulysses"* (Cambridge, Mass., 1976); Michael Groden, *"Ulysses" in Progress* (Princeton, 1977); Karen Lawrence, *The Odyssey of Style in "Ulysses"* (Princeton, 1981); and Sheldon Brivic, "Joyce's Consubstantiality," in Morris Beja *et al.* (eds.), *James Joyce: The Centennial Symposium* (Urbana, 1986), 149–57.

taking place everywhere in the latter part of the book unmistakably implies a manipulator, an artificer. The artifice includes hints of the imminent meeting of the two characters given by means of Homeric parallels (so that Bloom/Odysseus must finally come to Stephen/Telemachus), as well as by a host of other connections between them. Thus, for example, in analogies between chapters, many of Bloom's activities in the afternoon echo Stephen's in the morning.[19] Numerous details about the two characters coincide: both are dressed in black, both lose keys, both have an interest in Italian language and music, and both are men of thought and feeling rather than action. Likewise, their thoughts (often returning, for instance, to *Hamlet*) begin to run on similar lines more often as the book proceeds. This phenomenon reaches its culmination in the wild expressionism of "Circe," in which thoughts become actions and characters interact with each other's thoughts.

By the end of the novel, then, something important has indeed occurred in the meeting of Bloom and Stephen. There is a relationship between the two, but it exists in the realm of art. It is aesthetic rather than naturalistic. Presumably, therefore, Stephen will not be able consciously to cement the friendship with Bloom that is crucial to his development until he is able to do so in the only context in which it lives—the artistic. And so, although the young man does not find what he needs on June 16, 1904, this does not damage the efficacy of the artistic connection set up between him and Bloom (and the "happy ending" of *Ulysses*). It makes perfect sense that Stephen is not aware of the importance of Bloom, for in fact he cannot realize it *until he discovers it in his art.*

We have returned to the Shakespeare theory, with a few adjustments, and we can see that it is important to the novel not only because of the light it sheds on Stephen's character but also because it shows Stephen moving in his thinking toward concepts that underlie Joyce's novel. The paradox of a distant author and a work that is "true" in its revealed passions and actions lies at the heart of this book, with its conspicuous and detached authorial presence who exerts his creative control over heavily autobiographical material. Part of the function of the narrator(s) is to inform us that

19. See Kenner, *"Ulysses,"* 100.

the writer of *Ulysses* has the kind of relationship with Bloom (and with Stephen as well) that Stephen needs to have. That relationship depends as much on Bloom and Stephen's being created out of aspects of Joyce himself as it does on his distance from them. The autobiographical character of the text is clearly central to what *Ulysses* is "about" and what Joyce was "about" in writing it.

The answer to the question of whether or not Stephen will be able, one day, to write his novels, then, is both yes and no. To the extent that he is Joyce, he will. To the extent that he is only part of Joyce, the part that is not Bloom or Bloom's son, he will not. Ultimately the hero of the book, in the words of Lynch's cap in "Circe," derives from the sense in which "Jewgreek is greekjew," the son consubstantial with the father (411). This phenomenon occurs in the act of simultaneously fabricating and remembering and thus points to the authorial presence and, behind it, the actual author. Ulysses, the man of cunning whose homecoming—whose reconciliation with his family and island—the book represents, is finally Joyce.

5

A Giant's Wake and a Packing Crate

Thus far, this study has considered four books by Joyce and Wolfe as what I have been calling *autobiographical fiction*, a subgenre of the novel. I have suggested, basically, that the adjective "autobiographical" that we use to describe their work should make a large difference in the way we regard the form and purpose of these novels. But the last published books of both writers—Joyce's *Finnegans Wake* and Wolfe's *The Web and the Rock* and *You Can't Go Home Again*—cannot be easily defined as novels or discussed in novelistic terms. *Finnegans Wake*, with its extreme transformations of language and form, is designedly difficult to categorize. Wolfe's last books, which were posthumously compiled and heavily edited, even rewritten in parts, by an editor, are also difficult to regard as texts with a recognizable author or novelistic purpose, even though they were intended to be marketed and sold as such. Nonetheless, several of the prominent concerns and phenomena of these last books are derived from the issues of autobiographical fiction and social class that I have been considering in the previous chapters of this study. Even though the issues are not embedded in novels with necessarily linear plots, consistent characters, stable architectonics, or unified expression, *Finnegans Wake*, *The Web and the Rock*, and

You Can't Go Home Again have nevertheless inherited much from the books that preceded them in the close family of texts that autobiographical fiction makes of a writer's *corpus*. In this chapter I intend to explore what is made of that inheritance.

Despite the prodigious amount of criticism of *Finnegans Wake*, the distinguished Joycean Fritz Senn could complain as recently as 1983 about the widespread impulse to reduce the *Wake* to "the formula '*FW* is X'": it is, he asserts, "the prototype of the algebra that we are lured into using against better judgment" when we approach the book.[1] We misjudge *Finnegans Wake* as we do Joyce's other works, he maintains, when we insist on beginning any inquiry with pronouncements about what is, or is not, absolutely true about the texts. To eliminate doubt is to falsify, even if that doubt is over the simplest of matters, such as the genre to which the texts belong. As Bernard Benstock observed about another basic question that is equally difficult to answer ("But what is it all about exactly?"), with *Finnegans Wake* "it seems preferable to beg the question rather than beggar the work."[2]

Let us begin to look at the *Wake*, then, not by insisting that it is one kind of novel or another (or that it is not a novel at all) but by noticing, in basic terms, what we have encountered in reading this long, difficult text. The most obvious characteristic, of course, is its singular language: from the first word, which is not in any dictionary and is not recognizable by context as a noun or a verb, we recognize that we have been thrown into deep water.[3] Joyce has exceeded himself: the technical experimentation of *Ulysses* seems tame beside this practically unreadable prose with its profusion of allusive, expansive metamorphoses of words and phrases from familiar use into new frames of reference. What extratextual reality is being referred to is unclear, though. Little wonder that post-structuralist literary theory often uses Joyce's last work to illustrate

1. "Dogmad or Dubliboused?" in Fritz Senn, *Joyce's Dislocutions: Essays on Reading as Translation*, ed. John Paul Riquelme (Baltimore, 1984), 102.

2. Bernard Benstock, *Joyce-Again's Wake: An Analysis of "Finnegans Wake"* (Seattle, 1965), 3.

3. Or to use Jacques Aubert's metaphor, we are swimming upstream, against the current, from the first word of *Finnegans Wake*. See his essay "riverrun," in Derek Attridge and Daniel Ferrer (eds.), *Post-Structuralist Joyce: Essays from the French* (Cambridge, Eng., 1984), 69–77.

formulations about the gaps between signifier and signified in language: *Finnegans Wake* creates a world of language whose relationship to any extralinguistic, "real" world is always suspect.

Thus from the first page, the setting could be the Garden of Eden, Dublin city, or someone's bed.[4] It could be during the time of Tristan and Isolde, Napoleon, St. Patrick, the Hebrew patriarchs, or the recent past. As we might expect, characters in this world also bear little resemblance to the depictions of spatially or temporally distinct individuals that we find in most novels. Their identities are never allowed to congeal, so that one figure, for example, may be a Dublin pubkeeper (named Earwicker or Porter, perhaps), Tim Finnegan from a broadside ballad, a giant whose head lies under the Hill of Howth, Finn MacCool, Adam, Isaac, St. Patrick, the Duke of Wellington, one or two—or sometimes three—of the man's own sons, John Joyce, or John Joyce's son the writer, among many others.[5] Or the figure might be all of them simultaneously. In the essay mentioned earlier, Fritz Senn calls the language of *Finnegans Wake*, which "tends toward instant contradiction" of itself, "the microcosmic verbal integration of doubt." He correctly notes what such language allows Joyce to do with characters in this book: "Verbal options favor suggestive possibilities more than distinct identities. If we do not want to determine whether some person is a hunchbacked pubkeeper, or an English king, or a Shakespearean character, or the actor on the stage, in a pub, on a battlefield, or from a book or a nursery rhyme, there may be no more concise way than 'when Dook Hookbackcrook upsits his ass booseworthies jeer and junket but they boos him oos and baas him

4. Or, indeed, inside someone's head, as John Bishop asserts persuasively in *Joyce's Book of the Dark: "Finnegans Wake"* (Madison, Wis., 1986).

5. Tim Finnegan, "a gentle Irishman, mighty odd," is the tippling hod carrier whose story is told in the street ballad "Finnegan's Wake." He dies but rises again at his wake, thanks to the curative effects of *usquebaugh*, or "water of life," the Irish term for whiskey. One version of the song's lyrics appears in RE, 543n. The Hill of Howth lies at the outer point of the peninsula bordering Dublin Bay to the north. Finn MacCool (Fionn MacCumhail) is the giant warrior hero of one cycle of ancient Irish myths. The best guide to these multiple identities is Adaline Glasheen's aptly named chart, "Who Is Who When Everybody Is Somebody Else," in the three versions of her *Census of "Finnegans Wake": An Index of the Characters and Their Roles* (Evanston, Ill., 1956, 1963; Berkeley, 1977).

aas when he lukes like Hunkett Plunkett.'"[6] Luke Plunkett, we discover, was an amateur actor who rode a donkey on stage as Richard III and achieved notoriety for his outrageously bad playing of the death scene in a Dublin version of Shakespeare's play.[7]

The phrase quoted by Senn illustrates an important aspect of the *Wake,* since we will not be able to read it well without recognizing its unusually direct references to contemporary events in the "real world."[8] The book is full of seemingly trivial references gleaned from newspapers, city directories, history books, atlases, and actual conversations among Joyce's acquaintances. It is far from mimetic in the ordinary sense, since it deliberately avoids fabricating a literary facsimile of an intelligible world, but in another sense the book may be unsurpassed in the extent to which it draws upon the life outside its pages. Here, we recognize, is a new way to create art out of what Stephen Dedalus called "the reality of experience" (*P*, 253). Unique as it is, *Finnegans Wake* is also recognizable as the successor to *A Portrait* and *Ulysses* in many ways, not the least of which is its preoccupation with the joining of literature and life.

The controlling metaphors of the book suggest this theme along with a sense of expansion from the earlier works. *A Portrait,* as its title suggests, is an intensely focused likeness of an autobiographical character within the framework of his vocational role. The point of view is for the most part narrowly limited to Stephen's own; the novel's structural elements and its patterns of imagery are

6. Senn, "Dogmad or Dubliboused?" 111. The quotation is from *FW*, 127.17.

7. For most of my information about specific details of *Finnegans Wake* I am indebted to several reference books: Glasheen's *Census of "Finnegans Wake"*; Roland McHugh's *Annotations to "Finnegans Wake"* (Baltimore, 1980); James S. Atherton's *The Books at the Wake: A Study of Literary Allusions in James Joyce's "Finnegans Wake"* (New York, 1960); and Clive Hart's *A Concordance to "Finnegans Wake"* (Rev. ed.; Mt. Vernon, N.Y., 1974). For a helpful introduction to the book as well as a representative bibliography see Zack Bowen and James F. Carens (eds.), *A Companion to Joyce Studies* (Westport, Conn., 1984), 559–687.

8. One of the many fictions that *Finnegans Wake* makes apparent, of course, is the easy notion of a "real world": the information gathered from texts such as city guides, or even reported by eyewitnesses, is no more "real" in one sense than the most fabulous of fictions. For convenience, though, I will continue to speak of an extraliterary, extraperceptional reality, since to doubt the fidelity of reports about it is not to question its existence—a position I believe Joyce held as well.

as neatly fitted together as a Chinese puzzle box. Like a pictorial portrait, too, the novel presupposes a relationship between the artist and the subject, a relationship whose ambiguity provides much of the narrative subtlety of the work. *Ulysses,* like its title, is more nearly epical in scope, encompassing many more characters, points of view, kinds of discourse, and symbolic and thematic elements. Instead of being confined to the consciousness of the protagonist, the novel's range of vision is enlarged to include all of Dublin society. The autobiographical role has itself been divided, so that two characters claim our attention and, to some extent, share the weight of autobiographical identification as well. And the relationship we are meant to assume between world and text becomes more complex in this visitation of modern life by ancient epic material, as the narrative presence has become exuberantly ostentatious. The central myth used to illustrate the fictive representation of reality changes, too, from the story of Daedalus, a story of imprisonment and sorrow along with artistic skill, to the story of Odysseus, a saga of human relationships, cunningly successful undertakings, and a journey home.

Finnegans Wake uses not a homecoming but an archetypal fall and resurrection as its dominant mythic analogue, grafting onto the tale of a seemingly unremarkable Irishman not a mortal, even one as extraordinary as Odysseus, but instead Finn-agains, the legendary hero Finn MacCool and other figures, from Adam on, who fall and rise, sleep and awaken. The remarkable discourse, presumably reproducing the unconscious mind's freely associative patterns of fragmentary ideas, is tremendously inclusive.[9] The world of Joyce's dream book allows, as dreams do, for a nearly unbounded (though often confused) range of subject matter as well as many points of view from the continually shifting identities of its cast of characters. The relationship between author and text is flamboyantly exploited in the sound of the distinctive periodic style and the outrageously punning neologisms, as well as in numerous

9. This is not to say that for all its flamboyant misleading, *Finnegans Wake* cannot be approached using terms and concepts familiar to studies of narratives: see Jean-Michel Rabaté, "Narratology and the Subject of *Finnegans Wake,*" in Morris Beja *et al.* (eds.), *James Joyce: The Centennial Symposium* (Urbana, 1986), 137–46.

other devices that draw attention to the book as an artificial form. Among these are parodies of literary forms such as that in Book 2, Chapter 2, in which a lesson appears as scholarly or pedagogical literature with the main body of text, left and right marginal notes, and footnotes written in the voices of different characters. The first and last pages are joined by ending the book with the first half of the first sentence. Most notably, characters (if they can be called such) are identified by symbols such as Λ or Δ or even by the appearance of certain letters in the text—HCE shows up as Here Comes Everybody, Haveth Childers Everywhere, the Human Conger Eel, He Can Explain, and so forth.

Finnegans Wake is also directly autobiographical, even though no one character represents the writer as Stephen Dedalus did in *A Portrait* and, to some extent, in *Ulysses*.[10] We know that Joyce's family and friends were important models for the "charictures in the drame" (*FW*, 302.31–32) in many different ways, as Ellmann's biography reveals. In fact, Joyce often included in a day's writing recent activities or conversations in which he had taken part, so close were the correspondences between the "Work in Progress" and the progress of the writer's life. However direct the association between the writer's life and his book, of course, the *Wake* is hardly an "autobiographical novel" in the usual sense. It is at once more real than a novel and less so, in much the same way that a collage, a form of visual art that was popular among dadaists and other contemporaries of Joyce, is more faithful to visual reality than pictorial realism. Works of art such as the *Merz* constructions of Kurt Schwitters, for instance, are far more "real" than are traditional sculptural approximations of forms, even though they are more abstract.[11]

10. Interestingly, when Joyce spoke or wrote of his "Work in Progress," he consistently minimized its autobiographical nature. For instance, in Samuel Beckett *et al.*, *Our Exagmination Round His Factification for Incamination of Work in Progress* (1929; rpr. New York, 1972), a collection of explanatory essays by friends and associates "more or less" directed by Joyce himself, there is no mention of this pervasive aspect of the work. (See *LJJ*, I, 283, for Joyce's admission that he directed the symposium that produced the *Exagmination*.)

11. In this context see Danis Rose and John O'Hanlon's comparison of *Finnegans Wake* with Pablo Picasso (who developed the collage technique) and Georges

In *Finnegans Wake*, as in *Ulysses*, the autobiographical role is divided: this time it is split into many fragments, so that each of the male characters depicts part of Joyce's personality or experience. The main character, for example (whom critical studies tend to call HCE, Earwicker, or Porter, three of his many names), exhibits many anxieties that were probably Joyce's. He is middle-aged, growing tired of his wife with her "auburnt streams" of hair (the same color as Nora's), although the "pictures motion" of the two of them "eloping for that holm in Finn's Hotel Fiord, Nove Norening" can still elicit nostalgia for their early domestic life, when they "pulled down the kuddle and they made fray" (330.24–25). (Nora worked at Finn's Hotel in Dublin when Joyce met her.) HCE is tormented by conflicting emotions toward his daughter, who has a personality that splits in two as she looks in her mirror or is both Isolde of Brittany and Isolde of Ireland—characteristics that are painfully reminiscent of schizophrenia, the disease with which Joyce's daughter Lucia was afflicted. His vision is bad, "irismaimed," so that, with his "blackeyed lenses," he is compared with "bland old Isaac." He thus resembles the figure Joyce must have seemed to himself during the time of the *Wake*'s composition as, nearly blind from glaucoma, he deteriorated into "what remains of a heptark, leareyed and letterish" (590.2). His yearning for his daughter Issy is also connected with sight in the form of the colors with which she and her "rainbow girls" are associated. HCE's nameless crime may even have something to do with "why he left Dublin" (91.21–22). And of course, among numerous other correspondences, he loves to drink (hence the name Porter and his drunken fall from a ladder as Tim Finnegan).

HCE also has male progeny—perhaps one son (as Joyce did), perhaps two (as did Joyce's father).[12] Shem and Shaun, whether

Braque, in *Understanding "Finnegans Wake": A Guide to the Narrative of James Joyce's Masterpiece* (New York, 1982), x–xii.

12. See John Gordon, *"Finnegans Wake": A Plot Summary* (Syracuse, 1986), 50–52, for a brief discussion of whether Shem and Shaun are one figure, symbolizing the divided personality of HCE (and corresponding to Joyce's one son Giorgio), or two. As two, the standard autobiographical interpretation holds that they refer to James and Stanislaus (see, for instance, Benstock, *Joyce-Again's Wake*, 216–21), but Gordon

they are two sides of one personality or two separate characters, are also directly autobiographical in many respects, Shem especially, in that he seems to be the artistic side of Joyce's personality. Shem, called "Sunny Sim" (305.05), as Joyce was called "Sunny Jim" in his childhood, bears an uncanny resemblance to Stephen Dedalus and to James Joyce.[13] He hails from a genteel family who have severe financial troubles, who were "Ones propsperups treed" but are "now stohong baroque" (230.35–36). Shaun spitefully reports that Shem is "weird, I tell you, and middayevil down to his vegetable soul" (423.27–28). Shaun refers to Shem later as "Brother Intelligentius, when he's not absintheminded, with his Paris addresse!" (464.16–17). Although "barnacled up to the eyes," Shem has refused to marry because he has been "warmed off the ricecourse of marrimoney," and he has denied the church with a vengeance ("*Negas, negasti*—negertop, negertoe, negertoby, negrunter!") even though he once "went into the society of jewses" (423.22–23, 30, 33–34, 36). Indeed, Shaun calls his brother names and accuses him of declaring a self-serving *non serviam*: "Condemned fool, anarch, egoarch, hiresiarch, you have reared your disunited kingdom on the vacuum of your own most intensely doubtful soul. Do you hold yourself then for some god in the manger, Shehohem, that you will neither serve not let serve, pray nor let pray?" (188.15–19). Shem apparently intended to fly by the net of religion as well as those of nationality and race by exiling himself to the continent, but his flight out of Ireland may have been a mistake. The voice narrating Book 1, Chapter 7, the portrait of Shem, asks rhetorically, "Was liffe worth leaving?" and answers himself, "Nej!" (230.25).

Shem is a writer, a "penman." He not only reads the signatures that Stephen strived to decipher in "Proteus" but has also forged the conscience of his race just as an earlier Stephen vowed to do at

asserts that they may refer as well to James and his older brother, the firstborn, who died at birth (92–94). See also Clive Hart, *Structure and Motif in "Finnegans Wake"* (Evanston, Ill., 1962), for an explanation of the varying degree of distinction between Shem and Shaun, so that they are both one character and two (130–34).

13. Stanislaus Joyce's recollection of his brother's nickname is found in *My Brother's Keeper: James Joyce's Early Years*, ed. Richard Ellmann (New York, 1958), 23.

the end of *A Portrait*. But, in a fashion typical of the *Wake*, he has done so literally as a "sham," a forger (170.25). We hear "how cutely" he managed, instead of writing something useful for Irish housewives, "to copy all their various styles of signature so as one day to utter an epical forged cheque on the public for his own private profit" (181.15–17). We are asked rhetorically, "Who can say how many pseudostylic shamiana, how few or how many of the most venerated public impostures, how very many piously forged palimpsests slipped in the first place by this morbid process from his pelagiarist pen?" (181.36–182.3).

Shem's writing is autobiographical: he is known "to stipple endlessly inartistic portraits of himself" while "lit" with alcohol (literally, since he writes by the light of his red nose) (182.18–19). We hear that in his work "he scrabbled and scratched and scriobbled and skrevened nameless shamelessness about everybody ever he met" (182.13–14), using his pen to settle scores (as if BELLETRISTICKS [281.R1] and stones could indeed break someone's bones). He is compared, because of his autobiographical art and his pride, with "Nobookisonester" (Nebuchadnezzar/No book is honester) (177.14). He apparently wrote *Dubliners*, and he is mocked as a "shuddersome spectacle" writing *Ulysses*: "This semidemented zany amid the inspissated grime of his glaucous den making believe to read his usylessly unreadable Blue Book of Eccles, *édition de ténèbres*" (179.24–27).[14] Interestingly, as if Joyce's first autobiographical novel were indeed "just a poor trait of the artless" (114.32), *A Portrait*, for whatever reason, is scarcely mentioned by name in *Finnegans Wake*. Joyce's last work is being written, or so we are given to suppose on several occasions when "Work in Progress," as Joyce referred to *Finnegans Wake* before he settled on or revealed its title, is named. For example, Jaun is enjoined to "Work your progress!" at the end of his barrel ride in Book 3, Chapter 2 (473.21), and near the end of the book we are told that "a progress shall be made in walk, ney?" (567.20). At the conclusion of the *Wake*, ALP is enthusiastic about a forthcoming volume entitled

14. See *FW*, 186.19–187.15, in which the titles of the stories of *Dubliners* can be discerned.

Finglas since the Flood, exclaiming, "That'll be some kingly work in progress!" (625.13–14).

Finnegans Wake admits a far more active relationship between autobiographical writing and extraliterary life than did Joyce's earlier works. Still, however, the need to write about oneself is associated with a need to join an artistic aristocracy. Or to be more precise, in this book of mediated truths, one character insults another using this idea as ammunition for his diatribe. In one amazingly condensed passage, Shaun accuses Shem of being obsessed with self-writing—using his own blood for ink to produce works like Proust's autobiographical fiction—and of regarding himself as both a Christ-like martyr for his art and an uncomradely member of an idiosyncratic artistic elite. "Inkupot!" he exclaims: "He has encaust in his blood. Shim! I have the outmost contempt for. Prost bitten! Conshy! Tiberia is waiting on you, arestocrank!" (424.7–10). Shem's writing is anything but "pure" art (hence the famous description of him making indelible ink out of his own freeze-dried excrement).[15] His writing is affected by his spiteful temperament even if he wishes to be objective, and in turn, it may affect his life as he "sets up" situations that are "writefully right" for its sake: "He would jused sit it all write down just as he would jused set it up all writhefully rate in blotch and void, yielding to no man in hymns ignorance" (229.26–28). Consequently, black and white, in the business of autobiographical fiction, are "blotch and void." It is absurd to expect, as JUSTIUS (a type of Shaun) does, that MERCIUS (Shem) could separate the plain truth from the written form of it, even if he wanted to. JUSTIUS is tired of a fictional, third-person presentation of what he assumes could be simple and true, telling MERCIUS, "no longer will I follow you obliquelike through the inspired form of the third person singular and the moods and hesitensies of the deponent" (187.28–30). But truth cannot be so obtained: *Finnegans Wake* ultimately asserts

15. We are informed (in modest Latin) that Shem "*demum ex stercore turpi cum divi Orionis iucunditate mixto, cocto, frigorique exposito, encaustum sibi fecit indelibile*" (finally, from the foul excrement, mixed together with the sweetness of the divine Orion [urine], cooked up, and put out to cool, he made for himself an indelible encaustic [ink]) (185.24–25).

that Shaun-like straightforwardness can only be expressed through Shem-like art, the complex entanglement of the outer world, human perception (both conscious and subconscious), and literary fabrication. In other, Wakean words,

> The prouts who will invent a writing there ultimately is the poeta, still more learned, who discovered the raiding there originally. That's the point of eschatology our book of kills reaches for now in soandso many counterpoint words. What can't be coded can be decorded if an ear aye sieze what no eye ere grieved for. Now, the doctrine obtains, we have occasioning cause causing effects and affects occasionally recausing altereffects. Or I will let me take it upon myself to suggest to twist the penman's tale posterwise. The gist is the gist of Shaum but the hand is the hand of Sameas. (482.31–483.4)

The autobiographical writer, a Proust or a Joyce, both *invents* in the modern English sense of the word, making fiction, and *discovers* what was originally there, in the Latin sense of *invenire* (as if he were a Roman *poeta*). The forms of a fabricated code and its opposite, a documentary record, are both deconstructed as the provinces of history (cause/effect) and fiction (affect/altereffect) collide. Likewise, *Finnegans Wake* explodes literary form in order to represent stylistically and structurally what Joyce's long career of writing autobiographical fiction had taught him about his calling, like Stephen Dedalus' in *A Portrait*, "to recreate life out of life" (*P*, 172).

We see, then, where the writing of autobiographical fiction took James Joyce. The examining and remembering self that is at the narrative center of *A Portrait* and *Ulysses* has expanded into an artistic cosmos, just as its fictional representative has been diffused onto a vast canvas of impulses and relationships. In *Finnegans Wake* personal memory had become, in effect, human psychology and history on a grand scale.

A similar movement outward from the individual self of the protagonist, an expansion to include a wider range of concerns, can be seen in the books that represent Thomas Wolfe's last fictional writing: *The Web and the Rock* and *You Can't Go Home Again*. For Wolfe as well as Joyce, continuing development as an artist and a person necessitated a broadening in his autobiographical fiction. We can also see in these works that Wolfe was groping for fictional forms appropriate to express this shift of focus within an autobiographical mode, although his early death in 1938 prevented him from finishing the book that was to follow *Of Time and the River*. Thus the record we have of what would have been the unfinished work's structure and underlying patterns of narrative is sketchy at best. The fragments that were pieced together into the last two books cannot tell us much about how Wolfe would have tried to solve the problem of form in his fiction.

After the publication of *Of Time and the River*, Wolfe had some difficulty deciding which of several projects he should tackle next. Perkins and he had assumed that for his next novel he would finish the second half of the manuscript that had been cut in two to trim *Of Time and the River* to publishable size.[16] This material, still called "The October Fair," would pick up the story of Eugene Gant where it broke off in the inconclusive last scene of *Of Time and the River*, at the portentous meeting of the protagonist and Esther Jack, the character modeled after Aline Bernstein. The love affair of Eugene and Esther would unify the book, according to the scheme. But Wolfe also planned two other books, neither of which would be as conventionally novelistic as "The October Fair." One, tentatively titled "The Hills Beyond Pentland," would focus on Eugene Gant's ancestors and would be Proustian in organization, following the subconscious flow of Eugene's memories instead of a conventional chronology. The idea of experimenting with this form appealed to Wolfe, and he also developed a plan for a Joycean night-book, to be called either "Book of the Night" or "The Hound of Darkness," in which mosaiclike fragments of stories set all across the country during a single night would create a vast impressionistic portrait of America.[17] (Wolfe knew Joyce's "Work in Progress" well: he owned copies of "Anna Livia Plurabelle" and the March, 1928, issue of *transition*, which contained the beginning of Book 3, as well as *Our Exagmination Round His Factification for Incamination of Work in Pro-*

16. Indeed, a publisher's note attached to the beginning of *Of Time and the River* announced that "The October Fair (1925–1928)," one of the four projected volumes of the Gant story, was already written. This was far from true.

17. *The Hound of Darkness*, edited by John L. Idol, Jr., was recently published in a limited edition by the Thomas Wolfe Society (N.p., 1986).

gress [RSK, 301n].) At about this time, too, Wolfe began a short novel that was designed specifically *not* to be autobiographical, called "The Vision of Spangler's Paul." Gradually, the various projects coalesced into one—another long autobiographical work, to be experimental in style and universally inclusive in theme.

In all these projections we can see Wolfe casting about for the proper form to contain his future work. He was aware that years of work might be necessary for him to find his own way to expand his autobiographical art into an inclusive mature work, as Joyce had done in *Ulysses.* And he was worried that the exigencies of trade publishing (and an editor whom he suspected of "taming" his work into salable size and form) might not allow him the freedom he needed. In December, 1936, he wrote a long letter to Max Perkins in which he described at length Joyce's successful fight against conservative readers and publishers. He then announced: "I am now going to write my own 'Ulysses.' The first volume is now under way. The first volume will be called 'The Hound of Darkness,' and the whole work, when completed, will be called 'The Vision of Spangler's Paul.' Like Mr. Joyce, I am going to write as I please, and this time, no one is going to cut me unless I want them to" (*LTW*, 587).

Wolfe chose to compare himself defensively with Joyce at a crucial moment in his career: he also notified Perkins in this letter that he was leaving Scribner's to affiliate himself with another publisher. The two men who had worked closely to prepare *Look Homeward, Angel* for publication and had spent hours together every evening for six months to edit *Of Time and the River* had been close friends as well as business associates, but their relationship was badly damaged by the messy editing of the second novel and the increasingly common charges that Wolfe was unable to write his books by himself. The problem, as Bernard DeVoto saw it in "Genius Is Not Enough," was that "so far, one indispensable part of the artist has existed not in Mr. Wolfe but in Maxwell Perkins. Such organizing faculty and such critical intelligence as have been applied to the book have come not from the artist's feeling for form and aesthetic integrity but from the office of Charles Scribner's Sons."[18]

18. Bernard DeVoto, "Genius Is Not Enough," reprinted in Louis D. Rubin, Jr. (ed.), *Thomas Wolfe: A Collection of Critical Essays* (Englewood Cliffs, N.J., 1973), 75.

The split between Perkins and Wolfe may have been inevitable, given Wolfe's overreliance on his editor for emotional as well as critical support and his tendency to rebel against his own excessive attachment. Perkins, in turn, had tacitly encouraged the young writer to depend on him, perhaps needing to be cast in a fatherly role. But Wolfe's dependence, exaggerated in the public mind by critics such as DeVoto, had put the writer in an untenable position in relation to his future work. He had to prove that the form of his novels was his own. Such proof was of greater value to him than the closest of friendships or literary associations, so he severed his ties with his editor and publisher.

Wolfe lived a scarce twenty months after this dramatic and difficult break, and he did not finish his next full-length work. In May, 1938, he left New York for an extended trip to the West, leaving a wooden crate full of his manuscripts in the offices of Harper and Brothers, his new publisher. He had separated the sections of his new novel from the rest of the papers and had drawn up an outline to accompany them so that his editor at Harper, Edward C. Aswell, could read the rough draft in his absence.[19] The manuscript was bundled together and its sections were labeled according to their places in the outline, but it had only such unity as twine and the numbering of pages could give it. Wolfe told his agent, Elizabeth Nowell, that he was worried about letting Aswell read the manuscript, since "I know where I stand, but it is like presenting someone with the bones of some great prehistoric animal he has never seen before" (*LTW*, 764). He used another osteologic metaphor in a letter to Aswell, writing that his book was in "about the same state of articulation" as *Of Time and the River* was when Perkins saw it for the first time in December, 1933, and that "what he saw, of course, was only a kind of enormous skeleton." But Wolfe was careful to explain that he wanted the parallel between the fate of the two manuscripts to stop there. He insisted that he wanted to "proceed without any great assistance until I have brought it to a further state of development and completion," adding, "I do not believe that I am in need of just the same kind of editorial help at this

19. The outline is reproduced, with explanatory notes, in RSK, 415–37.

moment as Mr. Perkins so generously and unselfishly gave me in 1933, 1934" (*LTW*, 757–59).

We will never know, of course, whether Wolfe would have needed such help. He contracted pneumonia during his trip to the West Coast and died in September, 1938. Aswell, a junior editor, thus found himself in a precarious position at Harper, having offered a contract along with a generous advance for an unseen novel. He made a practical decision as he sorted through the vast quantity of Wolfe's material and began arranging, cutting from, and in some cases adding to the manuscript in order to salvage something for publication. The results of his ethically dubious labors were *The Web and the Rock*, published in 1939, and *You Can't Go Home Again*, which appeared in 1940. Aswell published a volume of Wolfe's short pieces, entitled *The Hills Beyond*, in the fall of 1941, and he finally acknowledged that he had played a part in the posthumous works in an appended "Note on Thomas Wolfe." He did not admit the whole of his contribution, though, and his massive editing later became highly controversial, as it will remain.[20]

It is probably best, then, to adopt a "packing-crate" method ourselves when we consider *The Web and the Rock* and *You Can't Go Home Again*, untying Aswell's unifying efforts and leaving the books as loosely joined as they were when he first read them. Only thus can we represent with any fidelity what Wolfe's last work might have been like if he had finished it. Only thus, in fact, can we do justice to his talent: for as wholes, *The Web and the Rock* and *You Can't Go Home Again* are not satisfying novels. They are more accurately regarded almost as anthologies (especially *You Can't Go Home Again*), aggregates of units of varying lengths in various states of polish that can nevertheless tell us much about Wolfe's unresolved struggle for artistic control over the material he was working to present.

The story that Aswell pieced together has roughly the same outlines as Wolfe's biography. In *Of Time and the River*, we recall, Eugene left America to rediscover and return to it through his art. *The Web and the Rock* begins the story of the autobiographical character anew, in a form that is in some respects more "fictional" than

20. See the afterword to Donald's biography, "The Posthumous Novels of Thomas Wolfe," for a description of Aswell's editing and an assessment of the re-

was the childhood of Eugene Gant in *Look Homeward, Angel*, and takes us through the first flush of his affair with Esther Jack and the composition of his novel to the trip to Europe he takes to escape her while he waits for publishers' decisions about his manuscript. In *You Can't Go Home Again*, the book is published, "through the kind of accidental happening which so often affects the course of human events," at the same date as *Look Homeward, Angel* (coinciding "almost exactly with the beginning of the Great American Depression" [325]). The young writer gets a taste of the fame for which he has yearned, writes a second book, and flees to Europe again, this time to put some distance between himself and the American literary scene, whose opinions he dreads, when the book appears.

Scattered through both novels is a good deal of talk about the problem of autobiographical fiction, in scenes that show the protagonist struggling with his own need to create. (The protagonist had an assortment of names in the manuscript, but for convenience I will refer to him as George Webber, the name standardized by Aswell.) Wolfe put into the mouth of this character a number of statements that perform the double function of Stephen Dedalus' Shakespeare theory: they tell us directly about George, who has not written well yet, and they tell us indirectly about the person who has written what we are reading. In fact, though, since Wolfe did not use the kind of ironic distancing by which Joyce separated the narrator's and the character's points of view, the two functions merge in these statements to a much greater extent than in any comparable sections of Joyce's work.

In the version of his college years that appears in *The Web and the Rock*, we see a difference between George Webber and Eugene Gant that Wolfe was concerned with developing. Webber is not interested in escaping from life into art, as was the romantic hero of *Look Homeward, Angel*. Rather, great art for him reveals the artist unabashedly. He makes his discovery of the personal in the aesthetic when he reads Dostoevski for the first time. As he tries to explain to his friends,

---

sultant controversy (DD, 464–84). See also Leslie Field, *Thomas Wolfe and His Editors: Establishing a True Text for the Posthumous Publications* (Norman, Okla., 1987).

It's like Pascal said—that one of the grandest surprises in life is to open a book expecting to meet an author, and to find instead a man. And that's the way it is with Dostoevski. You don't meet the author. You meet the man. You may not believe everything that is said, but you believe the man who is saying it. You are convinced by his utter sincerity, by the great, burning light of him, and in the end, no matter how confused or bewildered or unsure he may himself be, time and again you know that he is right. And you see also that it doesn't matter how people say things, so long as the feeling behind the things they say is a true one. (*WR*, 212)

The distinction between "author" and "man" for which George is groping in this passage resurfaces in an important section of *You Can't Go Home Again*, in which George and his friend Randy Shepperton discuss the problems raised by the writing of autobiographical fiction.[21] George has written, we have been told, "a *Ulysses* kind of book" about life in his hometown, in which he "had drawn upon the experience of his own life . . . in a manner of naked directness and reality that was rather rare in books" (326). In fact, however, the novel, called *Home to Our Mountains*, was more like *A Portrait of the Artist as a Young Man* than *Ulysses*, as George comes to realize.

The furor over the book in his hometown initially makes George regret that he ever set pen to paper. He has separated in his mind the artistic and the human aspects of himself, calling the one "Man-Creating" and the other "Man-Alive." As he worked on his book, "Man-Creating" disregarded any human consequences that might follow from what he wrote in the name of the quest for truth. Unfortunately, "Man-Alive" has the greater claim of the two now that George sees "all the pain and anguish I have caused to people that I know," as he laments in a letter to Randy. "For what has [the book] accomplished, apparently, except to ruin my relatives, my friends, and everyone in town whose life was ever linked with mine?" (354–55).

The ostensible answer to this question—"The integrity of the

21. The character Randy Shepperton, who was used by Aswell as an example of Wolfe's "free invention," refuting the charge that Wolfe had been "merely" autobiographical, was in fact created by Aswell. The scenes in *You Can't Go Home Again* with Randy originally featured another autobiographical protagonist's brother; since George Webber was an only child, Aswell made the brother into the friend. See Edward C. Aswell, "A Note on Thomas Wolfe," in Thomas Wolfe, *The Hills Beyond* (New York, 1941), 358; DD, 472.

artist" (355)—is unsatisfactory precisely because the artist cannot find integrity in the novel he wrote. George cannot hide behind the facade of his art in the name of naked truth: the fact that it is a facade gives the lie to his excuse. And the novel he wrote is not naked truth: "There was scarcely a detail in George's book that was precisely true to fact . . . there was hardly a page in which everything had not been transmuted and transformed by the combining powers of George's imagination; yet readers got from it such an instant sense of reality that many of them were willing to swear that the thing described had been not only 'drawn from life,' but was the actual and recorded fact itself" (356). It was not truthful enough, in other words. But how can George make his art adhere more closely to reality while also taking into account the aspect of reality he has just discovered—that it is neither moral nor possible to separate his own life, and the lives of others, from the world of art?

There is some indication that Wolfe intended for George to find the solution to his dilemma from the catastrophe that Libya Hill undergoes soon after George's novel is published in the fall of 1929. After the false boom economy of the twenties, the town's bank fails and the citizenry has to face the depression into which it has fallen along with the rest of the country. With this crashing return to the rock of reality, the impact of Webber's web of art is dissolved. Randy tells George: "Since the bank failed I don't think I've heard your name mentioned. They've got too much real trouble to worry about now" (*YCGHA*, 375).

Randy, who has lost his job, who will lose his family home, and who (we surmise from a passing reference near the end of *You Can't Go Home Again*) might have been intended to die young, is well chosen as the voice of wisdom who will illuminate for George his delusions about art. Randy has assured his friend, significantly, that "even if he *was* a writer, he still considered him a member of the human race" (*YCGHA*, 358). It is he who rebukes George for playing what he calls "the wounded faun." In a long dialogue between the two characters, Randy speaks the author's sentiments to his autobiographical representative and sets George on a different course from the one taken by Eugene Gant. George had been working under the assumption that an artist "was a kind of fabulous, rare, and special creature who lived on 'beauty' and 'truth' and had thoughts so subtle that the average man could comprehend them no more than a mongrel could understand the moon he bayed at." He thought that "the artist, therefore, could achieve his 'art' only through a constant state of flight into some magic wood, some province of enchantment," and that he had been "driven out by the tribe" of ordinary society (*YCGHA*, 383). But Randy reminds him that his exile from Libya Hill was self-imposed. Furthermore, "as for this idea of yours that a man achieves 'beauty' by escaping somewhere from the life he knows, isn't the truth just the opposite? . . . I mean, taking your own book as an example, isn't it true that every good thing in it came, not because you withdrew from life, but because you got into it—because you managed to understand and use the life you knew?" (384).

Webber suddenly realizes what he needs to do. The critics who accused his book of being "too autobiographical" wrote the opposite of the truth. It was "not 'too autobiographical.' . . . If the critics had just crossed those words out and written in their place 'not autobiographical enough,' they'd have hit it squarely," he says to Randy. He explains: "My young hero was a stick, a fool, a prig, a snob, as Dedalus was—as in my own presentment of the book I was. There was the weakness. Oh, I know—there were lots of autobiographical spots in the book, and where it was true I'm not ashamed of it. . . . [But] The failure comes from the false personal. There's the guilt. That's where the young genius business gets in—the young artist business, what you called a while ago the wounded faun business. It gets in and it twists the vision" (384–85).

Webber "was down to solid rock" now, the narrator tells us (385). In the service of greater truth, about himself as well as about the world outside the self, he needs to move outward, to embrace a "larger vision." But this revelation does not help him solve the essentially formal problem that autobiographical fiction presents when the first *Home to Our Mountains* has been written—the problem of where to go when you can't go home again. We hear not only Webber's frustration but also Wolfe's as the friends' conversation continues.

Webber's problem, which would be comical if the narrating voice did not so obviously sympathize with the character, is that his material threatens to leave him completely enveloped, like Shem the Penman's "squidself which he had squirtscreened from the crystalline world," in a cloud of his own ink (*FW*, 186.7). "With a note of desperation in his voice," he tells Randy, "'I've got too much material. It keeps backing up on me—' he gestured around him at the tottering piles of manuscript that were everywhere about the room—'until sometimes I wonder what in the name of God I'm going to do with it all—how I'm going to find a frame for it, a pattern, a channel, a way to make it flow!' . . . 'Sometimes it actually occurs to me that a man may be able to write no more because he gets drowned in his own secretions!'" (*YCGHA*, 386).

Thus Webber looks frantically for a way to order his new work. His tentative idea is to combine truth with fiction by means of myth. He continues: "I think it may be something like what people vaguely mean when they speak of fiction. A kind of legend, perhaps. Something—a story—composed of all the knowledge I have, of all the living I've seen. Not the facts, you understand—not just the record of my life—but something truer than the facts—something distilled out of my experience and transmitted into a form of universal application" (386–87).

These passages clearly show Wolfe's thinking about his own attempt to move away from romantic idealism in his fiction. There is little or no indication in the narrative that Webber's dilemma is not also the narrator's. In fact, the considerable resemblance that the discussion between Randy and George bears to Stephen Dedalus' thinly dramatized theorizing in *A Portrait* comes from the obvious relationship in both scenes between the artist and the characters' talk about art. Both dialogues are devices to connect events in the narrative with autobiographical authors, to tell us how to read the novel in our hands by giving us the history of its writer's artistic beliefs.

We know that one of the problems with which Wolfe was engrossed in his last years was how to universalize his autobiographical fiction. His experimentation with one partially autobiographical character after another is also reminiscent of Joyce: to a great extent, Wolfe tried to do with one character what Joyce had done with two in *Ulysses*, to take the measure of his earlier, "wounded faun" self-image. Stephen Dedalus is something of a *fin-de-siècle* aesthete;

Leopold Bloom, the "all-round man," avoids Stephen's priggish self-indulgence.[22] Webber, in these scenes, banishes the Gant from himself to become a different kind of writer and person. According to a long note in one of Wolfe's pocket notebooks, the new protagonist of the novel to follow *Of Time and the River* would have "no trace of Eugene Gant-i-ness" in his character. He would represent both the mature writer and all men. Like Bloom, he would in some ways be more autobiographical than his predecessor but would also play a very different role formally, thus allowing the writer to transform the apprenticeship form of autobiographical fiction into a new kind of novel. Wolfe's notebook entry is explicit about the formal implications of the change from Eugene to George.

> The protagonist—the central character, the Wilhelm Meister kind of figure—really the most autobiographical character the author has ever written about because he wants to put everything he has or knows into him—is important now because the author hopes he will be, or illustrate, in his own experience every one of us—not merely the sensitive young fellow in conflict with his town, his family, the little world around him . . . but all of these things and much more insofar as they illustrate essential elements of any man's progress and discovery of life and as they illustrate the world itself, not in terms of personal and self-centered conflict with the world, but in terms of ever-increasing discovery of life and the world, with a consequent diminution of the more personal and self-centered vision of the world which a young man has.[23]

The progression outward from a portrait of the artist as a young man to a broader depiction of "life and the world" is, Wolfe realized, a change in the kind of novel in which this character would appear. And that formal change occurs because the relationship between the author and the character has altered. The autobiographical *Künstlerroman* cannot be written again. Thus,

> since there is no longer a trace of Eugene Gant-i-ness in the mind and spirit of the creator, the problem should be a technical one rather than a

22. Frank Budgen recalled that Joyce called Bloom an "all-round man." See Budgen, *James Joyce and the Making of "Ulysses"* (1934; rpr. Bloomington, 1960), 15–18.

23. Richard S. Kennedy and Paschal Reeves (eds.), *The Notebooks of Thomas Wolfe* (2 vols.; Chapel Hill, 1970), II, 940–41.

spiritual or emotional one. In other words, this is a book about discovery, and not about self-justification: it hopes to describe the pattern that the life of Everyman must, in general, take, in its process of discovery: and although the protagonist should be, in his own right, an interesting person, his significance lies not in his personal uniqueness and differences, but in his personal identity to the life of every man.[24]

Unfortunately, one reason why *The Web and the Rock* is an unsatisfying novel is that the edited book does not contain the rhetorical tension of the relationship between protagonist and author that unifies and propels forward *Look Homeward, Angel*. As it stands, the first half of *The Web and the Rock* is another version of the author's youth, in which the change to a different form has not been carried out. Some of the Webber material is as full of what Wolfe called "self-justification" as the earlier books are (naturally enough, since sections of the manuscript were deleted from *Of Time and the River* and even "O Lost," the early version of *Look Homeward, Angel*). But the drama of George's discovering his vocation, in a narrative form that mirrors that drama, the form that provides *Look Homeward, Angel* and *A Portrait* with meaning, is gone. Self-justification in a character and in a novel that do not need to prove themselves is frustrating and tedious. Like George Webber drowning in his manuscript, Wolfe made the serious mistake of altering his rhetorical plans but not discarding his old material, much of which could not suit a new formal purpose. Passages that are well written, and that perhaps should not have been excised from an earlier novel, damage a later work.

In the newer material Wolfe meant for social conscience to replace Gantian self-absorption as a way to order the form and meaning of his novel. Thus the conversation about art takes place in the context of the bank failure in Libya Hill: George is made aware of the falseness of the "wounded faun" mentality by having his eyes opened to the very real catastrophe in his hometown. A much larger proportion of the material that was made into *The Web and the Rock* and *You Can't Go Home Again* focuses on social problems than did Wolfe's earlier work. In fact, the dominant impression given by *You Can't Go Home Again* especially is that Wolfe's range of

24. *Ibid.*, 941–42.

vision was expanding greatly in his last work. Hugh Holman, one of the book's most influential critics, expresses the view of many readers that this expansion represents artistic growth. Holman calls the book "the social testament of a maturing—if not fully mature—man."[25] In fact, Wolfe had been acutely aware of the lack of political and social consciousness in his fiction for some time. One of the reasons he gave for breaking with Perkins and Scribner's, an old, conservative publishing house, was Perkins' disinclination to keep material in *Of Time and the River* that Wolfe had written to be socially relevant, as well as his discouraging Wolfe from including such material in the next projected book. Wolfe was not immune from the pressures of the political climate of the thirties, but Perkins felt strongly that his talent lay elsewhere. As Perkins wrote another of his Scribner's authors, Marjorie Kinnan Rawlings: "That was one of the issues between me and Tom, and I kept telling him that what he felt would come through his writing, even though not specifically stated. And yet he wanted at that time to be a Communist, the last thing he truly was."[26]

Perkins was right, at least in part. Even at his most political, Wolfe could not relinquish the focusing sensibility of the artist through whose eyes the world of wealthy New Yorkers in "The Party at Jack's," the vicious and relentless exploitation of small salesmen in "The Company," or the veiled horror of nazism in "I Have a Thing to Tell You" is revealed, and because of whose personal weaknesses these scenes, and others like them, have their meaning. In "The Party at Jack's," for instance, the barrenness of the Jacks' luxurious apartment building, the fragility of the seemingly imposing lives within it, the simultaneously coddled and victimized servants, and even the fire (which presages the bigger holocaust to come with the crash of the stock market a week later)—all these signs of social evil are also lessons about art and work for George Webber to learn, told by a remembering narrator as lessons he learned in order to write about them.[27] As Louis

25. C. Hugh Holman, *The Loneliness at the Core: Studies in Thomas Wolfe* (Baton Rouge, 1975), 89.

26. John Hall Wheelock (ed.), *Editor to Author: The Letters of Maxwell Perkins* (New York, 1950), 179–80.

27. Wolfe's novella was renamed "The World That Jack Built" by Aswell (from

Rubin notices, the magazine version of this episode, which was not a part of George's story but a narrative unit in itself, was more economically written. Nevertheless, in Rubin's opinion "the gain in objectivity is at the expense of vividness; Wolfe's art depends upon the presence of that author-narrator, and without it the fiction tends to be flat and unexciting."[28]

Yet the later fiction that does not demonstrate an authorial interest in the world outside George's artistic self-consciousness is flat and unexciting as well. Perkins was not completely correct: he and Aswell did indeed steer Wolfe's work in an unproductive direction by trying to pattern it after *Look Homeward, Angel,* narrowly focusing on the protagonist's intense search for self-completion, free of "dithyrambs" and extraneous matter. It was necessary for Wolfe's autobiographical protagonist to widen his area of vision, and it was necessary for the expression of his story to mirror that shift in perception stylistically. As Holman suggests, Wolfe's search for a way to make his protagonist into everyman, replacing Stephen Dedalus with someone akin to the universal self of Whitman, was far from being merely a response to the political climate or one more deluded attempt to write the great American novel or epic.[29] It was, in fact, vital to the artistic task Wolfe had set for himself, the making of a life's work of autobiographical fiction. Joyce split his fictional self in two, then fractured it into many pieces, to maintain the balance between the art and the life from which it came. Wolfe found no such solution to his similar problem, but his last work clearly shows that a great part of his labor was directed toward finding one. It is for his equivalent to Joyce's success that George Webber cries along with his creator: "'The *way*! The *way*! Do you understand?'" (*YCGHA*, 386).

Joyce spoke of *Finnegans Wake* as "a mountain that I tunnel into from every direction, but I don't know what I will find" (RE, 543). He did not work from beginning to end to compose the *Wake*, as he had in writing *Ulysses*. Instead, he wrote it piecemeal, one epi-

---

a chapter heading in Wolfe's manuscript) when he included it in *You Can't Go Home Again*.

28. Louis D. Rubin, Jr., *A Gallery of Southerners* (Baton Rouge, 1982), 166.

29. Holman, *The Loneliness at the Core*, 80.

sode at a time.[30] Wolfe, too, wrote section by section after his first novel. He also revised in large units. Aswell was surprised to discover, as he explained in his note to *The Hills Beyond*, that "far more often than not I found that there would be at least two different versions of the same episode, and sometimes there were as many as four or five versions. . . . When [Wolfe] was dissatisfied with a scene or character he would not, as a rule, simply revise his draft and get it recopied: he would put it aside and rewrite it some different way from start to finish."[31]

This habit contributed to the fragmentary quality of Wolfe's books after *Look Homeward, Angel*, of course, for Wolfe was not as interested in the links between episodes as he was in the pieces themselves. In his last manuscript he had not even written many links, and Aswell joined many of the seams between sections of *The Web and the Rock* and *You Can't Go Home Again* himself, in italicized transitions written in imitation of Wolfe's style and without attribution. Indeed, Wolfe's mastery of individual episodes is in striking contrast to the quality of the last books as wholes. This contrast caused at least one of Wolfe's most sensitive readers to suggest that he should not be regarded as a novelist at all, but rather as a writer of long stories or individual scenes.[32]

Wolfe's difficulties in shaping a book-length narrative after *Look Homeward, Angel* resulted in part from his undiminishing attempt to present a genuine and therefore an increasingly complex literary analogue to self in his fiction. He bored into his subject from one angle after another, experimenting with varying points of view (the many names and personalities of his autobiographical protag-

30. Ellmann reproduces a chart compiled by A. Walton Litz showing the dates of composition and publication of the various segments of *Finnegans Wake* (RE, 794–96). Joyce's working materials for Finnegans Wake are published in Volumes 28–63 of Michael Groden *et al.* (eds.), *The James Joyce Archive* (63 vols.; New York, 1978–).

31. Aswell, "A Note on Thomas Wolfe," in Wolfe, *The Hills Beyond*, 356.

32. See Holman, *The Loneliness at the Core*, 43–44, 47–71; and C. Hugh Holman, Introduction to C. Hugh Holman (ed.), *The Short Novels of Thomas Wolfe* (New York, 1961), vii–xx. The recent publication of Francis Edward Skipp (ed.), *The Complete Short Stories of Thomas Wolfe* (New York, 1987), may increase the number of readers sharing this opinion, since it is now possible to see conveniently (and in a judiciously edited form) the many short pieces that appeared in magazines.

onists are the most obvious evidence of his continuing experimentation with versions of self) and other narrative and stylistic devices, from comic distance to declamatory rhetoric.[33] Richard Kennedy once coined a new literary term, *fictional thesaurus*, to describe the genre of Wolfe's fiction. More seriously, he perceived that Wolfe's insistence on lyricism and associative or organic structuring was bound to cause problems in long fiction. Lyric fiction must consent to some novelistic techniques, according to Kennedy: if it did not, "the order of art would dissolve into the disorder of human mental activity."[34] In fact, as we have seen, this hypothetical result is a fairly accurate description of the tendency of both Wolfe's and Joyce's art to strain against the boundaries of traditional form in the writers' increasingly elaborate autobiographical fictions.

The thesaurus of Wolfe's last work, then, turns novelistic representation into another kind, which operates by repetition and extension rather than chronology and which by its very insistence on these methods constantly draws our eyes back to the ordering, visionary artist-self out of whom this universe is created. The need that impelled Wolfe, like Joyce, to re-create his young life as the growth of an artist, moved him to re-create in his later work the larger world in which he lived as an artist's created cosmos. Wolfe and Joyce each tried to write, and rewrite, versions of himself with which to mirror reality, beginning in the squalor of his childhood and ending with the chaos of the universe, but ordered and made beautiful through the always preeminent creator—"thereby," as Shem says, "reflecting from his own individual person life unlivable, transaccidentated through the slow fires of consciousness into a dividual chaos, perilous, potent, common to allflesh, human only, mortal" (*FW*, 186.2–6).

33. Kennedy lists seven manifestations of the central figure in the last mass of manuscript (RSK, 388).

34. Richard S. Kennedy, "Thomas Wolfe's Fiction: The Question of Genre," in Paschal Reeves (ed.), *Thomas Wolfe and the Glass of Time* (Athens, Ga., 1971), 28, 26.

Index